I0637448

Lock Down Publications and Ca$h Presents

The Birth of a Gangster 4

Delmont Player

Delmont Player

Lock Down Publications
P.O. Box 944
Stockbridge, GA 30281
www.lockdownpublications.com

Like our page on Facebook: Lock Down Publications
www.facebook.com/lockdownpublications.ldp

Stay Connected with Us!

Text LOCKDOWN to 22828 to stay up-to-date with new releases, sneak peaks, contests and more…
Or CLICK HERE to sign up.
Like our page on Facebook:
Lock Down Publications: Facebook
Join Lock Down Publications/The New Era Reading Group
Visit our website:
www.lockdownpublications.com
Follow us on Instagram:
Lock Down Publications: Instagram
Email Us: We want to hear from you!

Delmont Player

THE BIRTH OF A GANGSTER 4
Frank Season

By Delmont Player

Dedication

This book is dedicated to Charles, Stephanie and Ms. Pamela. In memory of John E. S., and his sister Stephanie. For a long time, I did not understand what remorse was. So, I could never truly accept full responsibility for what I did. And although I know that this is too small a gesture, I hope and pray that you may find some peace in it.

I know that I can never erase what I have done, nor give back what I have so unjustly taken from your family. And I am ashamed of that. But I vow to you, from this day forward, that everything I do will be in the memory and spirit of John. I only pray that you may find it in your hearts to forgive me one day.

May Allah (God) have mercy on my soul!

Acknowledgements

First and foremost, all praise to be allah, the beneficent, the merciful. I thank Allah (God) for not only saving me from mental and physical death. but for also pulling me up out of my ignorance to shape me into a servant of his people.

And I would be remiss, if I did not acknowledge, the realest man and only true friend that I have ever had. Frank C. Lance, friend, brother, family. So many people have "self" prescribed these titles in my life. but cuz, you proved them "all" worthless! I pray to Allah that you may one day find it in your heart to forgive me for what I have done to you. what I have so selfishly taken. what I can never repay. I ruined your life too! I cost you more than any man should ever have to pay to be someone's friend. you sat in prison and rotted away, because I was too much of a coward and not "man enough" to step up and accept responsibility for my own actions. And for that, I am sorry! The man I am today could not have ever done such a thing. so, just like I told John's family. I plan to spend the rest of my life making amends. not only to you all. but to the entire world!

Prologue

Frank

The instant Dakaron's cousin Clyde found a secure place to pull over so that we could finish interrogating the task force rookie, I jumped out and tried to gather my thoughts. I needed a breath of fresh air. I knew that Dakaron's other cousin, Little Phil and his man, Billy Lo could handle the rookie from here. After all, he'd already given up the names and location we needed.

I couldn't believe that it had come to this. I mean, murking street dudes was one thing. Even if they were so called kids. But kidnapping and killing police officers was something else. There was no coming back from that.

Fuck! I thought, wondering how in the hell I'd allowed Dakaron to drag me back into the game. Especially after we'd just crawled up from underneath life sentences less than a year ago.

I'd paid the price for fucking with Dak before. So, I'd vowed to myself when we first came home that, if the price ever got as expensive as the price I'd paid in the past, I'd walk away. But, here I was as always, allowing my loyalty to Dakaron to cloud my judgement and put my life and freedom in jeopardy. And for what? Because Dakaron never knew when to quit? Because he never knew how to just let shit go and walk away?

"This nigga and his fucking ego!" I cursed out loud shaking my head. But honestly, I knew that Dak would do the same for me no questions asked.

I'm not saying that I'm an angel or anything. But being a gangster wasn't my dream. Don't get it fucked up now. I was far from a slouch, and it was well-known that I'd peel a nigga's wig back just as quick as Dak. But it still wasn't a dream.

I didn't run the streets behind my older brothers or sit around the house watching gangster flicks all day. That was Dakaron's thing. In all honesty, I'd initially jumped off the steps to help my mother with the bills after she'd spazzed out on her boyfriend and ended up losing everything fighting the case at trial.

However, what a lot of motherfuckers didn't know though was that I was the first one to pop his cherry in the murder game, not Dakaron. Yeah, I know he always told the story about how he'd slumped his cousin's boyfriend when he was real young. But nobody really believed that shit. I surely didn't. Still, either way, I always played it cool. Always kept quiet and played my position. If niggas couldn't recognize a killer when he was in their midst, that was on them.

Besides, I loved it when they slept on me. Because I always got a kick out of the looks on their faces when they realized that I was the one sent to put them on their backs.

After a while, Clyde hit the horn and broke my train of thought.

"Come on, we got the address!" He tilted his head out the driver's side window and shouted. "According to the GPS we're about a half mile away!"

I stood there and took a few more deep breaths. Had I not loved Dakaron's ass so much I would've been backed out.

"What's up, Jack?" Billy Lo questioned pushing the back door of the van open. "We doing this or what?"

"Of course," I assured quickly moving towards the van.

"Then, we need to move before somebody spots us and starts getting suspicious." Billy Lo looked around cautiously as he held the door open for me.

I knew that he was right. Not only was Hamden an historically white, working-class community. But it had a serious neighborhood watch program and heavy KKK roots.

I stopped at the door and took one last deep breath to let the cool night air fill my lungs. I held it for a few seconds and exhaled as I begged Allah for his protection and forgiveness for the massacre that I knew was about to take place and climbed back into the van.

The situation with Dak had gotten out of hand. In fact, it was now bigger then Dak. It was now kill or be killed—in one sense or another—because the gun trace task force knew exactly who I was.

The only good thing about my situation was the fact that because the gun trace task force were so corrupt and did a lot of things off the books, it was a strong possibility that the entire police force wasn't on to me yet. Either way, going back to prison wasn't an option. I'd hold court in the streets first.

"This a straight up suicide mission," Little Phil suggested the moment I got back into the van.

"Why you think I recruited a suicide squad?" I joked trying to make light of the situation with a devilish grin as Billy Lo secured the door. I began to ready myself for the 'Call of Duty' style gunplay that was sure to take place when we stormed the gun trace task force black site like it was the nation's capital.

Clyde slowly pulled off and headed for our final destination. I knew shit was about to get real. To begin with, there were no camera crews. Secondly, the unsuspected, off-the-record location where the rookie said they sometimes conducted illegal interrogations and other unethical activity was loaded with weapons.

"You hear this nigga, Cuzzo?" Little Phil laughed adjusting the straps on his bulletproof vest.

"I heard him. But you know I've been dying to do some shit like this since the Freddie Gray riot," Clyde confessed from behind the wheel.

"I don't know about all that. But if there's revenge to be had, I'm all for it." Billy Lo chimed.

I'd let Billy Lo in for one reason and one reason only. He was Little Phil's man from way back and I trusted Little Phil just as much as I trusted Dakaron. Little Phil had been solid since the first day I met him in the penitentiary annex. Of course, I'd heard all the legendary stories about how Billy Lo had went up against the community and survived. I knew a lot of brothers wouldn't agree with me dealing with him. But none of them had come to me about going against the police either. Besides, I looked at it like this, any man who was brave enough to go up against such odds and come out unbroken, was a motherfucker I needed on my team.

"Aight bitch, make the call," Billy Lo ordered snatching the duct tape off of the rookie's mouth before handing him the cellphone. "And you better not tip them off," Billy Lo warned pressing the business end of his gun against the side of the rookie's head for encouragement. He also waved a photograph of his wife and young children in front of his face for insurance. "Put it on speaker too!"

We sat in the back of the van and listened carefully as the gun trace task force rookie explained to his Sergeant that he couldn't make it to the 'The Barn' for their weekly poker game. Which was nothing more than a coded saying for their safe house breakdown.

"Ah man, all the guys are here," the Sergeant's braving voice cracked over the speaker phone. "And there's broads and brew all over the place," the Sergeant dropped another coded saying for money and drugs.

"Tell that Scout he better come get him some of this pussy before it's all gone," One of his task force partners could be heard in the background.

"There's always next week." The rookie laughed nervously.

"You know the rules, Scout," the Sergeant addressed him by the nickname he said the guys had given him, since he was the newest member on the team. "When it is poker night, it is poker night. There is no guarantee that the brew will still be here next week. And you know how these guys get with broads. They're going to tear these girls apart."

"I understand," the rookie assured. "But like I said, something came up with the wife and kids."

"I get it. The home front always comes first." The Sergeant agreed.

"Suit yourself, Scout." Another one of his task force pals encouraged. "That just means more pussy and drinks for us!"

"Aight then, I'll see you guys at the office in the AM," the rookie suggested when Billy Lo signaled for him to end the call.

"Try to get in about an hour early," the Sergeant recommended before the rookie could end the call. "The Captain wants us to tag along for a high profile raid in West Baltimore."

"Fucking babysitting is what I call it! "One of his task force guys remarked.

"Sure thing, Serg. See you then." The rookie agreed just before I reached over and swiped my finger across the phone screen, ending the call.

"So, just how many of them mother fuckers are inside house?" I inquired taking the cellphone out of his hand and tossing it on the floor.

"Four," the rookie replied without hesitation.

"Come on now, we're not stupid. I heard at least six voices. Plus, I know it's about twelve of y'all on the task force." Billy Lo stared at the rookie to let him know that he'd done his homework.

"You're right. But everybody is not on the take," the rookie retorted. "Everybody doesn't even know about the barn. There are some good cops left, you know."

"Man, all y'all bitches are crooked!" I spat punching the rookie in the mouth.

"Hold up yo, chill," Little Phil intervened. "Let him talk."

"Yeah Jack, fall back for a second. "Billy Lo seconded as the rookie checked his mouth for blood.

"He's lying!" I barked, ready to hit him again.

"I swear to you. There's only four guys inside," he reiterated. "Serg, Woodie and two uniforms out of the Eastern."

I studied the rookie for a moment, looking for any signs of deceit. He appeared to be telling the truth. After all, he had been telling us everything we needed to know since we'd gotten the drop on him not far from the after-hour police sports bar the entire gun trace task force frequented in Little Italy. Yet and still, I knew that looks could be very deceiving. I knew a lot of good men who had been tricked out of their lives thinking that things had been sweeter than they actually were.

"Are you sure?" Billy Lo looked the rookie directly in the eyes.

"I'm certain," the rookie replied with a head nod. "There's only four people in there. Serg, Woodie and the two uniforms from the Eastern. Today's poker day."

"Bet," I said mashing the duct tape back across his lips satisfied.

"What now?" Clyde checked the mirrors and continued to follow the GPS route towards the gun trace task force safe house.

"Since they want to act like gangsters," I reached into my pocket and removed the silencer that I'd taken from Clyde's house and screwed it onto the nose of my gun. "We're going to treat them like gangsters," I rationalized before aiming the gun at the back of the rookie's head and blowing his brains all over the interior of the stolen van.

"I like this shit already," Billy Lo exclaimed with a sick smile. "We're coming up on the house now," Clyde alerted over his shoulder. "The Camaro's parked out front."

"We're killing everything in that bitch!" I declared stuffing the gun back into my hostler before reaching for the SK. "We're not showing them bitches no mercy."

Once Clyde pulled the van in behind the Silver Copo Camaro and parked, we all began looking at each other as if to make sure we all understood exactly what we were about to do.

"This the last chance for anybody to walk away," Little Phil spoke up. "Nobody will judge you. Like Billy Lo said, these aren't no corner kids. They're police. So, these bitches train for this shit!"

Little Phil let his words sank in as he slowly examined us individually. Nobody spoke up. Nobody backed out. Our silence said it all. We were all committed.

"Enough said," I broke the silence and reached for the door. It was time to show motherfuckers how I really got down for my crown. "Let's go do this."

Hold up, before I take you there, I have to tell you how I got here.

Chapter 1

Frank

In October 1979, I would become the fourth of six children that my mother would eventually give birth to. I was well into my teens before my little sister and brother came along. By then, my father was already serving time in the feds for funneling twenty-seven million dollars' worth of heroin into the city for the Rice Organization Wiretap indictment and moms was sitting over courtside fighting for her freedom. Most people thought that I was from North Avenue and Longwood. But the truth was, I was from the heart and soul of South Baltimore. A well-known neighborhood called Westport. A neighborhood that had given birth to a lot of certified wig-splitters and penitentiary legends. My neighborhood was the shit HBO specials like The Wire and classic movies like Blood In, Blood Out were made of. But don't get it twisted. North and Long was just as cold. And the violence, murder and drug game was just as prevalent.

I could still remember when I'd first moved around Longwood like it was yesterday. I mean, the first day, I got my ass beat. And not just by one motherfucker either. Sure it started like that, one-on-one, head up. But once I started whipping Jamaine ass, Tybo and Quincy jumped in it.

The funny part is, after that, we all became as thick as thieves.

I mean, I fucked with Hook, Urtle, Dewitt and Chrisco too. But it was Jamaine, Quincy and Tybo who I did everything with. Hooked school, played sports, hustled, everything. In so many words, we stayed in some shit.

I would always remember the day that my sister Cindy's boyfriend, Efrem shot the police at the neighborhood convenience store. We were playing football on Rosedale when Jamaine suggested we head up to Se7en Stars to steal some chips.

I was cracking on Urtle for playing football in his Penny Loafer's when the sound of a loud cannon went off and a uniform Baltimore City officer came flying through the large store front window of Se7en Stars backward before smashing into the ground.

"Oh shit!" I uttered as everybody froze.

We watched in horror as the well-known rouge cop slowly rolled over, gasping for air and began to crawl towards his patrol car as my sister's boyfriend exited the store with a rusty, duct taped handled sawed-off carefully surveying the street.

"What you got to say now, nigga? Huh? Talk that big bad wolf shit now. Mister police officer. Baltimore City finest!" Efrem taunted walking up to stand over top of the wounded officer. "You should've just walked away," he warned spontaneously cocking the sawed-off shotgun. "But nahhhh, your bitch ass always got to fuck with a nigga." Efrem brought the shotgun up and carefully aimed it at the cop's head.

"Take your little ass home!" Efrem noticed me standing outside the store. "Now!" He directed a second before rapid gunfire exploded from across the parking lot.

"Run!" Somebody shouted and we all took off running.

I don't even remember glancing back. But somehow, when I got home, I was able to tell my sister about the other police officer, who'd been half hidden behind the open patrol car door firing.

My sister had a thousand questions. But I could only answer so much. I was absolutely sure that it was Efrem who'd shot the cop with a sawed-off. You know, things like that. However, my sister eventually got tired of my lack of information and decided to go investigate things for herself.

The next morning, a tact-team showed up at my house in full riot gear, demanding answers. They wanted to know who Efrem was to me, what I'd seen or heard and where my friends were.

Turns out, the Se7en Stars Clerk had given me up to the cops. It didn't matter though, I would never cooperate. Talking to the cops was like a cardinal sin in my house and my mother was more treacherous than the Pope. Besides, I hated the police. They had allowed my mother's boyfriend to get away with abusing her only to show up on the day she'd had enough and decided to toss a radio into his bath water and electrocute his coward ass.

So when my sister started threatening to call some big time lawyer who once represented my father, I just stood there smiling.

"Oh, you're one of them smart, little bitches who thinks she knows everything, huh?" One of the officers fired from the crowd as they backed off.

"Something like that," my sister retorted proudly before turning to me. "Don't you ever talk to the police, you hear me?"

"Man, fuck the police!" I shouted loud enough for the cops to hear me and grabbed my nuts like I was a member of N.W.A.

"That's right," my sister encouraged. "Fuck the police!"

"You're going to need us one day," another officer assured walking around his patrol car to open the door.

"Why would I ever need the police?" My sister inquired. "All you motherfuckers do is come into this community and use us like political footballs that you'll throw around, kick-off or run in for a touchdown when you'll

16

are trying to send a message," my sister continued before he could reply.

"Remember that when somebody is shooting that little motherfucker!" The officer gestured towards me and climbed into his patrol car.

"Don't count on it," my sister fired before pushing me back into the house, slamming the door.

Growing up in a house full of exceptionally beautiful women made me extremely overprotective. Especially of my little sister, Demecka. I mean, I want to be clear. My older sisters were my babies too. But it was Demecka who I felt like I had to protect the most. Probably because I was the man of the house. Then, there were the hustlers who showed up at my mother's door chasing my sister Cindy. Hustlers who I cursed out and threatened until Efrem showed up.

I went for Efrem because he changed something in my sister for the better. One thing being the tough girl exterior she used to fend off the neighborhood male predators. Dudes just didn't play with Efrem. Not only was he golden glove-nice with his dick beaters, but he was also trigger happy with that biscuit and everybody knew it.

I'm not even going to front. I loved the way niggas laid down for Efrem. That shit made me feel ten feet tall whenever I was with him. Which was one of the main reasons why I didn't have no respect for a lot of so-called gangsters around Longwood. Especially, the ones who'd waited until Efrem went off to prison to try and push up on my sister. To me, as far as I was concerned, they were all straight up bitches.

Chapter 2

Frank

I never really knew exactly what happened with my mother's trial or how the verdict had come down. All I knew is that one minute, my mother was being snagged up for murder and the next, she was in our living room surrounded by family and friends when I came in from school.

To be honest, I didn't know what to do or say. So, I just stood there staring at her in silence until my mother rushed over and wrapped me up in her arms before kissing all over me.

"Ma," I whined, looking around embarrassed. I knew she had only been gone about eighteen months. But she had to understand that I wasn't a little boy no more. I had been holding the fort down. I had even gotten my dick sucked by one of Cindy's girlfriends.

"Ma, my tail," my mother retorted kissing me again. "I missed you!" She confessed making me blush. "Look at my little man, getting all big."

"He got a little weight-set in the basement now," Cindy revealed. "Him and his little friends live on that thing."

"I see." My mother smiled squeezing on me. "My baby got a little chest too," she added pointing at my muscles. My mother always had a way of making me feel larger than life.

"Do you know that the most dangerous place in the world is between a mother and her children?" My mother explained and I shook my head. "That's right, doesn't nothing in the world mean more to a mother than her children, you hear me?"

"Yes." I nodded.

"I love you so much." My mother kissed me again and I could see the water increasing in her eyes before she pulled me back into her arms again.

"I love you too ma," I professed honestly. Everybody knew that I was a mamma's boy. I didn't care how big I got.

I stood there, wrapped in my mother's arms and cried. There was nobody in the world like my mother. Which was why my father use to always say, "Evon Johnson is in a class all by herself."

We sat around the house, eating, dancing and telling jokes, enjoying my mother's company until my little brother and sister showed up with their father and moms disappeared.

I knew that Demecka and Shawn's father would had custody of them while moms was away. But I also knew that they'd be home the moment my mother was released. Like my mother had said, she didn't play about her kids and everybody knew it.

When moms reappeared sometime later, she began getting on Pooch and Kimberly for not helping my sister Cindy keep my head tight.

"Who the hell been cutting my baby's hair?" My mother questioned but none of my sisters were forth coming. "And boy when the last time you brushed your hair?" My mother inquired running her hand through my knotty hair. "Your head is beady as hell. And what's this line in your head?"

"That's the new style, ma," I replied moving my head out of her reach to run my hand over my half-moon part.

"Not for Evon Johnson's son it's not," my mother argued confidently. "We don't follow trends baby, we set them."

For the rest of the night, we circled around my mother, infatuated with her courtside stories. It was my first history lesson about women and just how unstable they actually were. By the time my mother finished, I was curled up on the couch with my head laid across her lap next to Demecka asleep.

Chapter 3

Frank

Only a few months had passed when Cindy and my mother began getting into it. At first, it was small things like arguing about bills and responsibility. Then, it began to escalate to personal stuff. Things like decision making.

"Every time I turn around you're running over to that city jail, visiting that no good nigga of yours," my mother fired as I exited the basement to get some water. "Tell that nigga to pay some of these bills around this motherfucker."

"Why don't you tell one of them niggas you're chasing to pay a fucking bill!" Cindy retorted. "Better yet, why don't tell Demecka and Shawn's father to pay some rent since he's over here so much!"

"Why don't you get a job?" My mother countered with an attitude before mumbling something about Cindy being trifling.

"I don't see you with no job either, ma!"

Hearing my mother and sister fuss over money and their choice in men always broke my heart and made me wish that I could do more. I wanted so bad to ease the burden. Especially where it concerned my little brother and sister.

I mean, I knew that the phone had been shut off and that the rent was overdue. But I never wanted my little brother and sister to have to experience hardship. I never wanted them to know what it felt like to be without. After all, they were my family. And family had always been the most important thing in the world to me.

I shook my head, grabbed a glass of sugar water and headed back down the basement to finish fucking with the weights. My plan was to turn the music all the way up and do some reps until Tybo or one of them showed up.

I turned the music up and laid down on the bench to put in some work. I was so focused on tuning my mother and sister out, that I didn't realize how hard I was going until my arms started hurting and gave out.

***

It seemed like it was all good just a few months ago. Moms was fresh out of jail, Efrem hadn't started trial and my sister was still reaping the benefits of his power.

But things changed quick after Efrem was found guilty. Dudes started switching up and playing games. Yeah, they would still stop by and kiss the ring from time to time. But it was crumbs compared to before Efrem blew trial.

I can still remember the day I came out of the basement to find another neighborhood gangster, by the name of Monique, whispering something to my sister. I knew he said something crazy because I saw the look on her face before she pushed him back. Monique just smiled and handed my sister a stack of bills. Then, he warned her that her free ride was over.

"If you want to continue to eat at my table, you better learn how to show some appreciation."

I'll never forget Monique's words. And I never forgot how things instantly began to change soon afterwards.

When I heard the coded tap on the basement window, I carefully place the weights back on the rack and shot outside. My mother didn't play about niggas hanging on her front porch.

"What's up nigga?" Jamaine got up to give me some love the moment I came bouncing out of the house.

"Nothing," I replied checking the window for any sign of my mother. "About to go up Bloomingdale and pump some gas," I admitted honestly, knowing that if I got up there early and took down, I could help moms with the rent.

"Man, forget all that," Jamaine encouraged waving my idea off. "I got another way to make some cash."

"Don't you always?" I smiled thinking about Jamaine's last get rich quick schemes. "I'm not fucking with you."

"Nah, this easy money," Jamaine assured confidently.

"Yeah, that's what you said when we broke into old man Ransom's house up the village," I reminded him. "Then, we fucked around and got cranked on."

"This is different yo. I'm telling you," Jamaine tried to convince me. "All we got to do is watch somebody's back while they take care of something."

It sounded easy enough. "Who?" I questioned curiously.

"Oily," Jamaine revealed.

"The big New York dude who be on Clifton?" I inquired to be certain.

"Yeah," Jamaine confirmed.

"And all we got to do is watch his back?" I studied Jamaine carefully.

"Yep," Jamaine shook his head.

After a few more questions, I followed Jamaine over to the Clifton side of North Avenue to find out exactly what I'd signed on for.

We found Oily, sitting inside his gold, MPV Mini-Van, talking to a few of his runners and waited. Once he finished, we strolled over to the minivan to holler at him.

"What's up Oily?" Jamaine greeted him as we walked up.

"What's up, little Jamaine?" Oily reached out to adjust the driver's side door mirror. "Come around the passenger's side," he instructed when he realized that he couldn't see past us with the mirror.

Jamaine and I walked around the other side of the minivan as I checked out the gold BBS Rims.

"So, what's up?" Oily asked rolling the window down.

"Nah, I just wanted to holler at you about what you told me the other day," Jamaine revealed.

"Oh, you ready to step up to the big leagues huh?" Oily smiled, showing off a mouthful of gold teeth.

"Yeah," Jamaine replied.

"What about your man?" Oily gestured towards me with his head. "Shorty trying to get busy too?"

"Yeah, that's my man. We do everything together." "Jamaine shot me a confident glance and I nodded in agreement.

"No doubt, no doubt." Oily shook his head respectfully before removing his New York Yankee fitted cap from his head for what felt like no reason. "Aight, check it right," Oily readjusted his fitted cap with the same awkward twist and tilt and continued. "One of y'all going to watch the block and the other one is going to hold the pack while my runners slang."

The instant I heard what Oily said, I twisted my face up and expressed my position. "I ain't holding nobody's drugs." I looked from Oily to Jamaine because, he of all people knew that, if I was going to be in the drug game, it wasn't going to be as a fuckboy.

"Shorty bugging already?" Oily eyed me.

"Chill Frank." Jamaine shot me an irritated look.

"Chill Frank, shit!" I retorted. "I ain't holding no packs like a stash house!"

"I'll hold them," Jamaine volunteered. "All you got to do is watch for the police."

I looked at Jamaine for a moment. Every time he had a plan, it always went wrong. Yet and still, he was my nigga, so I always supported him.

"Alright," I agreed thinking about being able to help my mother out. "If you hold it, I'm in."

" We're good?" Oily looked from Jamaine to me and back.

"Yeah, we're good yo." Jamaine nodded and just like that, we were in the drug game.

Oily give us a spill about fucking his money up and I could tell that he was serious. After that, he handed Jamaine a couple of bundles and told me where to go stand and it was on.

The crazy part was neither Jamaine nor myself were smart enough to ask Oily when or how much we were getting paid.

Jamaine and I stayed out on Walbrook all day, holding the work and watching the block. My numbers could be a little off. But Oily re'd up at least fifteen times and the packs that Jamaine were holding, was in bundles of twelve, at ten dollars a pop. Which meant that we helped Oily secure close to two-thousand dollars. Yet, at the end of the night. That nigga only handed us twenty slugs apiece.

I was heated but Jamaine kept saying that we'd get more as long as we stayed down.

"Man, that nigga just pimped the shit out of us," I fired as we headed back across North Avenue. "We could've hit Bloomingdale and got more than this," I argued stuffing the money into my pocket.

That's exactly what I get, I thought to myself. I should've just called my uncle out Westport for the money. But I didn't want my mother to kill me.

Chapter 4

Frank

I wasn't exactly sure when Dakaron started being a regular around the way. But I knew it was the summer that I got real nice on the bikes because Quincy had ended up getting locked up for the gun charge after Dakaron crashed a stolen car down Chocolate City. When it was all said and done, Quincy ended up at Charles H. Hickey School for Boys.

Everybody was cheering as I stood the bike straight up and wheelied it from one end of Rosedale to the next.

I'm not tooting my own horn or anything. But when it came to them dirt bikes, I wasn't nothing to be fucked with. I was a twelve o'clock boy before that shit even existed. I used to lift my shit up and walk that bitch for six and seven blocks at a time, doing all kind of wild tricks; real wild-out wheelie shit.

The only nigga who could honestly get in my business was my cousin Moonie from Westport. And that was only because he knew how to do all that no handed shit.

"Ayo, let me ride that bitch," Tybo requested as I came to a stop.

"Nigga, you know you're not about that bike life." I smirked playing with the throttle as everybody began to gather around the bike.

I made the front wheel come up off the ground as if I was about to take off again.

"Whoa nigga!" Tybo snapped taking a step back like everybody else.

"Let me ride it though yo." Tybo begged but I knew that he only wanted to impress the girls.

"Nah nigga." I shook my head. "I'ma be the only one getting all the pussy." I bragged sincerely. The only nigga in the crew who could probably give me a run for my money was Jamaine. But that was only because he'd fuck anything. Plus, he was the only one besides me and Hook eating pussy.

"Nigga you bluffing," Jamaine challenged. "I sees more pussy than a toilet seat."

"Seeing pussy and fucking is two different things," I corrected.

"Nigga, you ain't hitting nothing but Keisha," Jamaine fired.

Just the sound of Keisha's name always brought a smile to my face. I mean, not only was Keisha the baddest thing around the way. She had the best pussy in West Baltimore. And I wasn't just saying that because it was hot, hairy and hell of tight. I was saying that because, out of all the females that I'd fucked so far, including the few older women, Keisha was the only one who could make me burst like a bottle of carbonated water the instant I got in it.

"That's sexy ass Keisha to you nigga," I teased knowing that Jamaine was still sour behind the fact that I'd stolen Keisha from him.

"I ain't going to lie yo," Hook interjected. "Just by fucking with Keisha, Frank got us all beat," Hook admitted. "Even the old heads be chasing her fine ass."

"Nigga, she ain't all that!" Jamaine fired waving Hook off but we all knew that he was lying.

"Shiiid, nigga you must be blind," Tybo argued. "Keisha fine as fuck!"

"Man, all them Paylor girls bad. Keisha, Pamela, Brenda, Sherly Maryland." Hook added and nobody argued because we all knew that it was true. The entire neighborhood was chasing after Urtle's sisters. But only a few of them had been caught.

"That nigga just fronting because Frank took his girl," Hook joked.

Delmont Player

"Chill yo," I looked at Hook sternly. It wasn't that I was tripping about him clowning Jamaine. I was all for that. However, I looked up and saw Urtle coming down Longwood and wasn't trying to hear his mouth.

For the rest of day, we just chilled around my front and played on the dirt bike until Urtle and them decided to go sell some newspapers for the Nation of Islam Muslims so they could have some money to play Tonk.

Chapter 5

Frank

By now Dakaron was living up 'The Junction' on Garrison Boulevard, going to Edgewood Elementary with Tybo and them. Efrem was home too. Again, I didn't know exactly what had happened or how his case had played itself out. But I did see something on the evening news about an appeal. Everybody thought that Efrem would've come home on some chill shit after being so lucky. But he came home on some goon shit. Robbing and pressing everything. He wasn't fucking around. He wasn't even fucking with my sister like that. My mother said that it wasn't that he didn't love her. It was just that prison relationships required more than Cindy was willing or able to give.

Of course, Cindy had a different outlook. She said, too much time and distance had gotten between them and equaled up to too many disappointments. However, I felt like it was more than what my mother or sister was telling me. Especially since I knew for a fact that Cindy had been creeping around with Monique. Yet and still, I kept my mouth closed and my thoughts to myself because Efrem didn't treat me any differently.

It wasn't until the day that Efrem beat Dakaron's hands with a book until they were swollen, that I decided to stay the hell away from him. Dakaron felt like he would gotten caught up in some personal shit going on between Efrem and Monique, and I wasn't so sure that he was wrong. After all, I knew about the love triangle concerning Efrem, Monique and my sister. But again, I kept my feelings to myself hoping that everything would work itself out.

However, little did I know how things were really about to get serious. First, Urtle accidentally shot Dakaron. Then, we all decided to jump off the steps headfirst and start getting work from Oily. No more corner watching and pack holding. It was time to carve out a lane for ourselves.

Our mentality was like fuck it. Since the old niggas around the way didn't want to put us in the drug game, we went to a nigga who would.

And shit was going good too. Oily was fronting each of us an eight ball a piece and we were killing it. Everybody except Jamaine of course. He fucked his pack money up the first week, tricking off with fiends and shit and ended up having to run off. Which was crazy because we all knew exactly what would happen when Oily caught up with Jamaine.

In the end, niggas came together and paid Oily off on Jamaine's behalf because we knew that he wasn't to be fucked with. Hook had witnessed him shoot one of his runners for coming up short on a *g-pack*, so we already knew how he was going to step to Jamaine.

We were all standing on the side of Jean's on North Avenue, waiting for Oily, when I spotted Jamaine in the passenger's seat of Monique's J30 Infiniti coming off of Longwood.

"There go your father," I joked Dakaron as Monique pulled over.

"Ayo, stop playing with me nigga!" Dakaron threw a lazy right that I easily weaved.

"Fuck is up with Jamaine?" I wondered especially since we hadn't seen him since he decided to run off with Oily's work again.

"I don't know," Dakaron admitted.

We watched in silence as Monique climbed out of the car alone, in the latest gear and approached us. "What's going on with y'all?" Monique inquired looking around.

"Nothing, chilling," Dakaron replied. "What's with Jamaine?" Dakaron looked towards the J30.

"Where Oily at?" Monique ignored Dakaron's question.

"W--wh-who? Oily?" Dakaron stuttered before looking at me nervously. Monique had caught him off guard.

"Don't insult my intelligence, Dakaron," Monique warned. "You think I don't know what's going on in my neighborhood? I got eyes everywhere." Monique continued. "Now, where's Oily?"

"In the store getting a soda," Dakaron revealed.

Monique walked off and strolled into Jean's without uttering another word.

"Why the fuck you tell him Oily was in the store dummy?" I snapped the moment Monique disappeared inside of Jean's.

"Yeah, that was stupid," Hook seconded shaking his head.

"You think he didn't know Oily was in the store?" Dakaron questioned rhetorically. "Oily's MPV is right there on Longwood."

"Still, now he going to try and tell Oily not to give us nothing," Hook added.

"Man, fuck all that," I fired. I wasn't worried about Oily. He wasn't like all the other dudes around way. Monique didn't pump no fear in his heart. So I was sure that Monique wasn't about to stop his money. "I'm trying to figure how that nigga not only know that we're hustling. But who we're hustling for?"

"Are you serious?" Dakaron looked at me strangely before continuing. "Look who's in the passenger seat."

"Jamaine ain't do no shit like that?" Hook argued but I wasn't so sure.

Jamaine had always been one of those selfish type niggas who only thought of himself. Still, I wanted to believe that he hadn't sold us out like that. "You think he would do some shit like that?"

Before Dakaron or Hook could fix their mouths to respond, Monique came storming out of Jean's dragging Oily across the ground by his collar like he wasn't two hundred plus pounds of solid muscle.

"Get your bitch ass up nigga!" Monique fired releasing Oily's shirt like he was nothing more than a bag of garbage.

"Ayo, I'ma murder you son." Oily scrambled to his feet. "I'ma split your wig kid. That's on everything!"

Oily got his feet and rushed Monique. However, Monique sidestepped and hit him with a combination so wicked that I didn't even notice the brass knuckles until Oily was stretched out on the sidewalk with his face busted open.

Monique removed the bloody brass knuckles and began wiping them off with the handkerchief he removed from his back pocket.

"That's the nigga you want to work for?" Monique tossed the handkerchief on top of Oily's body and directed his attention to Dakaron. Then, he walked back over to his J30 real quick and tossed the brass knuckles to Jamaine in the passenger seat.

"Huh?" He massaged his bruised knuckles before walking back over to the now slightly conscious Oily to squat down.

"They tell me that you're a killer." Monique grabbed Oily by his throat and flipped the front of his shirt up to reveal the shining, nickel plated .45 stuffed in his dip. "But I know a coward when I see one."

Monique snatched the .45 out of Oily's waistband and hit him upside the head with it.

"Open your mouth bitch!" Monique ordered, stuffing the gun into Oily's bloody mouth before he could completely comply.

"Please," Oily begged in submission before Monique jammed the .45 down his throat and made him gag.

You can't be that crazy, I thought to myself watching Monique cock the hammer back. It was broad daylight, and the entire avenue was watching his performance.

"You hear this coward?" Monique looked towards Dakaron again.

"Please, please," Monique mocked merciless. "Nah bitch, since you want to give my little brother drugs to sell. You're going to answer for that," Monique declared and began beating the hell out of Oily.

Monique pistol whipped Oily to within inches of his life. But nobody dared to stop him. They just all stood around in shock. I had never seen Monique get violent on the streets. But I'd heard that he could.

"Don't you ever put no fucking drugs in none of my little brothers hands nigga." Monique stood straight up, towing over Oily and carefully slid the .45 into the small of his back. "You hear me?"

Oily just laid there and shook his head like a housebroken pet.

"As a matter of fact nigga, you got twenty-four hours to skip town. If I see you after that, I'ma blow your brain out." Monique threatened before folding Oily up with a powerful kick to the ribs.

"Everybody in the car now!" Monique demanded looking at us. Hook and Dakaron instantly took off. But I remained still, unable to move for more reasons than one.

"Get in the car, Little Frank," Monique instructed. "I'm not going to tell you again," Monique warned opening the driver's side door to climb into the J30.

"Come on, yo." Jamaine got out and held the back door open for me as Dakaron climbed up front with Monique.

I took one more look at Oily balled up on the ground in pain, moaning like a bitch and vowed to never let another man put fear in my heart. Then, I walked over to the car and climbed into the back with Hook before Jamaine got in and closed the door.

"Put y'all seatbelts on," Monique instructed calmly as if he hadn't just beat a nigga half to and left him laying out on the pavement. "Double check them too because some time the lock don't catch," he added peeping at the side mirror before starting the car and pulling out into traffic.

I couldn't speak for Hook or Dakaron but I was leery as shit.

Monique was too calm for me. Especially after the way he'd fucked Oily around.

"Don't ever let me catch you hustling for a nigga like that?" Monique finally spoke up, breaking the uncomfortable silence. "Especially, no New York nigga. They're chameleons. All they do is show up with names they've given themselves, front some little nigga or start fucking one of these silly broads and the next thing you know, it's a thousand of them niggas on the strip." Monique kept his eyes on the road and continued to drive.

"That goes for the rest of you little niggas too," Monique glanced over his shoulder.

"Man, you ain't putting no food in my stomach," I mumbled before I could even stop myself and instantly regretted it.

I saw Jamaine look at me like I was crazy and slide over towards the door. Dakaron just continued to face forward, and Hook stared out the window. Monique cut his eyes at me in the rearview and laughed. Then, he admitted that I was right and jump on the expressway.

"The thing is though, there's a lot of different ways to eat out here," Monique explained. "You can eat the crumbs that fall from a nigga's plate. You can earn a seat at the table and break bread like a gentlemen or you can simply just take the whole fucking plate like a gangster."

"I want the whole plate!" Jamaine declared without hesitation.

"I want a seat at the table," I replied honestly because, if I was eating I wanted my niggas to sat too.

"Yeah, me too," Dakaron seconded. "Because I ain't eating nobody's crumbs."

"Yeah, that's what I was thinking." Hook shook his head.

"Fuck it, I'm sitting at the table too." Jamaine jumped on the bandwagon as always. "But I'm sitting at the head of the table."

"Aight then, it's time y'all little niggas start earning y'all seats." Monique cut his eyes at me again.

"How we supposed to do that?" I questioned curiously.

"By first taking the whole plate of the motherfucker who has been feeding you crumbs." Monique pulled up in front of a two-story home with a red door.

"That's Oily's mother house. Go knock on the door and tell that old bitch that if she doesn't give you all the money and work up in the there, I'ma get out of the car and kill everybody in the house."

"What, right now?" I questioned nervously looking at the house.

"Nah, tomorrow," Monique said sarcastically popping the lock on the back door.

"That's his mother though," I argued not wanting to do nothing to a nigga's mother. Not even for a seat at the table.

"So, it's a cold game," Monique retorted.

"Man, I'm not doing nothing to nobody's mother," I declared ready to face the consequences.

"You're in the wrong line of work, Frank. You're not going to make it very far in this game fighting lions over sheep," Monique explained.

"Man, I'll do it," Jamaine volunteered. "I know how cold the game is."

"I like your spirit, Jamaine." Monique reached in the small of his back. "Here's something that will always keep you warm." He removed the chrome .45 that he had taken from Oily and passed it back to Jamaine.

Monique kept the car running as we sat there and watched Jamaine make his way up to Oily's mother house and knocked on the door. An elderly, pudgy cheeked woman with salt and pepper hair opened the door with a friendly smile and began talking to Jamaine and within seconds, he was drawing the .45 forcing his way inside.

Jamaine disappeared inside for what seemed like hours but was actually only minutes before he came sprinting from the house with a bag and large envelope laughing.

"That old bitch tried to buck at first." Jamaine jumped into the backseat out of breath.

"Did you get everything?" Monique turned completely around to analyze the contents in Jamaine's hands.

"Yeah." Jamaine shook his head and held up the bag and envelope.

"I got a biscuit too," Jamaine disclosed.

"Aight, keep the gun and stuff everything else underneath the back of Dakaron's seat," Monique directed pulling off. "Make sure you put your seatbelt back on too. We can't afford to get pulled over," Monique added as Jamaine worked the drugs and money underneath the seat.

On the way back to the city, Monique laid out some ground rules, offered me some so called needed advice, suggested that we bring the rest of the crew in on the licks, and promised to line up some major moves for us as we pulled up on Rosedale, down the street from my mother's house.

"The next time I put you on a mission you're going to carry it out too," Monique warned with a threatening look as I climbed from the car and just like that, our new hustle was born.

Chapter 6

Frank

It seemed like we just started grabbing niggas out of nowhere. I mean, nobody was safe because nobody was off-limits. I even got Tybo and Hook to help me grab my sister Kim's babyfather after he threatened to put his hands on her. I couldn't kill him or nothing because he was my nephew's father. But that didn't stop me from throwing his ass into the trunk of his Maxima, duct-taped up and riding around with his ass until he shitted on himself and coughed up some money.

"Hold up for a second yo, turn the music down." I pointed at the stereo-system and looked up the basement stairs towards the door.

"What's up?" Tybo asked looking at me curiously as Hook hit the pause button on the Wu-Tang Clan 36 Chambers cassette tape.

"Nah, I could've sworn I heard something," I whispered listening closely for the squeaky sounds of the wooden first floor above.

"This nigga tripping," Hook shook his head. "That weed got you paranoid."

"Shhhh." I put my finger up to my lips to shut Hook up and continued to listen closely. "There it go again." I grabbed the .380 off the bed and shot to my feet, certain that I'd heard something. "Somebody's upstairs."

"Yo, I think I hear something too." Tybo perked up with his eyes darting all over the basement ceiling as if trying to pinpoint a certain location.

"You hear it yo?" I studied Tybo.

"Hold up." Tybo touched his chest. "That's my heart," Tybo confessed. "I can hear my heart beating," he joked making Hook laugh.

"Niggas always playing," I mumbled sitting back down on the bed just as the basement door eased open and I saw a foot carefully step on the first step.

I smiled to myself and slipped the .380 into my pocket because I knew it was Dakaron. He was the only nigga brave enough to wear some Wallebse's. But Tybo and Hook were so busy laughing and playing, trying to joke me that they didn't even see Dakaron until he scarred the hell out of them and damn near blew their high.

"That is what you silly niggas get." I laughed. "I told y'all I heard something."

"Fuck y'all niggas up to?" Dakaron inquired noticing the ski masks on the bed.

"Waiting on Maine so we can go hit that barbershop near Lexington Market I was telling you about," I revealed pulling the .380 back out of my pocket. "All the ballers be in there on Saturdays."

"Man, 6 might as well wait. Monique lining something real nice up for us now." Dakaron picked up one of the ski-masks and put it on. "I like this though."

"Yo, I'm not going to keep waiting on Monique. Especially when that nigga keep crumb feeding us," I argued honestly. "Plus, Maine already went to dent pull something."

"Yeah man, ain't nobody stunting that nigga Monique. He gonna fuck around and make a nigga grab him too," Tybo interjected jokingly as Dakaron shot him serious look.

The sound of a car horn interrupted us.

"That's probably Maine right there," I suggested walking over to peek out of the basement window. "Yeah, that him." I saw Jamaine sitting behind the wheel of a light blue Honda Accord.

"Let's do this baby." Hook stood up stuffing his gloves and ski mask into his pockets.

"What's up?" I turned to Dakaron. "You rolling or what?"

"Nah." He shook his head. "I'ma sit this one out and wait on Monique."

"Bet." I gave Dakaron some love and headed out the door behind Tybo and Hook.

"Let's ride," I encouraged, climbing into the stolen Honda.

"Where's Dak?" Tybo questioned looking towards the house.

"He's not coming," I replied. "He said he's going to wait on the move with Monique."

"That nigga crazy," Tybo said taking the words right out of my mouth. "Ain't no way in the world, I'ma pass up a sure thing for no crumbs."

"Aight, let's go." Hook tapped the back of Jamaine's seat. "That just means more for us."

The ride downtown was uneventful. We drove pass the barbershop twice to scope out the scene and sure enough that motherfucker was packed with ballers.

Hook and Tybo spotted the two Range Rovers and 500 Benz parked out front of the shop and went crazy with greed. They got all excited and started talking crazy. They wanted to just pull up outside of the shop and storm inside.

I didn't think that was good for various reasons.

Then, Jamaine thought that it would be a good idea to park the car near the projects, on the other side of Martin Luther King Boulevard and walk in. But that was too dangerous for me. First of all, Downtown Baltimore was like a breeding ground for police. Secondly, there was no way that we could go running across MLK with masks on and guns drawn. But if we didn't, that would put us at another disadvantage. Because too many people would see our faces.

In the end, we just decided to go with the original plan. Pull up down the street from the shop, mask up, wait until the coast was clear and stroll in. That way we didn't have to go far to get away and we never had to remove our ski masks.

By the time the coast was clear, there weren't as many people inside, but the dude with the Benz and one of the niggas with the Range were still present.

"Look at these little niggas man," a fat chump draped in jewelry alerted with a grin as we walked in masked up and began locking the door.

"Man, y'all motherfuckers better stop playing," one of the barber's warned as Tybo flipped the open sign to closed and started working on the blinds.

"This a stick up," I declared with my muffled voice looking around. "Check the bathroom!" I instructed gesturing towards Hook.

"What? Little shorty if you don't get the fuck out of here. I'ma get up and put my foot up your ass," another smooth cat threatened from his barber's chair and continued to get his shave.

I can only image how we must've looked strolling into the barbershop in probably the most colorful clothes stickup boys had ever worn. Not to mention the fact that, not one of us could've weighed more than a hundred and twenty-five pounds. We probably looked like a joke. But I assure you that we weren't nothing to be played with. Especially with guns in our possession.

"Oh, you think I'm playing, huh?" The smooth cat with the full bread snatched his barber's gown off and went to get up.

I closed the distance between us just as he got completely to his feet and began to crack slick again. I hit him so hard that he went over the chair. I may look and sound like a kid. But any nigga that I had ever put my hands on would tell you that I hit like a grown ass man.

40

"Anybody else think we're playing up in this bitch?" Jamaine paused to see if we had any more non-believers. "Aight then, start getting on the fucking floor!" He ordered and started snatching niggas out of their chairs.

Satisfied that we had everybody's attention now, I rolled the punch-drunk older cat over onto his stomach and ran his pockets. Then, I took his watch, pinky rings and necklace.

"Chump ass nigga," I learned over and mumbled into his ear before snatching the chain off of his neck. "You lucky I didn't knock your dumb ass out." I mushed his face into the floor and made my way over to the fat dude.

We ran through the entire shop with the quickness. Stripping customers and employees of their possessions. Fat boy was loaded too. I took at least ten grand from his pocket, another five out of his sock and a nice Rolex off his arm. Jamaine wanted to take his Benz. But I wasn't dying to joyride in a Benz that bad.

"Let me search it then," Jamaine begged.

"Nah man." I shook my head. "We don't got time for that," I lied.

The truth was that shit always went wrong when I want against my better judgement.

"Let's get everybody into the bathroom."

I already knew that there were no windows because my Uncle Cateyes had brought my cousin Moonie and I to the shop a few times to get our hair cut.

Once everybody was locked inside the bathroom, I told them not to come out for thirty minutes or I'd kill them all. On our way out, I had an idea and stopped to grab one of the barber boxes.

"What the hell are you doing yo? We gotta go." Hook stared at me like I was crazy as I began boxing up the first barber station.

"Hold up real quick." I continued tossing clippers, guards and all types of other barber stuff into the box. "Tybo, put all that shit over there in that bag right there." I pointed to the counter where all the combs, powder and things were.

"You is fucking crazy yo," Jamaine professed and headed for the door. "I'ma back the car up to the door."

Hook shook his head and looked towards the back of the barbershop.

"We're still out here!" He warned as someone rattled the door handle.

"Y'all niggas crying now. But y'all going to want me to cut y'all hair watch," I assured knowing that Hook's cheap ass hated spending money at the barbershop to get that big ass head shaped up.

Jamaine pulled up out front and started hitting the horn like a mad man.

"I'm gone yo." Hook peeped through the blinds. "This stupid nigga about to start making a scene."

I took a quick glance around the shop to make sure that I had gotten everything I needed to start my own backyard barbershop, grabbed a barber's smock off the coat rack and headed out the door behind Hook and Tybo. It wasn't a bad lick, if I had to say so myself.

Chapter 7

Frank

I wasn't exactly sure how my mother and sister found out that I was jacking niggas. I think it came out during the Oily situation. Especially after that nigga came back through Longwood with an AK-47 looking for Monique or any one of us. Whatever the case, they went the hell off. Moms even scraped up enough money to send me out to Florida to visit my father in federal prison. However, my Pops couldn't control me from the penitentiary, and he knew it. So, he just suggested that my mother enroll me in all types of big brother, scared straight programs and sent me home.

None of that program shit work either. I mean, I was already too gone. Already too addicted to the allure of the streets. Plus, I loved the power I felt when I had that biscuit in my hand.

Eventually, Cindy fell in line and my mother fell back. I mean, what else could they do? I knew they didn't want me in the streets but wasn't nobody else putting food on the table.

Before long, Monique came through with a nice little string in South Baltimore. Though not without cost. One thing I had learned about Monique was that he would feed our self-esteem to motivate our drive. Then, have us on a mission for his own benefit by the time we could count to five.

To make a long story short. Monique had us rob a nigga who turned out to be a cousin of his, that was fucking his baby mother.

After the home invasion, Monique decided not to line up anymore missions and suggested that we start hustling. I wasn't really feeling that. But of course, Dakaron always thought anything Monique said was golden and Jamaine was right along with him. Needless to say, we ended up opening up shop in South Baltimore, on Monique's cousin strip with the exact same color valves.

Monique said it was about money. But I knew that it was about power. It was Monique's way of showing his cousin that anybody who crossed him or got in his way, was fair game. Which was the main reason why after I found out that Tybo may have robbed a few of Monique's drug spots with Chrisco and Dewitt, I felt like Monique had something to do with his disappearance.

It just didn't make sense to me that right after we hit Monique's cousin, Tybo would come up missing. Dakaron keep trying to convince me, that I was tripping, and Monique had this theory about Oily. But I wasn't dumb. I hadn't forgotten the look on Dakaron's face when Tybo joked about grabbing Monique. I knew that Dakaron had probably mentioned it to him too.

The only thing that made me unsure was the fact that Oily disappeared too and nothing ever happened to Chrisco and Dewitt. Because I knew that Monique wasn't the type to take a slight to his gangster lightly.

Once we started jamming down South Baltimore, there was no looking back. Everybody was seeing paper, especially Monique. But I wasn't mad. The whole crew was eating. Plus, we were still pulling side licks with a dude name Big Al. He was an East Baltimore nigga with a fetish for home invasions and a wide repertoire of information on all the major hustlers, which made the moves so much easier.

"Ayo, I'ma need you to babysit for a minute." Dakaron came bouncing out of the stash house in a hurry.

"What? Man, hell no!" I leaned up off the car. "I been here all morning."

"I know, but Sweet Pea just paged me nine-one-one from the hospital," Dakaron explained coming towards me. "She had to take Delmonte to the emergency room."

44

What could I say about that? He had to go make sure his daughter was okay.

"Jamaine already on his way," Dakaron added as if he was reading my mind.

"You owe my big time nigga." I got out of the way.

"You know I got you dog," Dakaron assured.

"You finished getting everything together?" I inquired now more concerned about the work we had to move to another location because of an unexpected eviction notice and unnecessary heat.

"Yeah, everything's in the safe down the basement behind the furnace." Dakaron looked towards the house. "I left the biscuits underneath the living room couch."

"When they gotta be out?"

"By sometime early next week," Dakaron replied.

"Why don't we just move that shit this weekend?" I suggested, ready to just head home and lay down.

"I don't want to chance it. The spot too hot. Ain't no telling when the knockers might run up in that motherfucker," Dakaron rationalized. "Plus, I'm not dyin' to have a safe full of drugs just sitting."

"Where Miss Nia and her sister at?" I looked towards the house.

"I don't know where the hell Brontay went, but Miss Nia upstairs in the shower."

"I'm telling you yo, you owe me," I assured to make sure Dakaron understood that I would be cashing my favor in.

"I got you nigga." Dakaron opened the car door. "I'll hook you up with Samone's sister Margo or something."

Dakaron knew that the mention of Margo's pretty ass was enough to stop my resistance. There weren't too many females who could bring a smile to my face like Keisha or Margo. Everybody knew that I had a type. It was just that very few women fit it. But I'd been sweet on Margo since the day, Samone introduced her to me on her aunt's front.

Not only was Margo my type, she was caramel brown and thick just like Keisha. To top it off though, her beauty matched her sense of humor.

"Say that's your word?" I demanded knowing that Dakaron played about a lot of things, but his word wasn't one of them.

"That's my word," Dakaron declared sliding behind the wheel of his car.

"Say no more." I nodded stepping back. "I'ma hold it down," I added with every intention of holding him to his word.

Dakaron smiled, started the car and pulled off.

About five minutes after Dakaron pulled off, Miss Nia stuck her head out of the second floor window and began calling for him.

"Dak's gone," I revealed getting up off the steps before stepping out far enough for her to see me over the porch roof. "I'm the only one out here."

"Okay, lock the door and run up here real quick," She insisted.

"I got to wait for Jamaine," I explained.

"It's not going to take that long." Miss Nia disappeared from the window before I could respond.

I'ma just go ahead and be straight up with you. Miss Nia was another female that I was sweet on. I mean, to say that she was bad would be an understatement. Miss Nia was pretty like my sister Pooch, Thick like Cindy and gangster like Kim. Not to mention she was an old head. The only problem with Miss Nia was that she got high on the low.

I locked the front door and bounced up the stairs to see exactly what Miss Nia wanted. "Miss Nia!" I called out heading for her bedroom.

"Miss Nia!" I called out again once I noticed that the bedroom was empty.

"I'm in the bathroom!" She hollered out.

I turned around and headed down the hallway towards the bathroom. "Miss Nia," I tapped on the cracked bathroom door gently.

"Open the door and come in," she instructed.

"I'm coming in," I alerted slowly pushing the door open.

When I stepped into that steam filled room, I was met by the most magnificent sight I'd ever seen in my life. Sitting comfortably in a bathtub full of bubbles was Miss Nia. And just when I thought that it couldn't get any more beautiful, Miss Nia slowly stood up and handed me a washcloth.

I stood there frozen as bubbles cascaded down her curvaceous body.

Everything on Miss Nia from her full breast to her thick, gapped thighs was flawless. I mean, this women looked twice as good in the bathtub. Her pussy had just enough hair to show off her pretty pussy-lips and her small waist and lower back seemed to just melt into her soft hips and bubble-butt.

Miss Nia was straight up gorgeous. She looked as if she'd stepped off the pages of a Jet Magazine – straight beauty of the week material. "I need you to wash my back," Miss Nia turned around to reveal the nicest ass I'd ever seen on any woman.

My heart started beating real fast as I began to sweat. I was fucked up. My mind went blank and all I could do was stare. *She looks like an older version of Keisha*, I thought.

"What are you waiting for?" Miss Nia glanced at me over her shoulder.

I shook my head to snap out of my trance. Then, I bit my lip, carefully dipped the washcloth into the hot, bubble bath water and began cautiously washing Miss Nia's back.

By now, my dick was harder than a frozen pack of Now-and-Laters, so I had to turn my body awkwardly to hide it.

I slowly ran my eyes up and down Miss Nia's exquisite body, memorizing every inch. Each freckle, each curve and every tattoo. *Damn.* I licked my lips and took her in from the nape of her neck to the small of her back. I was in heaven as I gently washed Miss Nia's back.

When I felt Miss Nia's body shiver and saw the goosebumps on her on her skin after I ran the washcloth gently over her ass cheeks, I smiled.

"What are you doing?" Miss Nia looked back over her shoulder again and I instantly turned my head shyly and looked at the bathroom wall.

"Look at me," Miss Nia encouraged.

I took a quick glance and looked back towards the flower covered wallpaper.

"No," Miss Nia snapped. "Look at me good."

"I'm looking," I lied after stealing another glance.

"I'ma tell all your friends you were scared to look at me," Miss Nia teased with a giggle.

"I'm not scared," I declared forcing myself to stare at her.

I can't lie, I was scared to death. I'd never been in a situation like this before. I was used to dealing with girls my age or fiends. Females who knew I had something that they wanted. But this was different. Miss Nia was a grown ass woman. A grown ass, super sexy, aggressive woman at that.

"Wash me all the way up then," Miss Nia challenged bending over in front of me to grab the other side of the bathtub.

Again, I froze up. Miss Nia's pussy was so close that I could smell it. It was phat like a blowfish with curly lips. I dipped the washcloth into the bubble bath again and slowly wiped up the back of Miss Nia's tender thighs.

"Unh uhn, get my pussy and ass too," Miss Nia directed arching her back so that her ass cheeks opened up to expose more of her pretty pussy and ruffled asshole.

I was on cloud nine and my dick was about to burst through my jeans. I washed Miss Nia's butt cheeks first. Then, I took my time washing her pussy and asshole. I intentionally used my fingers to penetrate her pretty pussy a few times while I was washing her up. She was hot, slimy and sticky inside like a freshly baked bowl of banana pudding.

Miss Nia slid one of her hands in between her legs and began playing with her own pussy, teasing her pretty, pink clitoris. "You see that button right there." She hung her head low enough to see my face between her legs as she used two fingers to hold her pussy lips open.

I shook my head because I couldn't speak.

"Lick it for me," she instructed almost as if she was out of breath.

I gradually leaned forward until my face was between Miss Nia's ass cheeks. Then, I slowly extended my tongue until I felt her smooth, velvety clitoris with the tip of my tongue.

"Lick it!" She demanded, and I complied.

I didn't really know what I was doing. But Miss Nia appeared to be enjoying it. At least she kept crying out for more and telling me not to stop as her legs continued to shake.

"Take your clothes off," Miss Nia straightened back up and turned around detaching her tasty pussy from my mouth.

She didn't have to tell me twice. By now, I was horny as shit and would've done anything she told me to do without question.

I wiped my mouth and quickly got out of my clothes.

"I told my sister that your little ass had a big dick," Miss Nia confessed the moment my billy club popped out of my boxers.

"That motherfucker long too." She took my dick into her soft hand and began slowly stroking it.

I was already going out of my mind when Miss Nia, suddenly stepped out of the tub without warning and fell to her knees without releasing me.

"Ohhhh, and it's thick." She smiled up at me devilishly and kissed the head. "I'm about to fuck your life up, sugar," Miss Nia warned before going to work.

When she deep throated me, I was no more good. I wanted to marry Miss Nia. I didn't give a fuck how old she was.

I mean, Miss Nia did things to my dick with her mouth that could only be describe as debauchery. She used a lot of saliva, twisted her hands like she playing with a telescope and sucked on the tip like she had a popsicle in her mouth.

She basically ruined me for all other women. Because if a bitch couldn't follow that, I didn't even want to waste my time.

Good God Almighty, I thought when I finally began to stretch Miss Nia's tight pussy open. Pussy that hot, sticky and deep should be bottled up and sold over the counter. I tried to take my time because I wanted it to last. But man, after about four, long, deep strokes I was cumming.

It felt like my body was going into a state of shock. First, my legs buckled. Then, I got dizzy. After that, I just started seeing stars and shit. It became hard for me to breathe.

I mean, it felt so good that I didn't realize that I was being choked out until my eyes began to roll into the back of my head.

What the fuck? I snapped out of submission and went straight into survive mode.

I instantly started struggling, forcing my fingers in between the thick forearm around my neck, trying to pry myself free.

"What the fuck are doing?" Miss Nia spat. "Let him go!" Miss Nia commanded before I heard and felt her slapping the arm of the motherfucker who was trying to put me to sleep.

"Brontay, grab this bitch!" The nigga who had me in the chokehold directed.

"You can't kill him," Miss Nia argued while I was going in and out of consciousness. "We still need him to open the safe," she added a second before I crumbled to the floor, gasping for air.

"Now, look what you did," Miss Nia barked. "How the hell are we going to get to shit?"

"Bitch, go put some fucking clothes on," the male voice advised with an attitude. "You in here fucking that little nigga!"

"Tay-Tay if you don't get the hell out of my face," Miss Nia warned as I rolled on the floor choking, still trying to catch my breath.

"Your ass shouldn't have took all day getting here. Now watch out!" Miss Nia complained.

"Brontay, check his pockets," Miss Nia directed. "See if he got something on him."

"Man, bitch watch out," the male voice fired a second before I was hit in the face with warm bathwater. "Wake your little ass up nigga!"

I coughed, choked and spit because some of the bath water went into my mouth.

"What's the combination to that safe downstairs shorty?" The big nigga stood over top of me aggressively.

"You think y'all going to get away with this shit nigga? You's a dead man," I threatened between coughs, sitting halfway up. I opened my eyes in time to see Brontay going through my pockets.

"Shut your little ass up before I break your jaw," the big, old head Miss Nia referred to as Tay-Tay threatened yanking me up off the floor.

"What's the safe combination?" Tay-Tay jacked me up.

"Fuck you nigga," I hulk spit in his face and grinned.

If I was dying, I wasn't going out like no bitch. Trapped off in a stash house with my tail tucked between my legs.

Tay-Tay curled me over with a solid gut punch before tossing me out into the hallway. "Oh, you wanna play tough, huh? "He smiled storming towards me again. "I got something for your little ass."

"Hold up man, I'll give you the combination." I assured. Pulling my jeans up. All I needed to do was stall until Jamaine showed up or get downstairs to the couch. "Just take me to the safe. I got to look at it."

Tay-Tay grabbed me by my collar and smiled. Then, he began dragging me towards the stairs. I wasn't sure if he was going to toss me down them or not, but I didn't put up any resistance.

"No! "Miss Nia shouted. "That's what he wants. They got guns on the first floor."

"Damn, I forgot all about them guns in the front room," Brontay confessed. "Where are they at?"

"Underneath the couch by the window," Miss Nia revealed.

Shit! I sighed as Brontay dipped down the stairs. I had to come up with another plan because Miss Nia had just saved Tay-Tay's ass.

I still trying to figure out my next move when Brontay came running back up the stairs. "Jamaine's at the door!" She alerted.

"Fuck!" Miss Nia fired looking around. "Keep his ass quiet, maybe they won't know we're here."

"He already fucking seen me," Brontay admitted.

"How the hell he see you? Why the hell you let him see you?" Miss Nia started looking around like she didn't know what to do next.

"There aren't any curtains up bitch remember?" Brontay retorted.

"Tie him up," Miss Nia directed scrabbling into the bathroom to grab her tennis.

"Where the guns at?" Tay-Tay inquired stepping over top of me, moving towards the steps.

"Still underneath the couch," Brontay replied. "I couldn't grab them in his face."

"I'ma go grab 'em myself," Tay-Tay uttered. "Keep an eye on this little nigga," he instructed moving towards the stairs. "And find something to tie him up with."

I saw my opening and took it. I jumped up off the floor and ran down the hallway into the front bedroom with Tay-Tay and Brontay on my heels.

I dashed into the room looking for any type of weapon. Seeing none, I jumped across the bed and dived right through the second floor window.

The thing about the houses on Ashton Street, was the fact that they had front porch roofs. So after I crash through the glass I landed right on the roof and started screaming for Jamaine as Tay-Tay tried to pull me back inside.

I rolled onto my back and kicked Tay-Tay right in the face. "Bust that big bitch dog!" I yelled looking off the roof at Jamaine.

Everything was happening so fast that I hadn't even realized that Tay-Tay had released my leg and ducked out of the window until Hook waved for me to jump down.

I rolled off the roof and hung jump down just in time to see Tay-Tay storming down into the living room to flip the couch over.

"Go!" I broke for the car with Jamaine and Hook on my ass and jump inside.

Jamaine got behind the wheel and sped off before Tay-Tay could get outside.

"Ayo, what the fuck was that about?" Hook asked looking over his shoulder as Jamaine flew up the block.

"I'ma kill that junky ass nigga," I declared looking back one more time before Jamaine made a left. "They set me up to get robbed!"

"Ayo, you're bleeding like shit." Jamaine looked over at me.

I looked down at myself. I hadn't even realized that my side and shoulder was leaking. There was also a gash in my leg.

"How the fuck you get caught down bad like that?" Hook inquired but there was no way in the world that I was going to tell him about the shit with Miss Nia. I would never hear the end of it.

First they would clown me because I ate the pussy. It wouldn't even matter how bad she was. Then, they would ride me for slipping up and letting some women get the drop on me. And I just knew that they would've a field day if they found out that I had nut running all down my other leg.

"I don't know," I lied. "I went upstairs to use the bathroom and some big nigga jumped out of the closet with a knife."

"Where the fuck was Miss Nia and Brontay?" Jamaine asked.

"I told you they were with it. That's why we got to go arm up and come back," I explained. "The safe still in the basement."

"Man, that safe going to be long gone," Jamaine said. "Especially if Miss Nia and Brontay with that shit. Both of them old bitches gangsters."

"Nah," I challenged. "They aren't moving until next week some time."

"They may not have to be out until next week. But they're leaving today," Jamaine corrected. "Why you think we were grabbing the safe? All their shit already gone."

I thought about what Jamaine said for a moment. He was right, Miss Nia and Brontay had been emptying the house all week. "Man, I'm still strapping up and going back down there." I exclaimed still in my feelings.

One thing for sure and two things for certain though. Rather I was able to catch up with Miss Nia and her shiesty sister or not, I'd never be caught without my biscuit again.

Chapter 8

Frank

By the end of 1996, we were doing our thing. We had expanded and basically locked Sandtown down. Of course, I never did catch up to Miss Nia or her sister, Brontay again. But I did run across the big nigga Tay-Tay when we first branched out into Sandtown. Gave that nigga, a good old fashion beat down with a baseball bat too.

The only issues we seemed to be having now were from Quincy. He was finally home, but he was also off the chain. It was like he felt as if he had to make up for lost time. If that wasn't enough, for some strange reason, this nigga loved to play cowboy. It got to the point where nobody wanted to give him a biscuit. Because he was always doing some simple shit.

"You got to fall back sometimes dog," I pleaded with Quincy as we stood outside of the small, body shop on Bloomingdale waiting for Monkey-Wrench to finish working on one of my dirt bikes. He was having a lot of unnecessary static with Paul-Paul over nothing.

"Why you defending that nigga against me dog? We come up outta of the sandbox together," Quincy argued.

"I'm not defending nobody. You're my nigga. I'm just telling you what's right. Sandtown is his backyard," I clarified.

The crazy thing was that I didn't even trust Paul-Paul myself when Jamaine first decided to bring him to the table. Now, I realized that he was solid.

"And it's not just Paul-Paul," I maintained. "You and Dak need to kill that shit y'all on too."

"Here we go with the Captain Save-A-Hoe shit."
Quincy looked off and took a deep breath. "I knew you didn't
just pick me up to come around here and get this bike."

"See, there you go," I warned, knowing Quincy knew
that he was being disrespectful. "You need to get off that
bullshit nigga!"

"Nah, Dak need to get off that bullshit. He been on
some bitch shit ever since that Willie Bates incident," Quincy
retorted but we both knew that it was bigger than him not
showing up for a robbery. It was about Venus and how she
had his nose wide open.

"Y'all niggas just need to sit down and talk like men," I
suggested as Monkey-Wrench used the chain to lift the
garage door up so that I could grab my dirt bike. "After all,
it's a new year and Dak's birthday next month."

"He the one acting like he got his big hat on," Quincy
complained.

"Well, somebody got to be the bigger man." I climbed
onto my KX120 and kicked the starter. "Take my car back to
the house," I instructed handing Quincy my keys. "Just think
about what I said dog."

"Yeah, aight," Quincy mumbled nonchalantly.

"See you back at the house," I said cranking the throttle
before taking off dawn the alley.

Chapter 9

Frank

I was driving down North Avenue in route to my mother's house, listening to Quincy vent about Venus and how he thought that she was still creeping off with Dakaron. And even though I didn't believe that it was true, all it did for me was confirm the fact that bitches always thought that they were slick. It was the reason why I didn't trust them. They would cheat on a nigga for nothing, lie right to your face about anything, and leave you for dead the first time something better came along.

"You know Dak wouldn't do no cruddy shit like that," I defended Dakaron because I knew that he wasn't that nigga. Dakaron did a lot of wild shit. But fucking over his friends wasn't one of them. He took his honor extremely serious.

"Man, that nigga keep giving me this wild ass smile every time I mention Venus name," Quincy explained. "I'm telling you yo, if I catch a nigga out there fucking with my girl, I'ma melt his shit like a stick of butter."

I took my eyes off the road for a split second to glance over at Quincy. He couldn't be serious. I mean, I knew Venus was bad, and bragged about how good the sex was. But damn, I didn't think my nigga would be ready to put a motherfucker to sleep behind her. Now, I was curious.

"You tripping," I mumbled wondering if love was starting to blind my nigga.

"I ain't tripping. A lot of shit just changed since I been gone," Quincy spat falling silent as I pulled up in front of my mother's house and parked.

When I climbed out of the car, it seemed like everybody was watching me. I said something to Quincy to make sure that I wasn't geeking. But he brushed me off so, I just headed on inside.

The moment I stepped through the front door and saw my mother storming towards me with a butcher's knife in her hand, I got on guard.

"Whoa Ma! It's me!" I jumped back and snatched my hat off real quick so that she could get a good look at my face.

"Watch out," she demanded like she was on a mission.

"Hold up ma, chill." I laughed nervously, carefully grabbing her arm. "What's going on?"

"Go look at your sister's face," she declared pointing towards the kitchen. "That's what the fuck is going on."

"Aight, ma," I looked past her towards the kitchen. "I still need you to chill out," I advised reaching for the knife. Because if I didn't know anything else, I knew that my moms would kill something.

Glancing at Quincy, I said, "Go find out what's going on out there for me Cuz," I instructed before guiding my mother towards the kitchen.

When we got to the kitchen, Cindy was bent over the sink, cursing up a storm, trying to tend to her swollen face.

"Ayo, what the fuck happen to your face?" I rushed to my sister's side concerned, looking at my mother.

There were tears running down Cindy's cheeks and her nose was busted.

"Cindy, you don't hear me talking to you?" I snapped when she ignored my question. "What happened to your face?"

"Ma," I turned to my mother. "What's going on? What happened to Cindy's face?"

"Some nigga put his fucking hands on her," my mother fired.

"What nigga?" I demanded to know, ready to kill something myself now.

"Some nigga around the corner name, Shorty Bullock or something," my mother disclosed, and my head instantly began to spin.

I had to sit down for a moment. Shorty Bullock was a larger than life, North and Longwood legend who I'd grew up admiring. So, I didn't want to fuck around and do nothing too disrespectful. *Cindy must've done something crazy, I thought* because Shorty Bullock wasn't the type to just jump out there and put his hands on somebody's peoples. He of all people knew what that could bring.

Still, Cindy was my sister, and nobody fucked with my sisters and got away with it. Neighborhood legends or otherwise.

I looked around the kitchen and noticed my little sister, Demecka for the first time. She was over in the corner, hiding behind the trashcan. She looked so scared that it made my blood boil. I got up and slowly walked over to her and asked her if she was okay.

"I'm scared Franklin," Demecka whispered, breaking my heart. "That man hit Cindy and yelled at me."

"Come here." I pulled Demecka into my arms and held her tightly.

Shorty Bullock was going to answer for his sin against my family.

I thought about something my mother used to always say and knew what I had to do. I was the man of the house and I had to make sure that my family was safe. Especially the women.

"Ayo, Cindy got into it with Shorty Bullock." Quincy bounced into the kitchen with a strange look on his face.

"Yeah, I know." I informed.

"I tried to holler at him. But he around there on some gangster shit. Talking about Cindy disrespected his baby mother."

My mother's words echoed in my head again. "Any man who puts his hands on a woman deserves to have his ass beat."

I kissed my little sister on the forehead, took one look at the women I had vowed to protect and headed for the door.

"I tried to tell that nigga that Cindy was your sister, but he acted like he didn't give fuck!" Quincy explained following me out the front door.

"Just show me where that nigga at," I ordered because I knew for a fact that Shorty Bullock already knew that Cindy was my sister. The nigga used to drop money off at my house for Efrem.

"Come on. He around there near the hole on Longwood." Quincy lead the way.

"You got the biscuit on you?" Quincy peeped over his shoulder, and I just gave him the nod. Ever since the little South Baltimore situation I kept the heat on me. But I didn't think that it was going to come to that. After all, Shorty Bullock was one of the neighborhood OGs who'd schooled me up.

The situation with Cindy had to be a misunderstanding. Some female shit that had gotten out of hand. All Shorty Bullock had to do was apologize to my sister and throw her a few dollars and all could be forgiven.

When we arrived at the hole, I instantly got a bad feeling. I strolled over to Shorty Bullock and asked him to step off with me real quick. However, this nigga started making a scene, trying to clown me.

"Oh, you got a few dollars now. So you think you're a big boy huh?" Shorty Bullock grinned. "I remember when your little dirty ass was wearing Efrem's old clothes for days."

"What's up yo, what are you trying to do?" Quincy whispered in my ear.

I took a deep breath and stared at Shorty Bullock. I couldn't believe he was trying to carry me like a lame. "Just let me holler at you real quick like a man," I pleaded.

"Oooohh, yo said, let him holler at you like a man," One of Shorty Bullock's little, dick-riding, spectators instigated.

"Come on dog," Quincy tapped my arm. "Yo, ain't got no rap."

"I'm trying to keep this shit from going somewhere else." I mumbled more to myself than anybody making Shorty Bullock's audience laugh.

"Nigga's find that funny?" Shorty Bullock silenced everybody with a look, getting up off the steps. "You threatening me, Little Frank?" Shorty Bullock stepped into my personal space. "Because it can really get tragic, nigga!"

"Man, you gotta check that nigga," Quincy encouraged in my ear trying to gas me up.

I knew Quincy was right. But now wasn't the time nor the place.

It was broad daylight outside and Longwood was loaded with people. "I wasn't threatening you, yo." I humbled myself and took a step back. "I was just trying to talk to you on the one-on-one that's all."

"Yeah, well nigga, kick rocks," Shorty Bullock fired mushing me in the face.

I charged towards Shorty Bullock, but niggas got in between us.

"What nigga?" Shorty Bullock barked. "What the fuck are you going to do?"

I locked eyes with Shorty Bullock. If he was anything like the nigga they said that he used to be, he had to know that I was going to knock his head off the first chance I got. For the moment though, I humbled myself.

"I heard that big homie." I smirked, nodded my head and began backing up.

"Your sister got more heart then you nigga," Shorty Bullock teased as I turned around to walk away. "That's why I punched her in her fucking mouth! The next time I see you though I'ma slap your brains out."

I can't honestly say what happened or what Shorty Bullock had triggered in me. But it was like in that moment, I lost it. All the anger and frustration I felt bubbled to the surface, and before I knew what was happening, I zigzagged past everybody, drew the .357 Bulldog and shot Shorty Bullock directly in his face.

"Now that's how you suppose to check a nigga!" Quincy exclaimed after Shorty Bullock's head exploded, and his body crumbled to the ground.

I stepped over top of Shorty Bullock and looked down as everybody scattered. He didn't seem so large now with the center of his face knocked in and the entire back of his head hanging out.

"If any one of you bitches talk to the police, I'ma come back and kill your whole family," Quincy warned grabbing me by the arm. "Let's go dog."

We ran back to the car and got the fuck out of there because I didn't want to make my mother's house hot.

I flew up Rosedale, jumped on Bloomingdale, hit North Avenue and bucked a left on Northern Parkway. Then, we headed towards Quincy's sister crib.

It was like all the pain I'd been feeling since Tybo's disappearance was gone. The fact that I'd just blown a nigga's brain out in the middle of the day, on a crowded dope strip didn't even register.

"Ayo, you folded that old nigga!" Quincy broke the silence. "Got right up on him like, boom!" Quincy used his hand to imitate the way I had shot Shorty Bullock in the head. "That shit was graphic too. I'm talking about that nigga's brains, and everything came out the back of his shit," Quincy fired excitedly with a smile. "Did you see those niggas faces when his shit popped out? They..."

I hadn't even realized that he was talking because I was so zoned out.

When we got to Big April's spot, she wanted to know what was going on because motherfuckers were already talking. She had gotten two or three phone calls about how Quincy and I had shot up Longwood over some junky buying drugs from another hustler.

"Man, motherfuckers lying," Quincy declared rushing me towards the bathroom. "Plus, we been here with you all day remember?"

"Y'all asses ain't been here all day!" Big April corrected quickly.

"You sure?" Quincy questioned. "I could I've sworn I gave you five hundred dollars."

"Oh yeah, I am starting to remember." Big April agreed and Quincy smiled.

Inside the bathroom, Quincy instructed me to place my arms over the sink, so that he could make sure that I didn't have any gunpowder residue on my forearms and hands. But when I did this crazy nigga dropped his pants and pulled his dick out.

"Ayo, what the fuck kind of freak shit is you on nigga?" I looked at Quincy like he was insane.

I knew he had been locked up, but I'd never heard about no faggy shit. "Fuck you on up in here?"

"Man, shut your dumb ass up and hold your arms over the sink nigga!" Quincy snapped grabbing his dick as he stepped forward. "The acid in piss is the only thing that can remove gun powder residue without a trace," he explained.

I studied Quincy's face for a moment, trying to read him because I wasn't sure if I believed what he was saying or not. Him and Dakaron played so much that I didn't know when to take them niggas serious.

I shook my head and took a step back. "You're not pissing on me, Cuz."

"Aight cool." Quincy hunched his shoulders. "Let the police get it off of you."

That got my attention. I definitely didn't want to get caught down bad with gunpowder residue all over me if I got grabbed for a homicide.

I stepped back up to the sink, extended my arms and turned my head. "Cuz, I swear to God, if I find out this shit ain't true, I'ma kill your dumb ass."

"It's true yo, trust me." Quincy started laughing. "I learned it when I was locked up. My man Butt from Park Heights put me down when he was fighting his bodies."

"Nah yo." I pulled my arms back again. "Why the fuck you keep laughing?"

"I'm tripping off you," Quincy replied with a smile. "You always think somebody playing. Now come on, in case the police fuck around and show up."

Again, I extended my arms above the sink and turned my head. This time I closed my eyes and waited. When Quincy's hot piss hit my arms, I cringed. I felt like a freak in a low-budget porno.

"Rub it in nigga!" Quincy ordered and I complied.

After I basically took a golden shower in Big April's sink, I grabbed one of the new outfits I'd purchased for Quincy when he first came home and hopped in shower while he went to get rid of the .357 Bulldog.

I planned on checking into the piss theory as soon as I got a chance.

Chapter 10

Frank

The murder of Shorty Bullock didn't blow up in my face the way I thought it would. Especially since I'd knocked his shit loose in front of every bit of twenty witnesses. Instead, the streets bowed down to me because of who Shorty Bullock was. There were also so many stories circulating that it wasn't even funny. Of course, Monique had to put his hand in the mix too. Whatever the case, I was in the clear. At least for the moment.

I did, however, get snatched up and taken downtown for questioning by a couple of overzealous detectives, who for some reason, thought that they were slicker than me. Once they realized that their little good cop, bad cop, get me to tell on myself tactics weren't going to work, they threatened to nail me to the cross and released me to my mother's custody.

After that, I laid low for a while. I wasn't hiding or anything. I just wasn't as easy to see as I usually was. Especially around the way. I started playing South Baltimore a lot more heavier. Even finally got to hook up with Margo.

The only time I left Pigtown to go back up the way was for Dakaron's sixteenth birthday party and somebody ended up putting my sister's old boyfriend Efrem on Fox.

The streets immediately started whispering about me having something to do with it, because of the shit with Shorty Bullock. Motherfuckers thought that I was on some bullshit. Knocking off all the OGs for territory.

If that wasn't enough, Quincy had the nerve to steal from us and start rolling with the same niggas we'd been having static with since I could remember.

It all started when Dakaron got jammed up for a Glock-19 while I was out of town in early May. Still, nobody could've told me that all hell was about to break loose.

I remembered Jamaine and I picking Dakaron up outside of the jail after Quincy had taken everything out of the crew safe. Dakaron couldn't believe it. We argued, disagreed about the course of action and got nowhere.

In the end, I assured Dakaron that Quincy was dead to me and prayed that he stayed his distance.

Things were cool for a minute. Then, Quincy showed his true colors again when he stood by and allowed some little dusty hood rats to bring Chanae a move. Of course, I wanted to see Quincy about that in the worst way. But again, Dakaron went to bat for him.

"I don't know what it is about that bitch ass nigga that keep stopping you from letting me put the dirt on him. But you need to check that shit," I argued.

"He's family, dog," Dakaron confessed.

"Family don't do the shit that nigga did, Cuz," I retorted thinking about all the fuck shit Quincy had done. "And I know he didn't give that bread back nigga!"

"Yeah nigga, you aren't slick." I added when Dakaron looked at me surprised before explaining how I knew that Quincy hadn't given that money back.

Eventually, I convinced Dakaron that if Dana and them had to go, Quincy needed to go also. After all, he was the biggest threat of them all because he knew how and where to hit us all where it would hurt the most.

I would never forget the night we followed Quincy and them from the club. I watched from the car as Dakaron and Jamaine crushed Quincy and Chuck. It was bittersweet. I mean, on one hand it hurt. But on the other, it had to be done.

It seemed like things cooled down for a minute. Then, niggas ambushed Dakaron and tried to kill him outside of some bitch he was fucking house. Dakaron survived, but man, the damage was done. I could see the pain in my brother's eyes when I picked him up from the hospital and drove him to his mother spot. I would never forget the magical words he uttered before he exited the car. He said we're going at niggas. That was music to my ears. A wounded snake wasn't much different than a healthy one. They were both venomous and could still strike at any moment.

I rubbed my hands together excitedly as Dakaron climbed out of the car because I had been dying to lay my murder game down again.

I picked Dakaron up first thing in the morning and got straight to business.

We hit Poosie first. Then, went to clean up Dana and them. The curveball came when Monique summoned Dakaron to Dru Hill Park and told him to bring us along.

When we got to the park and climbed into Monique's new Benz. He instantly began talking some bullshit that I wasn't trying to hear at all.

He wanted us to squash the South Baltimore, Pigtown beef. Said it was causing too much heat.

Come to find out, Monique not only knew Bulleteye-Ty and Dana. But he was hitting them with work also. That wasn't enough for me to let up on the gas though. Them niggas had taken a shot at the throne and for that, they had to fall.

Monique and I went back and forth for a minute, until I had enough. "I'm not letting that shit go!" I got out of the Benz and slammed the door. Monique was out of his mind if he thought that he could tell me what to do.

I wasn't Dakaron. No nigga dictated my actions. I made my own decisions. I walked over to sit on the hood of the car as Dakaron and Jamaine continued to chop it up with Monique. *That nigga got me fucked up if he thinks that he can call shots for me.* I shook my head.

About ten minutes later, Jamaine climbed out of the Benz and made his way over to the car.

"What's up?" I inquired.

"Nah, yo wanted to holler at Dak real quick," Jamaine replied leaning up against the car beside me.

"That nigga a possum Cuz, but Dak so concerned with being his protege that he keeps sleeping on him," I vented.

"He may be right though yo. "Jamaine looked at me. "At the end of the day, it's about getting money."

I didn't reply to Jamaine's statement. I just stared at him and shook my head. Monique had him wrapped up in his web too.

It may have been about money for them. But it would always be about principle for me. Because I always valued principle over profit. A nigga couldn't buy me.

When Dakaron finally climbed from the car, I pulled straight up on him. I wanted him to know that I wasn't paying that shit Monique was talking about no mind. "I ain't squashing the beef!" I declared. "Not after the shit them niggas pulled."

For the first time, Dakaron agreed with me and decided to go against Monique's wishes.

"Ayo, you know that's going to change y'all relationship. So you're going to have to be careful around that nigga, Cuz," I warned. "Yo, the type to kill anything he can't control."

"I'm just not going to even tell him," Dakaron rationed like it was nothing, but I knew better. Monique wasn't stupid. He was one of them type of old niggas, who would do just about anything to survive and stay on top.

"Still, be careful, Cuz," I cautioned as Dakaron reached for his pager.

"I need a phone," Dakaron slid the pager in his pocket opening the driver's door. "Sweet Pea just paged me nine-one-one."

I slide off the hood of the car and hopped in the passenger's1st seat as Jamaine climbed into the back. I decided to leave the shit with Monique alone for now. At least until we found out what was going on with Dakaron's baby mother.

Chapter 11

Frank

The Park Heights indictment fucked a lot of dudes up. First, Dakaron's brother and them were swept up. Then, the feds started kicking in all kinds of doors. The entire operation eventually lead back to a high profile, informant that the feds had put up in a half million-dollar, fourteenth floor, waterfront, Beacon Condominium in Canton. During the initial hearing, after we poured into the Edward A. Garmatz United States Courthouse, it was discovered that the government's confidential informant had illegally placed a magnetic GPS tracker underneath Dakaron's brother truck to monitor his movement.

"Ayo, that shit was like a fucking movie in there," Jamaine exclaimed as we walked out of the federal courthouse. "I ain't never seen no shit like that."

"They're going to try to smash your brother and them, Cuz," I assured thinking about all the crazy charges the federal prosecutor had read off in the courtroom.

"Yeah, I know," Dakaron agreed. "That's why they hit them with that Rico Act. But Tauwn already got a trick for that shit. That's why my cousin Little Phil confessed to the murders." Dakaron continued. "All he worried about now is my daughter's grandmother, Creola."

"Ayo, your cousin a fucking soldier!" Jamaine declared. "Ain't no way I'm eating a murder for nobody."

"Nigga that's just what my bloodline breeds," Dakaron professed proudly. "That's how that Truesdale pedigree is cut."

"Niggas wouldn't even have to do all that, if that wild, bitch ass, rat nigga wasn't crawling underneath cars and shit like Robo-cop," Jamaine argued.

"I don't even see how they can use that shit," I revealed honestly. "That's why I'm telling you. If your brother and them take that shit to trial, they're going to fuck around and beat it."

"Man, niggas don't be beating no feds yo," Jamaine contended.

"Yeah, that is because they don't be trying them bitches!" I disputed.

I wasn't trying to get into a debate about it. But it was widely known that most dudes who went with the feds choose to plea out instead of going to trial and fighting.

"Yeah, but even still, let's forget about the rats my brother and them already know about," Dakaron interjected. "It's going to be the ones who they aren't aware of that's going to cause the most concern. The ones the feds haven't drew out of their holes yet. Them the ones who can cause more problems, even for us," Dakaron explained. "Because they're the ones who will know the day to day."

"Yeah, you're right about that." I shook my head. "It's probably best yo and them do take the dive and get out of the way."

Jamaine, Dakaron and I hung out downtown for a while. We even slid over to Baltimore Street and paid one of the bouncers to let us slip in the side door of a popular strip club. And man let me tell you, Baltimore had some of the baddest strippers on the face of the earth.

Yes, I'd heard about places like Atlanta and Miami, but I had to admit. If they had bitches that were half as bad as the ones I saw that night on stage, then, I needed to move there.

There was still a lot of tension between Monique and I but I wasn't stunting his old ass. I was too focused on stalking my next victim down South Baltimore.

Dakaron did say that Monique asked him a lot of off-the-wall questions, like he was fishing for information. Which made me wonder if Jamaine was playing the fifty.

Especially since, he began hanging out with Monique on the regular, promoting his visions and shit all of a sudden.

Dakaron thought that I was tripping, so I left it alone. Plus, everything seemed to be going good.

Then, Dakaron got ambushed again. Only this time, he was left for dead outside of his trade school. Of course, I didn't waste no time confronting that nigga Monique about his little peace agreement. I also hinted at the fact, that if my nigga died behind his bullshit, nobody was off limits. Especially, not his old ass.

Monique tried to talk me down. He started talking about Dakaron's brother and a possible ongoing investigation. He even tried to convince me to sit down with the Pigtown niggas. But I wasn't trying to hear none of that shit. The time for talking had passed and I was out for blood.

I called an emergency meeting with Hook and Jamaine, so that we could put our heads together and come up with a plan of action. Because retribution was a must. Then, we recruited a few of the Sandtown wolves, distributed a couple firearms and went duck hunting.

Chapter 12

Frank

We tore the city apart behind Dakaron. We hit old enemies, new enemies and anybody who we thought were a threat. I even went through the Village hanging off the back of my cousin Moonie's dirt bike and tore some shit up because I heard that Shorty Bullock had family up there.

Fuck all these police keep creeping through here for? I wondered, as I watched the third or fourth cop car float down Rosedale.

I was sitting on my mother's front, in between the legs of a little bitch that I was fucking, getting my hair braided.

"Am I tripping or is that like the third time that police car dipped pass here?" I looked over my shoulder hoping that I wasn't going crazy or being paranoid.

"I don't know." Mynesha hunched her shoulder and sucked her teeth like I was getting on her nerves. "I wasn't paying that shit no attention anyway," she added before turning my head back around, dipping her fingers into some kind of new, thickening shea butter hair food. Mynesha yanked my head back and began greasing my part as she continued to pop her chewing gum.

"Ouch." I turned my head sideways and cut my eye back at Mynesha. "Don't be pulling my fucking hair like that bitch!" I snapped ready to go off.

"Sorry," she apologized submissively, easing up a bit. "I was just trying to make sure that they were tight."

"I don't need them motherfuckers that tight," I assured facing forward again.

The only reason I continued to put up with Mynesha was because she had some bomb ass head. On top of that, her pussy was tighter than an airplane bathroom.

"It felt like you was trying to pull my shit up from the root," I added focusing my attention back on the vanishing police car as Mynesha gently began to tug at my hair again.

"If you don't want me pulling your hair, can you at least sit still?" Mynesha pleaded as I moved my head trying to watch another police car as it drifted by the top of the block.

What the fuck? I thought, noticing the white man behind the wheel. That's a whole different police officer.

I knew I wasn't being tripping now. Something was up. I started thinking about the shit I'd did since Dakaron got touched up. I mean, I knew that I had been extra careful. But was there any chance that I'd actually slipped up? *Nah*, I thought. I had been masking up real good every time I went to lay niggas down. Still, the game was so fucked up and full of bitch niggas nowadays, that I wouldn't be surprised if one of them whore ass niggas tried to put a case on me.

I had just told Mynesha to hurry up, when the unmarked car spun the corner and pulled over.

Shit! I thought seeing the two familiar detectives exiting the car as multiple police cars sped up to my mother's house from all directions. I knew exactly what was up. Bitch ass niggas had finally given me up about the Shorty Bullock shooting.

"Whatever you do, don't get up," I mumbled to Mynesha under my breath, knowing that my lemon squeeze .45 was beneath the cushion she was sitting on.

It never ceased to amaze me how niggas talked all that gangster shit, only to clam up and start name dropping the instant the heat was on.

"Hello Mister Lane," the male detective who'd been harassing the entire crew since Shorty Bullock's murder walked up followed by his partner. "You remember me and my partner, right?" He gestured towards the female detective. But I refused to respond.

"Well, I told you I'd be back, didn't I?" He smiled removing a piece of paper that I instantly recognized as a warrant from inside the breast pocket of his suit jacket.

Again, I remained silent. I mean, I wasn't no slouch when it came to encountering the police. So I knew that whatever it was going to be. It was going to be rather I talked or not.

"I always loved the ones who play tough, don't you detective?" He looked at his partner.

"Sure do," she replied. "They're always the funniest ones to break."

"Stand up and turn around," he demanded and handed me the warrant. I slowly got to my feet and complied.

I turned around and eyed Mynesha as the female detective reached down and picked up my coat. I was nervous as shit. If they told Mynesha to get up, I was fucked. Not only was the lemon-squeeze .45 fully loaded. But I'd just dogged a nigga with it down Pigtown the night before.

"Place your hands behind your back," he instructed removing some handcuffs from his back pocket. "Franklin Lane, you are under arrest for the murder of Darryl Diggs, on the night of July twenty-first," the detective began. "You have the right—"

"Hold up." I pulled at the handcuffs and tried to turn around. "Who you just say?" I questioned confused because I knew Shorty Bullock's whole name and it wasn't Darryl Diggs.

"Resist again," the detective warned holding my arm while he secured the other handcuff around my wrist. "If you can't not afford an attorney,"

"Resist?" I repeated looking over my shoulder with my face twisted up. "Man, you locking up the wrong person," I argued sincerely.

"Aren't we always?" The female detective taunted. "Tell it to the judge."

"I'm telling you man. I don't know no Darryl Diggs," I confessed as the detective lead me to the unmarked car.

"Man, this some bullshit!" I snapped as he opened the back door, told me to watch my head and forced me inside.

"You're probably going to need this," the female detective joked with a satisfied smirk tossing the coat across my lap. "It tends to be cold where you're going," she added before securing the door.

I wasn't tripping through. I knew it was a bluff tactic. They wanted me on the Longwood body but couldn't get me. So they came up with some bullshit to try and scare me into telling on myself. But they had a better chance of finding Tupac's killer.

Chapter 13

Frank

I couldn't believe the bullshit the homicide detectives were doing. These wild bitches had actually booked me for a murder that they knew that I didn't have nothing to do with. If that wasn't enough though, when they got me downtown, they swore up and down that Dak was cooperating.

"I'm telling you, after your boy Dakaron got shot, he started singing like a birdie." The detective looked me straight in the eyes. "How else you think we got you?" The detective added sitting across the table from me inside the interrogation room. But I just looked at him like he was stupid.

People could say what they wanted about Dakaron. He was a coward, an opportunist, arrogant, whatever. They could even call him a bitch. But one thing he damn sure wasn't, was a snitch.

In the end, I just used my rights to remain silent. I also refused to say or sign shit. I just requested a lawyer and got comfortable.

Within an hour, I was cuffed up again and transported to the Central Booking Intake Center on Madison Street to be formally charged with first degree murder.

Central Bookings was a cold motherfucker. Especially since the bitch ass guards on duty took my Colombia Coat on some hating shit. When I hit the section, or rather dorm, I dropped my bedroll into the makeshift bed I was assigned to. I tossed the bullshit ass bag lunch into the garbage and headed towards the phone. I looked around the dorm for any familiar faces. Then, I scoped out the refugee camp type scene.

The dorm was overcrowded and understaffed. I mean, there were niggas everywhere and I hadn't seen a guard since the fat, funny looking, cross-eyed clown with the high pitched voice escorted me in. I stepped over a few dudes who had somehow managed to sleep through all the noise, unnecessary activity and an extremely strong odors of ass, feet and nuts.

"My bad yo." I made a mistake and kicked the side of a dude's tub as I maneuvered my way toward the phones.

The guy rolled over, looked up, mumbled something under his breath, pulled the blanket back over his head as he curled up and farted.

"Man, don't pay that old, miserable nigga no mind," the tall light-skin cat I'd first noticed when I entered the dorm voiced his opinion strolling up. "He knows he's not supposed to have that tub right there in the middle of the afternoon anyway."

I kept my thoughts concerning when, where and how dudes slept to myself. I had my mind on other shit anyway, like, first trying to find out who the hell Darryl Diggs was and if Dakaron had been grabbed up.

"They keep stuffing guys in here. That's why it's so packed," he explained. "The dorm only hold like fifty motherfuckers. But they got niggas in here sleeping all in tubs. Then, they housing dudes in the gym. Got them sleeping on cots, boats and shit. We can't even get no rec because of that."

"What's up with phone?" I pointed at the two currently preoccupied phones. "What we got to get on a list or something?"

"Nah," he smiled like he was amused by my greenness. "We run the phones ourselves over here."

"Oh, aight." I nodded. I was used to training school. "I'm trying to get in line."

"That's a bet. I got you," he assured. "You can go after me," he added and continued. "So, what they grab you for?"

I already knew this song and dance. I'd encountered it before out Boys Village. But I wasn't on that 'Friendly Fred' shit.

"Listen yo," I began. "I don't mean no harm or nothing. But I'm not here to make no friends. I'm just trying to go next on the phone," I explained respectfully as possible.

"I hear you bruh." He shook his head as one of the dudes using the phone, flipped it upside down and hung up.

I noticed that nobody else was moving to grab the phone and inquired about it.

"Don't nobody touch that phone after one but Isreal," he disclosed.

"Who?"

"Isreal," he repeated noticing the confused look on my face. "See the big dude over there near the shower with the kufi on?"

I looked in the direction he referred to and saw this big, Iron Mike looking, George Forman sized joker, hanging a towel and washcloth over the shower rail. "What he about to get in the shower?" I questioned, sizing him up. "*Damn, yo is a big boy!* I admitted to myself.

"Probably," he replied. "He usually get in the shower around this time."

"So, what the phone just going to stay empty until he get out of the shower?"

"Yep," he assured like it was a normal thing.

"Where you at in line?" I asked curiously.

"It's still like four or five people in front of me," he replied.

"Oh man, hell no." I looked towards the big dude again. I wasn't about to wait for no four or five niggas to get on no phone when it was one open.

"I'ma jump on that one real quick," I pledged.

"I wouldn't fuck with that phone if I was you bruh," he warned me with a sincere look of concern on his face.

I considered his advice. I definitely didn't want no static. But I had to call my folks. All I needed was five minutes. "I'ma be off before he even get out of the shower." I assured moving towards the phone.

When I picked that phone up off the hook, it seemed like the entire dormitory got quiet. I mean, even the guys who were sound asleep stopped snoring. Dudes stared at me like I'd lost my mind. But I just flipped the phone right side up and began dialing my mother's number.

Damn, I thought leaning back looking around for the dude who'd just hung up the phone.

He had that bitch rocking like he'd had the whole mouthpiece up his ass. *What the fuck was that nigga eating before he got locked up?* I shook my head and tried to wipe the phone off with my shirt because the smell was making me nauseous.

"Ayo, who the fuck told dude that he could touch that phone?" I heard somebody snap across the dorm and looked over to see Isreal's head hanging out of the shower between the two shower curtains.

"Nah yo, my bad." I spoke up on my own behalf. "I was just trying—" I began to explain when he cut me off.

"Nigga, I ain't trying to hear that shit! Hang the fucking phone up!" He ordered.

"Yo, you tripping. I'm not even going to be two minutes," I rationalized.

"Nigga, if I got to put my tennis back on, I'ma crush you!" He threatened.

I closed my eyes and tried to humble myself. It was always the big niggas cracking slick. "Yo, I only need two minutes," I pleaded.

"Aight yo, go ahead." He waved me off and pulled his head back into the shower.

"Thanks yo," I mumbled, shook my head and smiled at all the nonbelievers and began to dial my mother's number again.

The next thing I knew, Isreal was in my face. "Nigga, I don't care if you only need two seconds," he fired snatching the phone out of my hand. "Don't touch this fucking phone!" He flipped it back upside down and slammed it on the hook. "What nigga?" He barked threateningly when he saw me still standing there with my face twisted up. "Act like you want it and watch me break your fucking jaw." Isreal took another step into my personal space, balled his large hands up and went on. "Have your bitch laid out in the hospital, eating apple sauce through a straw nigga!"

I swallowed my pride and took a step back. "I didn't mean no harm dog," I confessed honestly because the truth was, I didn't want no trouble. I just wanted to go home.

"That's what I thought." Isreal smirked and headed for the showers again.

"I told you not to fuck with that phone, bruh. That nigga crazy," the light-skin cat reminded.

I stood there knowing that every time I gave a nigga an inch. He always took a mile. Yet and still, my focus was on getting on the phone. So, I could see what was what, because somebody was playing games.

It took me every bit of an hour and a half to get on the phone. But I was able to get straight through. My mother didn't know nothing, and Cindy was already making calls.

I assured them that everything would be alright and promised my little brother that I would be back home, cutting his hair again before the week was out. I know that it was just a big mix up.

Once I got off the phone, I started scheming of a way to settle the score with Isreal. I mean, regardless of how big he was and no matter how hard light-skin kept trying to convince me that he hit, he had to answer for the way he carried me.

The crazy thing is I hadn't even gotten the chance to stalk Isreal for real, when he came my way.

"Ayo, what's your name?" Isreal inquired.

"Frank," I revealed honestly.

"Where are from Frank?"

"Westport, but I be up North and Longwood," I replied.

"Yeah, my man from up there," he exclaimed with a pause. "Anyway, my bad about that shit earlier," he apologized. "I just be having to keep these niggas in their place, you feel me?"

"Yeah." I shook my head.

"Anyway, what I be doing is charging niggas ten dollars a week in commissary for ten phone slots," Isreal explained. "But I don't let niggas get too out of control because I be having to call my baby." He held up his wedding band. "Check it out though. Since, I fucks with a few of them Longwood niggas, I'll let you get a ten dollar slot."

This nigga has to be kidding, I thought with a smile. First, he cold blooded disrespects me. Now, he turns around and tries to extort me out of a phone fee like he worked for AT&T or something.

"Nah, I'm good yo." I laughed because he was funny. "I appreciate it though."

"No problem." He nodded like he was really looking out. "But I still don't wanna catch you on my phone yo, straight up," he warned. "You know how the game go. If I let you slip through the cracks, everybody going to want a free pass, you dig? So, if you're not paying in commissary, you're paying in blood."

"You ain't got to worry about me yo," I held my hands up in surrender. "I don't even plan on being here long."

"Say no more." Isreal turned to walk off.

I couldn't help myself. I cracked him right in the back of his nugget.

Come on now, you couldn't have possibly thought that I was going to let that shit be? Not Evon Johnson's son. Not after the die had already been cast. I'd smashed niggas for less. Plus, I hated bullies with a passion.

When I hit Isreal on the back of his cranium between the ears, he instantly dropped to knees and fell face first into the concrete as I backed up and leaned up against the wall. A lot of niggas wouldn't have even realized that I'd knocked him out. If it wasn't for the fat ass, lazy guard who just so happened to be making his rounds. And I still could've gotten away with it, if my hand hadn't swollen up when I hit Isreal on the back of his hard ass head.

"Damn bruh, I didn't even realize that you had put slim to sleep until they called the code," the light-skin cat disclosed, basically dry-snitching on me as the guards escorted me from the dormitory. "I thought that nigga was offering salat," he continued to talk freely as I exited the dorm.

I can't lie, that was funny, and I couldn't help but to laugh. Because Isreal definitely looked like he was offering salat. Especially, when his body unconsciously went into prostration.

Chapter 14

Frank

Time was flying, especially after I was moved over to the Baltimore City Jail for the dormitory situation. Isreal was a straight pussy. Bitch ass nigga had me placed on his enemy's list.

The jail wasn't so bad though. Especially after you got use to the politics and stuff. Plus, there were dime pieces on almost every section. House up on O, Patterson down on K, Sippeo in the dorms and Ms. Long's pretty, old ass around traffic.

Before I knew it, five or six months had gone by, and I was still being held on 'no bond' status for the first degree murder of a motherfucker I swear that I didn't know. By now, Dakaron was also over the jail. Of course, as always, trouble seemed to find Dak. So, he wasn't over the jail a hot second before he ended up getting stabbed.

Now, Dak told me that the East Baltimore niggas tried some sucker shit. But I suspected that Dak was on his best bullshit as always. Whatever the case, I grabbed my bone chipper and went hunting.

I hollered at my man, Lamont McGinnis or Money as most niggas called him, to get the low-down on the niggas I was looking for. Money gave me the 411 on the Chapel Hill dudes Dak had gotten into with without hesitation. Not only was he family but he was on the Inmate Counsel Board, so he knew everything and everyone who was moving or shaking over the jail.

Like I said, Money was like an uncle to me. I'd known him since I was a kid and he used to come out Westport to my house with my father and Uncle Cateyes back in the day. So, I knew that everything he said was straight up.

I mean, despite the fact that Money was rumored to have put a few dicks in the dirt. I knew that he wasn't with the dumb shit. Money was about his paper. Nothing more, nothing less. However, he loved my father and respected me. So, at the end of the day, I knew that he would give me the guidance that I needed.

Money told me about the Chapel Hill Crew. There were about ten or fifteen of them over the jail on a federal indictment. I appreciated the heads up. But I was solely concerned with the ones who'd tried the clown shit with my nigga.

See, what a lot of niggas didn't know was that even through Dakaron and I were like night and day. In fact, Dak was the type to go with the flow of things. Whereas me, I never simply just adapted to my environment because my mother had always told me that the key to true manhood was the ability to remain who you truly were, no matter where you find yourself. Furthermore, I wasn't wilding out like Dak, running around trying to be a jailhouse legend. I was trying to get home. All that other bullshit meant nothing to me.

Yet and still, Dakaron was my heart and righthand man. So, I wouldn't hesitate to tear a nigga's ass up for violating him in the slightest form.

Once I found out who all the players were, I laid low and waited for them to come off of lockup. It was crazy because I was finally beginning to understand why the administration labeled us *animals.* I mean, I didn't know if it was because the jail shit was starting to get to me. But when you really considered how we acted without thought and fed off of our lower desires. You could truly see the comparison.

We even talked about tearing the fur off of each other. And you had niggas over the jail, throwing feces on each other.

Another thing that being over the jail was quickly teaching me was that niggas weren't real. I know that you couldn't adequately judge a person until God put that period on their life. But man, when it came to Jamaine, that nigga was so phony that it wasn't even funny. It was actually sad.

I mean, this nigga would sell you a dream like it was nothing. On top of that, he never showed up when you needed him. He just kept spinning you. Like he kept spinning me about the lawyer, money orders and everything else.

It got so bad that I just decided to stick with the court appointed, Public Defender Chip Johnson because I couldn't count on Jamaine to do nothing but bluff. What hurt the most though was the fact that I loved Jamaine like a brother and would've gladly given my life or freedom for him.

I wanted to scream on Jamaine so bad over the phone for the way he was acting towards me. Especially after all the jams I had pulled his greedy ass out of. Not to mention, all the shit I was pulled into behind his ass. I even sided with his bluffing ass against niggas from out Westport. Yet and still, he refused to play fair.

But I kept my cool because I knew that the police and or prosecutor on my case could easily sign into the computer program that allowed them to monitor my phone conversations, to gather evidence to use against me at trial. Plus, I knew that when it came to jumping on a nigga's case and snitching, it was a very popular I thing over the jail.

On the streets, it was different. Most people were more than ready to talk, if it meant that they could escape custody and nothing was ever written on paper or recorded on tape. Especially, younger niggas who would give their own mothers up if they knew that it would help them out.

In the joint, it was worst though because niggas didn't care who knew if they told – they just wanted a *get out of jail free card* and they would hop on any case to get it. To make matters worse, the Baltimore City Police Department was already involved in one of the most ambitious mass incarceration programs that American had ever seen.

"Lane?" A pretty, peanut-butter-brown correctional officer called my name cautiously as I was coming off of a visit.

"Franklin Lane?" She inquired again noticing my curious stare.

"Yeah, what's up?" I hesitantly looked around, hoping that I wasn't about to get strip-searched or nothing because I kept the bone chipper on me. Especially, after Dakaron came off and got to pushing with a few Chapel Hill niggas inside the gym. Him and his crazy baby mother's brother. They were the talk of the jail and according to our big homie, Willie Bates, everybody now knew that Dakaron was my rap buddy.

"You're not in trouble or nothing." She giggled like a shy, little schoolgirl.

"Oh, I didn't know what was up?" I relaxed, licked my lips and smiled all while sizing her up.

"You got some pretty ass eyes," I confessed ready to shot my jumper. Shorty was bad and thick just like I liked them.

"Thank you." She appeared to blush. "You're Truesdale's cousin right?"

My antennas went up again. I knew that the Chapel Hill Crew had some pull around the jail. So I decided to play it safe. "Who's Truesdale?" I questioned.

"Dakaron, your co-defendant," she stated matter of factly.

"Yeah, yeah. That's my peoples," I declared. "Why?"

"No, I just wanted you to know that he made out on his infraction," she explained. "He should be off soon. Probably before the weekend."

"I heard that, good looking out." I nodded truly appreciating the heads up.

"I hope you can keep him out of trouble this time." She smiled.

"That is a tall order." I assured. "But I'll try. What Is your name though?" I inquired curiously.

"Officer Glover," she revealed, and it instantly hit me. She was the CO that Dak was talking about being sweet on when we'd went to court.

"Thanks, Miss Glover." I sized her up one more time and went on about my business. *That nigga Dak always finding a dime.* I thought heading back to the section.

"Let me see your pass."

I turned around to find this wild, bitch ass C.O. that I couldn't stand. This chump loved popping up out of nowhere, patting me down and shit.

I didn't even respond. I just waived him off and continued walking towards the section.

"Are you disobeying a direct order?" He asked, and I could hear his keys jiggle as he removed something from his belt. Most likely, his mace because he had to know that I'd beat the brakes off of him if he tried to put some cuffs on me for nothing.

I just shook my head, spun around, pulled out my visiting slip and handed it to him. I wasn't about to let him spoil my day. I'd just gotten finished seeing the strongest mother and prettiest little sister on the face of the planet earth.

"I saw you down there on post fourteen talking to Officer Glover." He took the visiting slip out of my hand. "What was that about?" He questioned surveying the visiting slip.

I started to go in on his bitch ass for even insulting me. But then, I decided to humor myself. "Who G?" I fired as if I knew Miss Glover personally. "Nah, she use to fuck with one of my old heads out Westport," I lied.

"Who?" His head snapped up like a pigeon. "I mean, oh. Ummmmm." He tried to gather his himself, but it was too late. I was already on to him. I knew an insecure nigga when I encounter one.

In fact, he reminded me of this lame named, Kelechi who I use to go to school with. A real wild buster, with some kind of hair disease that marched around the school playing tough, while myself and at least two other dudes from the school that I knew of, were secretly blowing his girl's back out.

"Yeah, I know 'G' real good, you feel me?" I hinted to something devious with a knowing look.

"Nigga what? Man." He stepped forward and paused as if he had to catch himself. But I was ready for whatever.

I stepped back and squared straight up. I wasn't even going to give him a chance to call the code for assistance. I was going to knock his bitch ass right out.

"Look," he seemed to calm down a bit, "when you're coming off a visit, you don't need to be worrying about talking to nobody." Backing up, he added, "You need to make your way back to your cell."

"Man, I can't help it if a guard stops me," I argued.

"It doesn't matter. You need to get back to your cell," he spat handing me the visiting slip back. "Next time, I'ma write you a ticket for holding up the institutional count," he threatened and walked off.

Wild bitch. I stared at the back of his head for a second and thought about Isreal. I hated when a bitch ass nigga had some authority because they never knew how to act.

I shook my head and headed on to the section.

***

The only time Dakaron and I got to really get in tight was during our court trips. We would update each other about the streets and things like what was going on with our love lives and shit.

What tripped me out the most was how different motherfuckers were acting towards me and Dakaron. They were hanging up the phone on me, talking crazy and playing games. But when it came to Dakaron, they had their minds right. Which was crazy considering the fact that I played fair and Dak treated them like shit when we were home. Keisha was even accepting Dakaron's calls and rejecting mines and he'd robbed her boyfriend while we were in the streets.

"Yo, when we get in the bullpen, I need to holler at you about the case," Dakaron mumbled one day while we were on the van going to court and I just looked at him strangely and nodded, because we rarely ever discussed the case. I'm talking about trial strategy, plea agreement, guilt, innocence, nothing!

Once we arrived at the courthouse and went through all the normal bullshit, Dakaron and I found a corner in the bullpen and sat down to talk.

"What's on your mind, Cuz?" I inquired curiously.

Dakaron stared at me for a moment before he spoke. Almost as if studying me, "Ayo, did you have something to do with this shit?"

"What? Nigga are you serious?" I challenged.

"Yeah nigga," Dakaron retorted. "I ain't stupid, everybody else be sleeping on you. But I know how you get down."

"Cuz, I don't even know who that nigga is," I spat sincerely. Then, I studied him, wondering if he was involved. Especially since I knew that he would do just about anything to appease or protect Monique. "What about you? This your work? This some shit you did fucking with Monique?"

"Yo, you know I ain't never been shy about claiming my skeletons," Dakaron declared. "That's why I thought it was your work. You know, I'ma ride out with you regardless," Dakaron added.

I knew that he was telling the truth. Dakaron was just that type of nigga. When he was with you, he was with you. Win, lose or draw. "I'm telling you, Cuz, I don't know who the fuck Darryl Diggs is. I did find out that he's supposed to be from up Park Heights though."

"I never heard his name," Dakaron assured shaking his head. "But I'ma ask my brother about him."

That was all I needed to hear. If Dakaron didn't murk dude and I know damn well that I didn't do the nigga, there was no way that we weren't going to beat this shit. The police were playing games.

"Pernell Green, Issac Truss and Muata Jones, let's go gentlemen," One of transporting guards popped up with three bailiffs behind her. "Your verdict's in."

I looked up and saw a tall, dark-skin, slim, lanky joker with corn rolls, a stocky brown-skin, hairless faced kid and a clean shaved, bald head older cat with the meanest bop I'd ever seen. They all had red, black and green African medallions hanging from their necks.

"Man, them fools going down," One of the dudes in the crowded bullpen fired loud enough for everyone to hear the moment the three codefendants disappeared. "Do you know who that was?" He questioned no one in particular and continued when someone took the bait.

"That's them Pan-African brothers who exposed all that government corruption, murdered a couple agent provocateurs and freed two of their comrades," he explained and for some reason the Inner City Blues by Marvin Gaye jumped in my head and made me want to holler. "Ain't nobody went that hard since them Fatiu brothers Diop and Ajamu stormed the courthouse and went nuts."

Chapter 15

Frank

"...It's a thin line between love and hate, friends and snakes, nine-millis and the pearly-gates. I destined to come, predicted, God son. He blew breath in my lungs." I was in the cell, rapping my man Nas latest single, Hate Me Now featuring Puff Daddy, getting ready for a visit.

Over the last few months, the game had gotten so pitiful that it was hard to even smile. First, I discovered that a few bitch ass niggas were running around, mumbling under their breath, trying to throw dirt on my name. Then, I had to come to the realization that dudes whom I once looked up to in the streets, and wondered what it was like to be like, were fake. I mean, not only had they not addressed the false rumors about me when they first surfaced but, they knew the truth because they knew my case. Yet and still, they laid back and let that shit spread although they knew that the cruelest lie was the one told in silence.

I wasn't surprised though. Especially, when I considered how they were over the jail getting the treatment. In the end, it all came out and got cleared up though. Some chump name, Tank from around near Longwood was over the jail telling on his brother, and somehow our names got crossed up.

When the cell door opened for my visit, I took my headphones off, slid them under my pillow and headed for the visiting room. You already know I was fresh to death.

"Who's that, your little girlfriend?" our regular tier officer inquired with a slight attitude the moment I walked up on the desk to get my visiting slip.

"I don't do girlfriends," I assured with smile.

"Un-huh," She rolled her eyes and handed me the pass. "Just make sure you're back in time to clean my tier," she instructed with a look I knew all too well.

"Yes, ma'am." I winked. Yeah, Dak wasn't the only one doing him over the jail. I was getting my dick wet on the regular basis too. I just kept my shit under my hat. I didn't even call my folks by their name. "You're the boss."

"Boy, go ahead on your little visit." She blushed at the hidden suggestion. So, I knew exactly what time it was when I got back.

When Mynesha strolled into the visiting room looking all good, followed by Hook and sat down, I just smiled at her and shook my head.

Every time I put her on a mission, she carried it out. That was one thing I always respected about solid bitches. They always knew how to play their part.

"What's up, Cuz?" I checked Hook out. He was fresh as usual.

"Ain't too much. Waiting on you and Dak to come home," he replied.

"You and me both." I seconded sincerely. I couldn't get home fast enough. There was so much fuck shit being done while we were over the jail that it nearly broke my heart. Especially, when it came to Jamaine. Dakaron kept telling me to be patient, saying that Jamaine and Monique had our backs. But I was steady seeing signs of betrayal.

"So, what's going on?" Hook inquired, and I immediately began giving him the run down on all the foul shit Jamaine had been doing since I got over the jail.

I told him about how Jamaine was playing money games with the lawyer. I told him about how niggas were really over the jail starving. "It's like all the shit I did for that nigga when I was in the streets vanished," I continued praying that Hook could see the light.

I even told Hook about how Jamaine tried to crack on Mynesha for some pussy while he was supposed to be

94

dropping off some bread. The fucked up part was that Hook didn't seem the least bit surprised.

"Yeah, I already know how that nigga get down." Hook admitted. "I used to let him tag along with me to see this chick I was dealing with up the Junction. And this nigga doubled back one day and tried to holler at her," Hook explained. "When I pulled him up about it, he started talking about he was testing her and shit."

I just shook my head. It was painful what so called real friends did when you weren't around. Now, I understood why niggas hearts turned cold. "I'm starting to think that nigga allergic to loyalty," I confessed.

"I don't even think it's that dog," Hook challenged. "It's just a rough business being a real, stand up dude out here nowadays."

"Hmph," I grunted looking at Hook. What he said made a lot of sense. Niggas just weren't cut like they used to be. "Fuck that shit though. I ain't stunting that nigga. I'm pass that." I waved the topic of Jamaine off. "The reason I got Mynesha to come scoop you though was because I'm trying to get this lawyer shit straight."

"Man, what you thought I was lying on the phone when I told you I was fucked up out here?" Hook eyed me curiously.

"Nah Cuz, I figured you just didn't want to talk over the phone." I lied. The truth was that pain always made you question honor.

"Nah, I'm really fucked up," Hook admitted without shame. "Jamaine out here crumb feeding niggas. Especially since Monique running everything though him now." Hook revealed. "I be having to step on my shit two, three times to really see a profit. Fiends be coming back complaining and shit saying my shit garbage. That's why I really thought you wanted to see me. A nigga about to get back on his shit!" Hook looked at me knowingly. "And you already know what's up!"

I know exactly what Hook was hinting at. But just in case I didn't, he made it very clear. "I'm going to ride for you and Dak regardless. So, if you tell me to go get him. I got him," Hook fired.

Damn! I stared at Hook. Jamaine was really starting to create a lot of unnecessary bad blood, disappointment and dissatisfaction and the only thing it was producing was treachery. Yet and still, I couldn't send Hook after Jamaine like that. Because even though, I knew that Jamaine was a selfish motherfucker, he was still family. Besides, I knew it was the shame that hurt Hook the most. The shame of having to beg a nigga you called your brother for crumbs from his table.

"Just sit tight for now. Let me look into something." I thought about my cellmate crying about how his brother, who was getting all this money, wasn't doing right. "You got a lot of dudes over here that like to run their mouths about shit."

I spent the rest of visit talking about how the police were playing games. Explaining how the election season and crime spike in Baltimore was playing a part in our case.

When I got back to the section, the whole tier was already locked in. So, I grabbed the broom and got to work. Once I knocked the top and bottom tiers out, I slide into the closet and waited until my bitch showed up.

Once she snuck into the closet, it was on. I didn't waste no time. I pushed my jeans down to my knees and whipped my dick out. Like I said, Dakaron wasn't the only nigga over the jail getting his dick wet.

"Damn, I needed this baby." I looked down and ran my fingers through her long   hair as she masterfully bobbed her head back and forth, in a slow but steady motion. She was driving me crazy. I didn't know what it was, but I always ended up fucking with a pretty ass bitch, who gave top-shelf head.

I watched in amazement as she worked her magic, holding my djck with one hand as she took turns gently massaging the head with her mouth and other hand. When she cupped my balls and deep-throated, it was over. My toes curled and my eyes rolled into the back of my head as I nutted straight down her throat.

"I'ma have to wife your pretty ass when I get uptown," I whispered stumbling into a mop-bucket on shaking legs. I hadn't nutted that hard in a long time.

Now, I really wanted to fuck her thick ass. But I didn't want to blow the spot up. Especially since, she'd cried about me being too big the last time I tried to get up in that tight pussy. The crazy thing was I had only put the head in.

"I bet that little girl who came down here today, doesn't suck your dick like that," she fired confidently as she stood up and wiped her mouth with the palm of her hand.

I couldn't even lie. Mynesha wasn't no slouch in the neck department but her old ass was a head doctor. It was like she was making love to the dick with her mouth. "Nah, you definitely got shorty beat," I admitted pulling my jeans back up.

"You ain't seen nothing yet. Wait until we find a spot where I can really take my time sucking your dick." She smiled satisfyingly. "I'ma show you why I been able to keep my husband all these years." She bragged. "See, the young girls don't know how to keep a man. They don't cook. They don't clean. And they damn sure don't suck dick like they are supposed to."

"Come here." I pulled her into my arm after buttoning my jeans back up. Then, I stuffed my tongue down her throat as my hands went to her phat ass. I wanted to get up in that pussy so bad it was killing me.

"I can't wait until we can find a spot so I can get up in this pussy," I confessed before sucking her bottom lips and sliding my hand in between her thighs to cup her pussy. I could tell that motherfucker was wet and hot through her uniform. I mean, I could literally feel it.

"I don't know boy," She shook her head and reached inside the front of my jeans. "Mmmhhh, mmmhhh, mmmhhh," she moaned before biting her bottom lip as she squeezed my dick. "Your shit so much bigger then my husband's," she confessed. "Sucking it is one thing. But if I let you stretch this pussy open with that big motherfucker, he's going to know."

I didn't respond. There was no need to. Instead, I just began kissing her again. Because I knew just as well as she did, that before it was all over, she was going to give up that tight pussy. Rather it was on this side of the wall or the other.

We stood there tongue kissing and groping each other, lost in the moment until one of the clowns, on the tier started banging on the grill, calling her name.

I patted her on the butt and let her dip out first. Then, I waited for about ten minutes until the coast was clear, grabbed my shower gear and headed back to the cell.

"You enjoy your visit?" My cellmate inquired with a curious grin.

He knew what was up, but he didn't know what was good for real. If that makes any sense.

"I always do." I smiled with conviction. "But yo, remember you were telling me about your brother?"

"Man, fuck that sucker ass nigga!" He fired. "Yo, out there getting all that money and won't even send a nigga a couple of dollars."

"What if I told that I could get to him for you?" I stared at him seriously. I mean, I knew that a lot of niggas talked that gangster shit like they were really about that life but, when it was time to set their folks up to get grabbed, they back off the gas.

"Then, I would tell you to get to him and ask you what I needed to do." He perked up.

"You know where he lay his head at?"

"Absolutely." He nodded confidently, jumping off the bunk to fold his mattress back. "I got both of that nigga's addresses right here." He assured picking up a black phonebook.

"That's all we need." I smiled as he thumbed through the book looking for his brother's addresses.

I knew once I gave Hook the information. It was curtains.

Chapter 16

Frank

I hadn't even really gotten started lining niggas up for Hook when he fucked around a got himself hemmed up for some Sandtown bullshit. I was mad as shit too. Especially after we hit my cellmate's brother and two other niggas on the tier peoples and came off sweet. If that wasn't enough, Monique popped up over the jail on some federal charges. So, Jamaine was really showing his ass now. Even Dak was starting to see exactly what I'd been talking about now that Monique wasn't out there to hold Jamaine's hand.

None of that was the real kicker though. The real kicker came when the paperwork on Monique's surfaced. I was one of the first nigga's to read it too. All I could do was shake my head because, I'd known it all along. I just felt it. I mean, I'm not saying that I thought Monique was a rat. I just knew something about his slimy ass wasn't right.

Yet and still, after reading the paperwork, I told Willie Bates that he had to be the one to tell Dak because I couldn't get to him. Plus, I knew that if anybody else, pulled up on Dakaron with paperwork on Monique, he would butcher them. But he respected Willie Bates. And he knew that Willie Bates didn't play no games when it came to a man's name.

When word first came down that Monique had been rushed to the outside hospital, I knew what was up. Dakaron had went ham. The tier rep confirmed it for me when he came back and informed me that Dakaron had been placed on administrative lockup, pending investigation.

The weeks that followed were crazy. The cell got shook down two or three times. One time, I almost got into with one of the administration flunkies for tossing my shit around disrespectfully, looking for God knows what. Dakaron sent kite after kite. The 'snitchuation' with Monique really fucked him up. He was hurt because he really looked up to and admired Monique. For a minute, Dak seemed to blame the police for everything that happened. Even with Monique. It was almost to the point where it was like Monique hadn't had anything to do with it. As if he hadn't been in the streets.

By the time we got to trial, and Monique jumped on that stand, he had his mind right though. Our trial was a comedy show. It seemed like everybody was telling jokes. The judge basically allowed the state to get away with any and everything. Monique's bitch ass was the real main attraction though. And after he performed there was no way that we were beating our case.

The state even found some wild ass, jailhouse snitch nigga to prance into the courtroom, talking about a nigga confessed to him. I cannot remember exactly how long the jury deliberated. But I know that it wasn't that long before they were saying guilty, guilty, guilty.

After that, the judge ordered a pre-sentence investigation, set a sentencing date and brought us back up in the courtroom to bust our heads with life sentences. All that suspended sentenced shit did not mean nothing to me at the time. All I heard was life and the Patuxent Youth Offender Program recommendation.

When we got to D.O.C, we got the shift commander to place us in the cell together. It was crazy that we'd blown trial. Two friends who had done just about everything together, ended up going down together. All I kept thinking about was my family. Especially, my mother. She took the verdict hard. She said that the system was designed to fuck black people.

Me and Dak went over all the lies that came out at trial and vowed to fight our way back. "Ayo, when we come back from this one, everybody going to jump back on our dicks," Dakaron said just before I dosed off.

The next morning, right after breakfast, our cell door was opened by none other than Ofc. Patterson, the finest, redbone to probably have ever worked courtside.

"Damn, how you doing Ms. Patterson?" I smiled. I hadn't laid eyes on her sexy ass since this wild, Uplands dude beat her and her boyfriend up on the section over the jail.

"Fine," she replied.

"You ain't never lied," I admitted making her blush.

Ms. Patterson told me to pack up. I threw the little bit of cosmetics I had into a bag, gave Dak some love and headed downstairs to traffic to be shipped out.

I'm not even going to front. When I first arrived at the penitentiary annex, I was nervous as fuck! Especially, after a nigga rushed out of the cell slinging something that resembled a sickle the first time the doors opened. I knew that I had to get a bone chipper quick.

My cellmate turned out to be a Muslim dude from Park Heights name Jewels. He didn't know Dakaron, but knew his older brothers, Detauwn and Antauwn. I didn't gave a fuck about none of that though. I was trying to get right. But all this nigga wanted to talk about was Islam and the Deen.

It took me about a week to get my hands on a good piece of steel. I lucked up and ran into my man Alphonso "Butt" Spencer from over the jail. He'd gotten found guilty for two bodies a few months before me and was now in the penitentiary annex in D-building on A- tier.

"You get that?" Butt inquired the next time I saw him in the big yard.

"Ain't no question." I nodded gratefully as we began to walk the track. "That was good looking out," I assured thinking about the murder weapon he'd blessed me with.

"Make sure you keep that motherfucker on you at all times," Butt instructed. "It gets crazy around here every now and then."

"You already know, I'm trained to go Cuz." I smiled. I felt a lot more at ease now. "Ayo, what's up with my cellmate though Cuz?"

"Who, Jewels?" Butt questioned rhetorically as I nodded. "He a good nigga. He's from up my way. Yo just be on that Muslim shit all day."

"Yeah, what's up with that?"

"That shit a gang if you ask me," Butt replied. "They be talking all that righteous and sacred shit. But a lot of them niggas the biggest hustlers in the jail. And they be using that Muslim card as protection," he added. "That is why I don't pay that shit no mind." Butt spit on the ground. "The funny thing is though. I be going up the Moor Science Temple and they always talking about how the Moors and the Nation of Islam aren't real Muslims because they be allowing gang members to attend service. But I don't ever see none of them FOI's (Fruits of Islam) running around carrying knives, selling drugs or clicking up on motherfuckers. Especially, not the ones who done already told on somebody. And don't even get me started on the rapists."

I took heed to everything Butt said and stayed the fuck away from my cellmate and his Muslim brothers. I had never been the "get with" type in the joint anyway. Gangs, religion, neighborhoods, it all seemed the same to me. Besides that, I minded my business and stayed out of the way. It didn't take me long to settle into a nice routine. I found me a good workout partner and got put on the legal library list.

After that, I basically had two cells. The one I was sentenced to and the one that I created for myself. In so many words, I was housed in the penitentiary annex, but I lived in the law library.

The only time I ever really showed my face on the compound was on my way to workout, going on a visit or when I was sneaking around, trying to find an alternative route to freedom. Because I didn't give fuck what the judge or any other court of law thought. Evon Johnson's son was not dying in prison.

I wasn't really for sure exactly what Dakaron was up to over the Cut, but I heard stories. Of course, he always professed to be studying case law, looking for loopholes so that we could regain our freedom. But before long the cat was out of the bag and Dakaron ended up getting into it with some old penitentiary vets. Dudes who were well-known for slinging that knife. But I didn't give a fuck! Dak was my heart and I would go up against any and everybody for that nigga.

So, the moment them old niggas hit the annex, I started stalking the compound war ready. Patiently waiting for them to hit the compound.

I told my workout partner James to fall back. But he armed up and follow me to the yard. To be honest, the nigga never left my side. What I didn't know at that time was that James wasn't nothing to be played with. But I would bear witness to that soon enough.

By the time Dakaron hit the compound, the situation with the old heads from over the Cut was dead. Squashed by a few penitentiary legends who understood the stakes. Oh yeah, did I mention the fact that, South Baltimore, Cherry Hill and Westport, to be exact, had a stronghold on the joint? Yeah well, my Uncle Cateyes and his brothers names held a lot of weight in the joint. On top of that James' cousin, Charles Jackson moved mountains.

Time seemed to fly by quick for me. Days faded into weeks; weeks faded into months. I did mess around and end up on lockup for some simple shit during a mass shake down while they were taking our street clothes. The tier officer, Miss Sellman and I got into it over a missing pair of brand new, peach colored Timberland Boots. On the real, I wasn't really tripping until she started running her smart ass mouth, cracking slick and shit. That's what made me mad. So, when she came around for count, I grabbed my crotch and told her to eat a dick.

In hindsight, I realized that I was tripping. Especially, when I called her out of her name. Her chocolate ass was pretty as shit too. Under different circumstances, I probably would've pushed up on her but, her lying ass wrote me a bogus ass ticket talking about a nigga jerked off on her. I ended up getting thirty days for that bullshit.

It was my first real lock-up experience. And man, let me tell you, it was crazy. I got housed on C-tier with all the zap outs, shit slingers and trash talkers. The tier was so off the chain that I thought my neighbor had a cellmate the whole time I was there. I mean, it wasn't until I was actually coming off of lockup, that I went over to his door to leave him some old magazines and looked inside before I realized that he didn't have a cellmate.

That fucked me up for real because I had heard these niggas having conversations and arguments. I couldn't believe it. I scanned the entire cell to be certain. But there was only one bunk. I even asked the working man where his cellmate was at, and he looked at me like I was C-tier material and told not to ask nobody else that question. I never wanted to go back in A-building on lock-up again.

I ended up right back in E-building. On the exact same tier. My workout partner James was happy as shit and so was I until me and Dak lost our Direct Appeal. Soon afterwards, Dakaron got shipped back over to the 'Cut' behind some wild shit that happened in D-building. Still, it was the news about Monique that fucked me up the most.

I was sitting on the bunk, watching the evening news when Monique's name rolled across the bottom of the television screen. At first, I thought I was tripping. So, I waited for the sports, national news and weather to stroll by and read it again.

A fifty-plus year old inmate by the name of Stebastian Monique was found stabbed to death in the Maryland House of Correction west wing showers just before afternoon count, I read.

I instantly knew that Dakaron was somehow involved. He'd always been the type to settle a score. I just couldn't figure out how in the hell Monique had landed in the 'Cut' with Dakaron after being on both of our enemy list. I just hoped that Dak's crazy ass hadn't gotten caught.

The next morning, after peeping the news about Monique, I pulled up on my little home girl Hope from Cherry Hill after yard. Because I knew she had a sister that worked next door. I figured that Hope could holler at her little sister and find something out for me about Dak.

"Nigga, don't try to play the homegirl card with me," Hope bucked when I asked her about hollering at her sister for me. "Your ass ain't been acting like we cool."

"Come on with the bullshit, Hope. You know it's always Southside love." I smiled but Hope wasn't biting. "Oh, I know what I got to do," I assured when it hit me. "I gotta go get my man Jay!" I used James nickname.

"Boy, please, ain't nobody paying Laury ass no mind," Hope retorted but I could clearly see the lust in her eyes.

"Ay, Jay!" I yelled, looking upstairs towards the shower to get James' attention.

"Yeah, what's up bruh?" James leaned over the rail.

"Come here real quick." I looked back towards Hope as she rolled her eyes.

A few seconds later, James came bouncing down the steps in his shower shoes with no shirt on, smiling at Hope as she shook her head. He already knew what time it was.

"What's up bruh?" He inquired cutting his eye at Hope.

"Hope down here acting crazy," I revealed. "I'm trying to get her to call next door and check on my rap buddy but, she tripping," I explained. "I know that you can handle her though."

"Boy please, can't nobody handle me," Hope snapped. "My man can't even handle me."

"That's because that nigga a lame," James fired.

"Whatever." Hope sucked her teeth. "And you need to put your shirt on," Hope ordered stealing a glance at James six pack.

One thing about James was that nigga was shredded. I mean, don't get it twisted now, I was V12 up underneath the hood too. But James looked like a fucking action figure toy and everybody, even Hope's coworkers knew that she was sweet on James. And I wasn't hating on Hope or nothing. She was definitely a looker. Her little sister was just more my speed.

"Come on Hope," James pleaded with a soft look. "Check on bruh rap buddy for us."

"Oh, it's us now?" Her eyebrow shot up.

"Yeah, why you think me and bruh so tight? His rap buddy, Dakaron is my cousin," James lied.

"Well, I ain't making no promises." Hope shook her head defeated. "But when I go on my lunch break, I'll see what I can find out. What's your rap bubuddy'sast name?"

"Truesdale," I replied. "Dakaron Truesdale. I just want to know if he's okay."

"I got you." She agreed uncontrollably cutting her eye at James stomach again.

"Make sure you tell your sister I said hi." I smirked teasingly.

"Boy, we aren't kids no more." Hope fired probably knowing exactly what was on my mind.

"I wasn't saying it like that." I lied with a smile. My mind was definitely in the gutter.

"Damn yo! I wish y'all little niggas go the fuck on somewhere!"

James and I turned towards the bottom tier shower at the same time to find this wild, big, black, older nigga who went for bad, standing there naked, sneakily jerking off.

"Ay bruh, what the fuck!" James exclaimed immediately turning his head as I just stood there staring in shock.

"Yeah nigga, you in the line of fire!" He snapped making no attempt to cover himself up, nor hide what he had been doing.

"Fix the curtain Blakq!" Hope ordered. "Don't nobody want to see your old ass," she added strolling off the tier.

Still, I remain there frozen, wondering if this nigga had a death wish. "Ayo, what the fuck kind of shit you on?" I balled my face up. "I know you see us standing here talking."

"Man, shorty, I'm not trying to hear that shit!" He waved me off. "Niggas know what it is with me when a bitch working the tier," he justified.

Is this nigga crazy? I wondered. I mean, I didn't knock what no man did. That was his business. But I wasn't about to let no nigga disrespect me either. "So, what you saying? You gonna bust shorty head while we standing right here?"

"Man, shorty, I'ma do what I do. I don't give fuck if Jesus Christ right there." He began soaping his washcloth up. "Nigga in the way, he getting hit too," he declared before turning around to step underneath the shower water and get wet.

Again, I stood there, lost in my own thoughts.

"You know what a lot of y'all young niggas problem is?" He spun back around and started washing up. "Y'all be trying to protect these bitches too much. Talking about they're from around your neighborhood and whatnot. But I'm from the old school shorty. So if a bitch not breaking law or fucking, she's definitely getting this dick put on her. And ain't nobody going to stop that! I don't give a fuck if that's your homegirl, your sister, daughter or none of that other shit," he spat.

"Shiiid nigga, for all I care, she can be your mother. If she work this tier, I'm busting her head," he added.

"Come on bruh." James grabbed my arm.

"Nah Cuz, this bigger than Hope." I pulled my arm free and moved toward the shower. "It's a respect thing," I argued.

I wasn't trying to protect Hope. I wasn't trying to defend her. I mean, I wouldn't just let anything happen to her in my presence. But at the same time, she knew what she was signing up for when she accepted the job. However, I still wasn't just about to let no nigga get away with standing in the shower, jerking off on Hope or no other woman while I was standing there. I didn't give a fuck if he was out that mob or not.

"Don't write a check your little ass can't cash shorty," he warned and continued to wash up.

"Chill bruh." James pulled me back. "You got too much going on right now." He rationalized. "You just filed something in court."

James was right. I did have a lot going on. But still, it was hard to swallow my pride. Even if it was only for the moment.

"I'm telling you, bruh. Let that shit go." James looked at me cautiously. "That nigga always doing that shit. That's his MO. It's only going to be so long before he do it in front of the wrong nigga."

I allowed James to lead me back up the steps. I hopped into the shower and tried to wash off my ego because it was truly bruised.

Chapter 17

Frank

Even after Butt and one of my Uncle Cateyes homeboys, Black Junior — a gangster from Eastport, Naptown — pulled up on Blakq and got him to apologize, I was still feeling some type of way. Especially, after Blakq continued to disrespect niggas on the tier on some bully shit. James told me to just stay away from him and he'd stay out of our way. But it was hard because I despised bullies.

Eventually, Blakq and I ended up getting into again. This time over a conversation that didn't have nothing to do with him. Blakq just felt like he could say whatever he wanted to say, whenever he wanted to say it without consequence.

"That's it! I'm putting that knife in this nigga Cuz," I declared stoutly storming into the dayroom ready to discard everything I had in court.

"What's up?" James shot to his feet.

"Nah Cuz, this bitch ass nigga Blakq keep trying me!" I spat.

"Bruh, I told you to stay away from that nigga." James reminded.

"Man, I been staying out of that nigga's way," I argued. "But yo think he like that because he got a jail-house body; like he the only one that gets down for his crown."

"Calm down a little bit." James looked around cautiously before gesturing for me to follow him over in the far corner of the dayroom. "You got to watch these nosey ass niggas," he fired once we were out of earshot of everybody.

"Aight, what happened?"

"This wild ass nigga put his self in my conversation," I revealed. "Then, started talking all this gangster shit about how we ran to Butt and them."

"Hold up," James paused. "He said what?"

"He said, niggas ran to Butt like he was our father or something," I disclosed.

"So, what he trying say?"

"I took it like he's saying niggas need protection or something."

James just shook his head and took a deep breath before exhaling.

"Yeah, that's how I felt," I admitted. "I got to get this bitch."

"Aight, that's what's up." James surrendered. "Let me put Charles on point."

The stage was set. I didn't say nothing to Butt or none of my uncle's homeboys because this was one of those situation that had to be addressed, and I didn't want nobody trying to talk me down or intervene.

When we spilled into the dayroom that evening, I shot straight upstairs to play the phone as usual. After I finished kicking it with moms, I dipped back downstairs and waited for my moment.

Blakq was running around the dayroom as usual, fucking with people, being disrespectful. Around seven, he slid upstairs to use the phone and James followed suit.

I walked over and hopped up on top of the dayroom table with my feet hanging off the side. I kept my eyes trained on the stairs, waiting for James to give me the green light.

"Phone bruh," James appeared at the top of the stairs giving me the signal. I slide up off of the table and headed up the steps.

For a moment, I considered backing out. Or at least, going with the hot-pot and baby-oil move I conjured up. Because I felt butt naked without my bone chipper. Like I

Delmont Player

was at a disadvantage. Especially, since Blakq was known for getting down. Yet and still, I kept moving because I trusted James. Besides, if his plan went south, he'd be forced to jump into it anyway.

There were about five guys on the telephones engaged in conversation. Blakq was on the very last phone near the window. He had his chair turned the opposite way, so that he could use the back of it to lean forward and rest his head and arms on. He wasn't even paying attention to what was going on around him.

A nigga should never be that comfortable in prison. I thought stalking him like prey. I'd learned a long time ago that the worst motherfucker in prison was the nigga who couldn't sense danger.

I wouldn't classify Blakq as a hyena because he did his own thing. But I wouldn't equate him as a lion either. At least not the strongest.

I slipped into the bathroom and quickly took off my boots. Then, I removed the extra-long socks I had on and slipped my boots back on.

After that, I pulled the two large D batteries from my pocket and dropped them to the bottom of one sock before tying it down. Then, I repeated the same process. This time wrapping the excessive length of the sock around my right hand extremely tight before exiting the bathroom.

This nigga still sleep, I thought wondering who Blakq had his head down talking to. I looked at James and he simply gestured towards Blakq with a nod.

I adjusted the sock, letting it hang down by my side and began easing towards Blakq.

When I got within striking distance, I peeped at James again. He was watching me like a hawk. Blakq was still oblivious to the approaching danger. But one or two other

112

dudes sensed what was about to take place, hung up their phones and hauled ass downstairs.

I brought the D-batteries up, cocked my arm completely back and swung them bitches with all of my might.

When they made contact with Blakq's head. I heard something crush and something else crack as the top of Blakq's head opened up like an erupting volcano. Blakq fell out of the chair onto the floor. The rest of the guys on the phones instantly started moving.

"Oh shit," I said to myself backing up, praying that I hadn't killed Blakq.

"Give me that!" James tried to snatch the bloody sock out of my hand. "Let it go!" He ordered, snapping me out of my zone, so that he could unwrap the sock from around my fist.

"Go downstairs, make sure you don't have no blood on your clothes," he directed. "Go!" He snapped, and I started moving.

When I got to the top of the stairs, I turned around to make sure James was good. Then, I saw the most gruesome thing I'd ever witnessed in the system.

James reached down, rolled Blakq over onto his back and strategically sat on his stomach. Then, he withdraw the murder weapon that Butt had given me and started slaughtering Blakq. Raising the knife high in the air with both hands before slamming it into Blakq's chest repeatedly, like he was trying to kill him.

Now, I finally understood what James meant when he constantly talked about how we worked out for different reasons, with different things in mind while we were in prison. Things like pain, betrayal, abandonment, release, frustration and anger. All he talked about was preparing for physical and mental war within the system.

By the time one of the guards in the bubble peeped what was going on and called the code for assistance, I had managed to get Hope to let me out of the dayroom for a shower. However, I knew that once they ran them cameras back it was game over.

Chapter 18

Frank

I had just began to drift off into an impromptu nap when the cell door popped opened. "Mannnn," I sat up shaking my head. One thing about prison was there was no peace, no quiet, no rest and no warnings.

My cellmate stuck his head out the door to see what was going on.

"One of us got a visit," he said turning back around.

"It's definitely not me," I assured rolling back over, trying to get comfortable. I didn't get surprise visits. I knew when any of the few people who came to see me were coming.

"They took my visits for a year, so, I know that, what the fuck!" I heard my cellmate shout a split second before I looked up and realized that the cell was empty.

The next thing I knew the cell was flooded with CO's and I was being snatched out of bed and dragged out of the cell.

"Man, get the fuck off me like that!" I bucked, swarming to get free of the knee placed in my back.

"Keep still," Another C.O. barked as I was being handcuffed.

"Man, what the fuck is going on?" I questioned no one in particular looking around. I spotted my cellmate pressed up against the wall in handcuffs.

"Don't play dumb, you know exactly what this about." The half slick intel officer emerged from the crowd. "What you thought you got away? You know how many CI's I got on each tier?" He walked over to the cell and looked inside like he was surveying it.

The funny thing was I'd actually thought I had gotten away. Especially when they hadn't come and grabbed me immediately after Blakq was flown out to shock trauma and James was peeled off of him.

"What you thought we weren't going to run the cameras back?" He questioned before turning around. "Got you and Laury stabbing and beating Blakq," he exposed his hand, and I instantly knew that he was bluffing. "You know he might die right?"

By this time, I had already decided to remain silent. Rental cops, mall security, correctional officers, homicide detectives, housing authority, et cetera. They were all the same to me— information seeking enemies. Looking to box me up, box me in or in some cases box me out. Whenever the case, whenever I ended up in a situation being controlled by them, I kept my mouth shut. Because I knew that the less I said, the less I had to take back or defend.

"You don't have to talk, Lane. I got everything I need," he declared before turning his attention to the COs. "Tear that motherfucker up." He gestured towards the cell. "Open up everything in the there too," he instructed stepping out of the way.

Me and my cellmate, a laid back Christian dude named, Curtis Brown, sat there and watched as the guards tore our cell apart, looking for something that I knew they would never find.

The pity ass intel officer made them open up all of our shit too.

Boxes of soap powder, brand new food items, cosmetics, everything. They even called the maintenance men and plumping crew.

They had to have stayed in the cell for every bit of three hours.

By the time they finished, it looked like a hurricane had ripped through the cell. They really fucked Curtis shit up.

If that wasn't enough, they informed me that I was being placed on administrative lockup pending investigation.

I was livid, picking through the cell, trying to separate Curtis' things from mines.

After a while, I just said, 'fuck it', tossed my most important shit in the cart, cuffed up and let the COs escort me to admin.

I landed right back in the cell with Jewels, the weird ass Muslim dude from Park Heights who knew Dakaron's brothers. Jewels was on admin for allegedly promoting some inappropriate radical Islamic shit.

"Just think about it ock," Jewels was on one of his religious rants again. "Being in prison already shows you that there's a big difference between men and women."

"Yeah, niggas aren't shit!" I interjected.

"Nah, seriously ock. Men are power driven. They always want the crown. They never want to play their position. So, they're quicker to undermine, overthrow, scheme, plot and eventually betray the brother on top," Jewels explained.

"Mannn, women aren't no fucking different," I argued thinking about all the bitches who'd left me or other dudes I knew for dead. "That's why I just got to the point where I don't want no woman and I don't need no nigga. Honestly, if it's not my mother or sisters, I didn't even give a fuck about no woman. I use them for whatever I can gain."

"That's because you're hurt."

"Shiiid, I ain't hurt. I just want a fresh start when I get home." I defended.

"I hear you," Jewels said nonchalantly. "But still, even with all that being said, you're still going to need a loyal person in your corner. And who are more loyal than woman?" Jewels paused as if giving me time to consider his question. "Nobody! That's who," he continued. "Just think about it. Women never follow men of power with the intentions of crossing or replacing them. Look at Jesus and

Prophet Muhammad, peace be upon him. The women never failed them."

"Man, I don't know nothing about all that biblical shit," I confessed. "All I know is that I done seen the closest of friends snake each other out over a bitch. I done seen niggas go to war over pussy. And I done been right there fucking with a bitch while she's lying to some guy on the phone."

"I'm not talking about no hood rats, ock. Women who ain't got no damn sense, "Jewels retorted. "I'm talking about women like the ones who were around Jesus when he took his last breath. Women who remain loyal long after we fall."

"Yeah well, I don't know no women like that besides my mother."

"Aight then, so you know they exist." Jewels attempted to prove his point. "Men aren't like that. They argued about who would replace Jesus before he was even gone. And every last one of them with the exception of John I believe, turned their backs on him for one reason or another."

"So, what are you saying?" I questioned, looking for clarity. "All women are real, and all dudes are fakes?"

"Come on now ock, there's always an exception. But for the most part, you can count on women a hell of a lot more than you can depend on men," he explained but I still wasn't convinced.

"I hear you," I mumbled. "But all them motherfuckers fake in my eyes. Bitches and niggas."

"When you always do what you've always done, you always get what you've always gotten."

"What's that supposed to mean?" I inquired curiously.

"That you not only need to change how you pick and choose the men and women in your life. But you also need to figure out why you gravitate towards them and ask Allah, to guide you in the right direction. Because that's the only way you're going to find the right woman or the sincere brother you need in your life."

I stared at Jewels for a long moment. I could tell that he really believed his own bullshit.

"Yeah okay." I laughed and threw my headphones on because he wasn't talking about shit.

Chapter 19

Frank

I stayed on admin for just about as long as Blakq remained in the Intensive Care Ward at Maryland University Shock Trauma Center. By the time intel informed me that I was going off, Dakaron had been transferred to the Baltimore City Supermax for the Monique incident and James had been shipped out of the penitentiary annex to some unknown location.

"Ay CO." I ran to the door to catch the tier officer who'd just strolled by and looked into the cell. "Ay CO!" I repeated.

"Yeah," he acknowledged and continued to look into cells.

"What they say about me coming off? I questioned impatiently.

"Who is that? Lane?" He inquired.

"Yeah," I confirmed.

"Lane, if you don't lay your ass down!" He fired. "I told you they had a code in F-building," he added. "Be patient man, it won't be long. As soon as traffic call."

"Yeah, that's easy for you to say. You go home every day," I mumbled getting out of the door. I was trying to hit the compound bad. I mean, I couldn't wait to show my face. There had been a lot of whispers about rather or not I was scared to come off. So, you know I couldn't wait for the door to pop.

I walked over to look out of the window to see if there was any movement on the compound. I couldn't sit still. I felt like I had too much to do. "Man, I ain't trying to get stuck over this bitch until after count," I vented staring out the window.

"Allah knows best," Jewels interjected.

Here this nigga go. I shook my head and continued staring out the window. I thought about telling him what I really felt about the community. But decided to keep my thoughts to myself.

"Insha Allah, you give some thought to what we talked about, ock," Jewels continued.

"Concerning what?" I looked at him curiously, hoping he wasn't talking about no Muslim shit.

"Concerning you taking your shahadah," Jewels replied referring to the acceptance of Islam.

"I'm good on that," I assured thinking about all the things that were wrong with prison Islam.

"I'm telling you ock. It ain't nothing else around here for you," Jewels proclaimed.

"Man, that Muslim shit is a joke," I fired unable to bite my tongue any longer. "Y'all talk all that brotherhood shit and be the main ones around this bitch back biting and gossiping. Slandering each other's character and shit. And for what? Position, oil, jealousy."

"Damn ock, that's how you feel huh?"

"Yeah, I don't be with the fake, phony stuff," I declared thinking about all the Muslims who I knew that used the community to play games and shield their dirty practices. "The funny part is since we been cellmates all you talk about is how fucked up the gangs are. But the community doing the same shit!"

"First of all, I don't look down on no gangs. Because I don't believe in bad organization. I believe in bad leadership," Jewels corrected. "Secondly, you aren't ever going to see no real Muslims operating like a gang."

"That's a lie," I challenged confidently. "Niggas locking phones down, building tiers, storing weapons, selling drugs and everything else. What's different?" I stared at

Jewels, but he didn't respond. He couldn't. Not if he was being truthful.

"Then, you keep telling me how the blood of a Muslim is sacred," I added.

"It is," Jewels assured.

"Well then, what about the Muslims that hustling? The ones oppressing niggas and being aggressive? Is their blood sacred?" I asked rhetorically. "Like the Muslim dude that got beat up in the kitchen last week. This nigga dips his waffles into another man's syrup on some gangster shit. And what the community do after this man fucked him up huh?" I questioned with no intentions of allowing Jewels to answer. "Send two Muslims to stab the man half to death. If that's not no gang shit, I don't know what is."

"I'm not saying the community perfect. Not even close," Jewels admitted. "But there are a lot of brothers around here acting in accordance with the true folds and principles of Islam. Everybody in the community not looking for protection."

"Okay, so those are the ones whose blood should be sacred," I argued.

"I agree." Jewels nodded. "This is why brothers like you need to be in the community. Brothers who are serious. You can help clean the compound up. You know they say he who is worst in the dunya, will be best in the deen."

"I'ma independent head buster." I smiled. "Plus, I ain't got time to be babysitting no grown ass men." If prison hadn't taught me anything else, it taught me that, you couldn't teach an old dog new tricks.

Jewels and I continued to go back and forth until they came around and popped the door. "Be safe out there, ock. Keep your ears open and your eyes up."

"Ain't no question." I gave Jewels some love and bounced.

Even though, I wasn't with that Muslim shit, Jewels was still my nigga. I fucked with him because he was authentic. That was rare in prison. Especially, the penitentiary annex.

This time I landed in D-building on A-tier. Which was cool with me because, one of my Longwood homeboys sister ran the building and Butt was on the tier. You know, Butt hit me straight off with a bone chipper.

"So what now?" Butt inquired after giving me another vicious knife.

"I'm wait until they call this yard, so I can go out here a pull up on a few niggas," I explained looking around the dayroom.

"You know your man suppose to be in the infirmary over the 'Cut'?" Butt revealed.

"Yeah, I'm hip," I replied. "That's why these old niggas running around passing kites like they're going to do something."

"Man, fuck these niggas," Butt barked. "Chop these old niggas up."

"You already know. That's why I'm waiting for them to call yard."

"I'm rolling with you."

I nodded in appreciation. There was nothing else to say. I knew that as soon as niggas heard that I was on the compound, they were going to try to click up and stack the deck against me.

"You know I can't leave you out there by yourself," Butt grinned wickedly. "Let me go grab my baby."

I looked behind Butt as he dipped off to get further armed up and prayed that, we didn't have to wear one of these old niggas out for pump faking. Because the joints we had were really going to fuck something up.

Chapter 20

Frank

I'm sure you have guessed by now, that nobody had to get gutted. The two things about prison that you should never forget, was the fact that niggas gossiped like schoolgirls. Then, turned around and tucked their tails like bitches. Especially, when a man who they knew would push that joint hit the yard. Needless to say, it came down to a bunch of, *he said, he said* with nobody willing to stand behind that shit.

After all the dust settled and niggas knew that I wasn't ducking nothing, them old bitch ass niggas decided to let Blakq settle his own score.

So, prison life as I now knew it, went on. I got back in the library, working with a good brother name AbrasX. He was schooling me to the law and teaching me how to really find loopholes.

I did almost fuck around and get caught up about some off the wall shit though. An older convict came to the library and tried to swipe the entire *Yellow Pages* on some creep shit. Talking about he wanted to play *phone lotto*. Simply meaning that he wanted to use the book to sit in the dayroom, at the phone, dialing random numbers until he got lucky and found a woman willing to talk, but I wasn't trying to hear none of that shit.

First and foremost, all of my female cousins' telephone numbers were registered. Secondly, dudes used the book to take care of legitimate business. So, I deaded that shit.

The longer I stayed in prison, the more I learned that there were some real weird motherfuckers floating around. The situation truly made me overstand why AbrasX refused to help everybody get out of prison.

I got my first letter from Dakaron talking about the super max. It was rumored to be underground and some more shit. Butt told me that the supermax was off the chain. But not for the reasons I initially thought. Despite the fact that DOC housed their most problematic inmates there for everything from manipulation to murder and making money, the supermax was out of control. Dangerous due to the slew of female officers who loved to play mind games.

Butt said a lot of good men had entered the supermax and never made it back in one sense or another. Simply put, they got mentally or physically stuck there.

I knew Dak was straight though. His ass would probably fit right in. Because what a lot of motherfuckers didn't know about Dak was that his retarded ass had been over the jail on lock up, throwing piss, slinging shit and creating new freak-ass cocktail concoctions to threw into dudes cells.

Time began to fly by again. It seemed like nothing I filed in court held up. I stayed the course though. Like I said, I wasn't dying in prison. So, I keep on grinding and searching for legal violations in the case. It was an uphill battle though. Especially, trying to come up with lawyer fees after every defeat.

A couple of my uncle's older homeboys looked out. But hustling in prison just wasn't my thing. It was a gateway to unnecessary drama.

Before long, Dakaron was transferred up into the mountains to a spot called Ultramax. Word was the showers rolled up to the cell doors, mail was read on a screen and some more shit. It was serious. Niggas also said that the guards were extremely racist. Playing with inmates food, calling them niggers and stuff. Whatever the case, it wasn't long before some shit jumped off and Dakaron was right at the center.

I could still remember reading about the riot in the Baltimore Sun Newspaper like it was an insurrection. It was

January 6th, 2006. Dakaron ended up getting sent out of state with a bunch of rioters. All of this was during the same that I found Islam. Rather it found me.

I had ended up mistakenly being transferred over to the Cut's infirmary for a whole week. Somehow my vital signs came back completely off. I mean, it was almost as if my heart wasn't even beating. They said that my blood had essentially stopped flowing. Needless to say, they rushed me over to some top flight heart machine in the Cut.

Yet and still, once it was determined that it was a false alarm and I was good, the medical staff still decided to hold on to me for a few days. You know I found something to defend myself with in case it was a setup and Blakq was able to get to me.

The normal buzz of the Cut had just began to fade into a comfortable silence when my room door burst open, and this super muscular guy was pushed inside and ordered to stay put.

"What's going on?" I questioned a little paranoid as the guard secured the door.

"A bunch of guys just stabbed each other up out on the yard," he replied trying to see down the infirmary's hallway. "I think a guard got attacked too."

"What you got caught up?" I sat up and slipped my tennis on while he still had his back turned just in case he was on one.

"Who me?" He shot me a quick look over his shoulder. "Nah, the Baltimore, DC days were over a long time ago for me," he added. "I work up here."

"Oh." I fell silent.

"My bad brother," he turned around and walked towards me.

"Mudhabdhad," he introduced himself extending his hand.

"Say it again." I shook his hand.

"Mudhabdhad," he repeated his name extra slow to make sure I caught every syllable.

"Mudhabdhad," I repeated just as slow, and he nodded his head.

"Frank," I informed.

"Nice to meet you brother."

"Likewise," I assured.

To make a long story short, Mudhabdhad and I got to talking and he began to make a lot of sense. His whole approach to explaining Islam was different. He made me see it. He got me to feel it. He had me taste it. However, it was a question that altered everything I thought about what I was doing, how I was living. Why I wasn't at peace.

"You know how you love somebody, but they don't treat you right?" Mudhabdhad asked.

"Absolutely," I assured thinking about Jamaine, my so-called old girl and a few family members.

"Yeah well, that's how the street life or game as we call it is," Mudhabdhad said before going on to explain how I would never find peace, until I submitted my entire will to do the Will of Allah.

He talked about the disadvantages of going back out into the streets without a spiritual foundations. He made me think about something my mother use to always say about faith being the substance of things hoped for, the evidence of things unseen. Then, he pulled out a pocket-sized Holy Quran and showed me how I was born a Muslim.

In so many words, Mudhabdhad convinced me into giving him my word, that I would attend Jummah at least once.

Eventually, I was moved back over to the penitentiary annex and the rest became, as the say, 'Islam'.

Chapter 21

Frank

Dakaron sent me some flicks from out of state. I really hadn't believed this nigga when he said that they had shipped him to the federal penitentiary in Pollock, Louisiana. But when I got the flicks of him, Lil Ache and Willie Bates. It was a wrap! The governor had really placed my nigga in federal custody with no fed time.

Of course, Dakaron fed right into the hype. He was writing dumb shit like, you ain't got to drop bodies like Itchy Man or move bricks like Gorgie to end up in the feds. All you got to do is cut up in the system.

It didn't seem like we had been locked up for as long as we had, until we finally got a court date. That's when it hit me. That's when I really began thinking about it. So much time had lapsed. So many motherfuckers had fallen off or just straight up disappeared on us. And I always wondered if they realized that, there came a time when silence or abandonment became betrayal.

I had watched the whole system shift. Men who were once giants began to die off or curve out. The gang culture rose, snitching basically became *legal* because there was no longer certain punishment. And this was before the guard who got attacked on the yard during the Baltimore/DC war died in the hospital and the administration clamped down like 'Homeland Security'.

The thing that hurt me the most throughout my bid though, was the fact that niggas had questioned my integrity and falsely accused me of possibly doing something out of order. This was despite the fact that, I rose to meet every fucking challenge. I never backed down nor cowered in the face of adversity. My track record was impeccable.

When my lawyer came to see me about possibly transferred back over to the city jail to await the outcome, I immediately told him that I was good. A lot of dudes thought that I was crazy for choosing to stay in the penitentiary annex and Dak said I didn't know what I was missing. But the truth was, I had an extremely, bad, West Indies looking nurse with an extra tight pussy and magical mouth that I was fucking with. Plus, I thought about all the shit that I heard about was going on over the jail. Gang members acting like *junior COs* locking dudes in, talking reckless with guards and shit. Especially the women. Guards being gang members, getting guys stabbed and shit. Everybody getting high, turning into old and young junkies.

I even heard the Muslims were out of pocket over there. Clicking up like parasites. Acting like they were entitled to certain things because they were deep. There was no Islamic law, so there was no order. Dakaron had even said that they were starting to be just as hated as the Bloods before the NBA—Money No Bloods Allowed—Money alliance was formed. So, I had more than enough reasons not to go.

My lawyer explained to me over the telephone that the state had placed a deal on the table. Thirty or thirty-five for me and fifty for Dakaron. But I just smiled because I never even considered taking a dive. And I already knew where Dak stood.

When we went up in that courtroom and lost with all that we had in our favor, I was crushed. I mean, that shit really hurt. Especially, after being abandoned by the world and tossed around the pits of prison. Yet, I knew we would survive. We always had. We never crumbled. And no matter what, I always stayed focused on freedom. Even when my inner struggles of doubt and personal grief were at their peak, I remained tall.

So, when Dakaron and I got back into the bullpen. I told him to stay strong because, this too would pass.

Chapter 22

Frank

After we lost our court hearing and I went back to the penitentiary annex, my lawyer re-filed the trial judge's Patuxent 'Youth Offender' program recommendation and started pressing the administration to get me on the transfer list. But I just wanted to go home. I was tired.

It was at this same time that I started to feel heavy burdened. I felt weighed down, forgotten, isolated, lost and helpless. I went into a slight depression. My fucking hair even started to fall out. Islam was the only thing that kept me going. Because I swear by Allah, if it wasn't for His mercy and the practice of Islam, I would've murdered something.

"I just don't understand how these peoples can intentionally disregard their own law," I argued to one of my Muslim brothers as we walked down the compound, coming from the library. "It's personal ock, I know it is."

"Well, I don't want you to feel that special ock." He teased. "Nah, seriously though. Rather you're as innocent as you claim to be or as guilty as I confessed I was, the system will play games. It just designed that way."

"Yeah, but it is not supposed to be like that," I retorted. "Now, I'm fucked up. My folks broke and niggas in the streets acting like they ain't got no money. These lawyers still trying to get paid though. That shit got me thinking about hustling again." I continued, admitting how I truly felt.

"Fear Allah!" The brother warned staring at me for a long moment. "Now is not the time to lose faith."

"I ain't losing no faith," I assured. "I'm just talking about hustling. Changing my own conditions."

"Look ock, I know I can't tell you how to get your lawyer money. Especially, since the hunger for freedom is already there. But I will say this, it's normal to doubt one's faith in the face of tragedy or what seems like defeat. But Allah knows best, ock." he explained.

I really considered what the brother was saying because I knew that he had my best interest at heart.

"I can promise you this from experience though," he continued. "If you don't stand firm in your faith now, you will never stand at all. Because Allah tests us for a reason."

I knew what he was saying was dead on. But at the same time, the thought of dying in prison was a reoccurring nightmare that I refused to let materialize.

"You're right, ock, having only two, three people that you can truly depend on is a fucked feeling though," I admitted shamefully. "Especially when you have done so much for people."

"Yeah, I remember when reality first hit me," he confessed and continued. "My pops had just…"

I thought about reaching out to Paul-Paul about the lawyer money.

He had been one of our biggest supporters when we first fell. Making house calls, sending money orders and naked flicks, showing up in court and all. Then, I remembered that he too, in the end, had shown his true colors and left us for dead.

Plus, I hadn't spoken to him since all that crazy shit happened with Jamaine trying to rob Slick Webb and Veney and a real pet parrot gave his ass up.

"… that was what messed me up the most, you feel me?" The brother looked over at me as if he expected me to respond.

"Of course," I replied, unable to elaborate.

"Whatever you do ock, just don't forsake Islam for the dunya," he pleaded. "A lot of brothers been doing that lately. Leaving the community to gangbang."

"Imagine that!" I retorted thinking back to how bad dudes had wanted Dakaron and I to be down. "I didn't join that shit when it was at its strongest. So, you know damn well, I'm not about to join it while it's at its weakest."

There was just no way in hell that I would ever join a gang.

"Plus, that's the Willie Lynch syndrome," I added. "Niggas aren't doing nothing but feeding off of each other."

"Before I first met you, brothers were saying that you were affiliated." He studied me. "That was supposed to have been the reason why nobody ever stepped to you behind Blakq."

I couldn't help but laugh. "Guys come up with all types of reasons to justify not doing nothing," I said knowing that the only people who had probably been pushing some foolishness like that, were Blakq's so called homeboys. Old penitentiary negros who were afraid to jump out there and get the fur tore of off their asses.

"They don't be knowing that slander can get you slaughtered."

"You're right." He shook his head in agreement. "That's how brothers end up in something or on admin behind something they're not even a part of."

The brother and I continued to talk until we got to the building. Then, we salaamed each other and headed our separate ways. I really had a lot to think about.

Chapter 23

Frank

Hustling just wasn't going to do it for me anymore. I had come too far to essentially began going backwards. I knew too much and that alone required something. I thought back to all the programs I had completed. Friend of a Friend, Men in Transition Towards Success, Thinking for a Change and AVP. I knew that the two cutie pies, Adventurous Andy and No Nonsense Nina from the Alternative Violence Program would probably tell me to stay patient and persistent. Whatever the case, I simply just decided to keep my library gig and buried my heads in the law books.

AbrasX and I were over in the fiction section of the library, restocking books when the librarian hit the worker assistance button.

"I got it, sir," AbrasX volunteered getting to his feet before I could even respond. So, I just continued to stock books as if it was nothing.

But truth be told, I had been hot on Ms. Watkins heels from the first day her pretty, red ass strutted down the compound. I wanted to fuck her in the worst way. I took every opportunity I could to be in her personal space. I knew how old she was and how many kids she had. Shiiid, I even knew where to find her around the Whitelock area when I touched down.

"Don't forget to keep them in alphabetical order, sir," AbrasX instructed walking off.

"Yes, sir," I mocked peeping over my shoulder at the back of his bald head.

AbrasX was a good brother. Probably the most solid and conscious one I knew. But sometimes he just got in the way. I knew he didn't mean no harm. But still, Ms. Watkins was a target on my radar that I was trying to hit. Especially, since the nurse I was dealing with had clammed up on me after my case got denied.

I ran my finger across the back of the books already on the shelf, reading the titles and author names to make sure that they were all in alphabetical order. *If You Cross Me Once* by Anthony Fields, *Bonded By Blood and Trust No Man* by Cash, *Raised as a Goon* by Ghost, *Bodymore Murderland…*

"You good, Sir?" AbrasX walked back over with a look of brotherly concern on his face.

"Yeah," I glanced up at him strangely and continued fixing the books. "Why you ask me that?"

"Because Ms. Watkins just said they want you back in the building," he revealed.

"What now?" I stood up.

"Yes Sir." He nodded. "She's in there writing you a pass."

I instantly began thinking, wondering if I had done anything to get myself placed on administrative lockup. I wasn't hustling. I wasn't pressing up on nobody. The nurse girl had cut me off. And I definitely wasn't beefing. At least not with nobody that I could think of.

Oh shit! I thought when it hit me. I had put my hands on a nigga a few days ago. Lumped him up pretty good too. *Man, I know this nigga didn't show his face.* I shook my head because he was supposed to be hiding out in the cell on voluntary bedrest, so that we didn't get locked up.

Nah, slim a cold-blooded man. I told myself. If it was an admin move, I didn't know what the fuck was going on.

"What they shook my cell down or something?" I pried.

"She didn't say," AbrasX replied. "But they can't search the cell outside of your presence." AbrasX added knowing all the laws, DOC polices, and more.

"And Ms. Watkins didn't say nothing else?"

"No Sir, she just told me to let you know that they were calling you back to the housing unit so you could grab your stuff," AbrasX explained. "You good Sir?"

"I hope so," I replied knowing like AbrasX did that the building never called you back from work early unless something was wrong.

"You need me to do anything Sir? Make any calls?" AbrasX investigated like the true law-scholar that he was because he knew the ropes. He'd seen the same thing repeated so many times that he said he lost count.

"Nah, just make sure I get my job back, if they grab me."

"That goes without saying Sir," AbrasX assured.

I went into Ms. Watkins' office, got my pass, flirted a little bit and then headed on back to the building. *How in the hell the lame ass hearing officer get a shot at a woman like that?* I wondered curiously walking down the compound.

"Hotep," my man Angola from the tier offered me the signature Pan Afrikan greeting.

"Hotep," I greeted him back. I wasn't caught up on the bullshit. Besides, The Holy Quran says that, when someone gave you a greeting. Give them a greeting equal to or greater than. "What's up on the tier? They grabbing dudes or something?"

"Not that I know of." Angola looked back towards the building. "Why what's up?"

"Nah, they just called me back," I revealed. "They're probably about to bring me a move or something."

"You know they been sending a lot of brothers out too," Angola said.

"Yeah, I know." I paused for a second. "I hope that's not the case."

"Me too," Angola seconded. "But if you do go. I just hope you don't go over M-C-I-J. Especially not with all that slick shit you got."

"Why you say that?"

"You know how some of them property officer suckers be when they can't be a man. They're like women who can't keep a man. So, when they encounter a man, they don't know how to treat a man," Angola explained. "Although secretly, a lot of times, them suckers be wishing they could be that man."

Angola had never lied about that.

"If you go over there though, it's a beautiful sister, name Ms. Lawrence that work down the property room. Man, shorty fire! I'm talking about crazy bad. Red, thick, mean walk, soft voice, super sexy face. All that!" Angola spat excitedly and I knew Ms. Lawrence must really be bad, because Angola didn't even curse. "L. Lawrence. You won't miss the gap in her mouth."

"I heard that," I continued heading for the building to find out what was going on.

"Don't forget yo, seriously. L. Lawrence. Tell her Angola hollered at her!" Angola yelled.

When I hit the building, the Sergeant stepped out of the control center bubble and informed me that I was being transferred to the Patuxent Institution for the Youth Offender Program.

Chapter 24

Frank

When I first walked into the Patuxent Institution, I felt strange, like I was walking in a dream or something. I mean, this was the same prison where I had attended the 'Scared Straight' Program my mother had forced me into almost twenty-years ago. On top of that, I'd read 'The Master Plan' book by the guy Chris Wilson.

Damn! I thought wondering to myself, if any of the guys who'd tried to guide me in the right direction back then were still around. I inquired about the old head who used to talk the most trash because his name was the only one I could remember. Nobody appeared to recognize his name though. But shiiid, he'd had been about sixty years old back then. So, his old ass was probably dead. Then again, prison did preserve a motherfucker.

One of the first things I noticed about Patuxent as a resident, was the bullshit ass, little kid, mind games that everybody seemed to be playing. Officers and inmates alike. Then, the guards don't wear vest, nor possess radios. Some didn't even carry mace because there was virtually no violence. Therefore, disrespect that niggas usually got wore out for went unchecked like it was nothing. It was crazy. All I kept thinking about was how a lot of Patuxent residents, guards included was going to be in for a rude awakening when they arrived at another institution.

However, I stayed focused. I was only there for one thing and one thing only. Evaluation. Once that was finished, I knew I would be on the first thing smoking because I was now too old for the youth offender program. Another game the system played.

It took me a few weeks to get into the groove of things. Like I said, Patuxent wasn't like anything I had been use to for the last sixteen or seventeen years. I was used to spots like the 'Cut', Penitentiary annex, Supermax, etc. Spots where codes were called without warning. Spots where anything could jump off and somebody was always putting some work in. Spots where niggas were almost always on edge because the drama stayed heating up and the bodies stayed dropping. In so many words, prisons that weren't so watered down.

Of course, I was happy to run up on a few good men whom I hadn't seen in years. Men like Gregory Gaither, Henry Barksdale, Wyman Ushry, Darren Lee, Shakim Shabazz and Edmndson's Village very own, Ransom 'Rock' Williams III. Men who had guided me through one time or another. My pops homeboy, Lamont McGinnis was even on location during a risk assessment or something for parole. But if that wasn't enough, my old workout partner, James was on deck, and you know I hadn't seen him since the dayroom incident in the penitentiary annex.

We reminisced about how we'd almost killed Blakq and got away with it. But the thing we both wanted to do the most was put each other to the test on the workout tip. You know, to make sure each other still had it.

We started getting it in like we use too. A thousand of this. A thousand of that. Stomach, chest, back, running, the works. Niggas were looking at us like we were Martians or something because of the type of workouts we were putting down. Plus, I jumped in the boxing program.

Besides, the three amazing beauties, Ms. Tee, Ms. Toni and Ms. Sophia in the medical department, the only thing that was sweet about the 700 Club was this pint-sized, dimepiece named Tolbert, a fine, little, sassy thing named Chase, and the prettiest rookie I had ever seen, hands down; a slim, young beauty with curly dreads and the sexiest gap-toothed smile ever by the name of Ekeh. Beyond that, Patuxent was garbage. A straight circus with a bunch of clowns in it. I couldn't wait to get up out of that motherfucker.

Hold up! My bad! There was no way in the world that I could forget to mention the super bad, earth tone, facility ARP coordinator, C. Sheilds. Shorty was right on a grown and sexy, sophisticated level. She had serious body too with deadly curves.

Other than that, the only thing that kept me focus was James, freedom and the boxing program. I can't lie though, when I first started fucking with Darryl Newsome. My entire body use to ache. I'm talking about every fucking muscle. I mean, don't get it twisted though, your boy was already in blast. But training with Darryl Newsome was a whole different monster. Yet and still, I stuck with it because it was well worth it.

I wasn't sure exactly how long my evaluation was going to take. But if niggas thought that I was nice with my dick beaters before, Darryl Newsome was turning me into a fucking animal. After all, Darryl Newsone was one of the guys who kept the heart of the city – Antonio Jackson – sharp when he was doing his prison time. before he went home and claimed all the titles in his weight class.

Chapter 25

Frank

I didn't make the cut after my Patuxent evaluation. It wasn't no fault of mines though. Like I said before, I was just too old for the program now. Once I learned that the evaluation was complete, I wrote everybody I could, trying to get up out that motherfucker. But they were just determined to hold me hostage.

However, Allah always knows best. I ended up discovering the jury poll issue that got us back in court.

This may sound crazy. But once I realized that there was no way for the courts to get around the issue. I started feeling funny, strange even about going home. "Don't get me wrong," I paused for a second to make sure what I was trying to explain to James made sense. "I want to go home, believe that," I assured wanting to be clear. "It's just that so much has changed. I don't even really know my family no more," I admitted. "They're all grown up. My little sister was even out there protesting during the Freddie Gray riot."

"I understand exactly where you're corning from. It's a whole new world out there bruh." James agreed.

"Shiiid, in here too," I fired, thinking about how much shit had changed since I came to prison. Damn near all the women use to be bad. The food was good and the men moved in silence. You had family days and some more shit. Now, most of the women were busted up with big guts and flat butts, or they were overweight, funny-looking or funny-built. Even the male officers were out of shape. And the SRT — Special Response Team wasn't much better. It was taking these fat motherfuckers five and ten minutes to respond to codes for assistance. Add to that, the fact that the food was trash. Most of the family oriented programs were gone and the system had changed for the worst.

I mean, everybody wanted you to know their business. Dudes were throwing up gang signs and basically using drugs right in front of the police. The craziest thing though was the fact that, as deep as the gang members were, they had absolutely no real power. Because all they did was eat the flesh of their own. And no house divided against itself could stand.

"Don't even get me started on this watered down ass shit!" James warned.

"Yeah, I know right." I smiled knowing exactly how he felt about the game. "I just be thinking about all the motherfuckers who left me for dead, crossed me out, lied, thought I was finished or just straight said fuck me." I paused. "Like, how do I address them?"

"One of my former friends got killed by a fucking kid! And I mean, I honestly understand why the kid killed him. He was a piece of shit!" I admitted. "But still, he was my friend and I loved him like a brother," I vented. "I don't know how I may feel if I run into this kid."

"You got to stay focused. Remember who was there and who wasn't." James challenged making a lot of sense. "You definitely can't come back to this shit!"

"I know." I nodded in agreement remembering the days when the first thing a dude asked for, when he hit the yard was a knife. Now, it was drugs. "Insha Allah, these peoples don't play no games."

"For them to play games now, would be a straight up miscarriage of justice."

"Let's hope they see it like that," I mumbled optimistically.

It was September 16th, 2017, my little sister Meek's birthday to be exact, when Dakaron and I walked out of the courthouse free men. It was a feeling that I would never forget nor ever fully be able to explain. Something like Jonah coming up out of the whale's mouth.

I immediately fell to the ground and offered salat.

"They can't keep a fighting man down, Cuz!" I kept repeating over and over again. It felt so crazy. I mean, I had never laid down, given up or surrendered to life in prison. Never stopped fighting or looking for loopholes. But I also wasn't for sure if the day would ever come. Yet, there I was surrounded by the only people that truly mattered to me. My little sister had a theory about a birthday wish. But I knew that it was only by the grace of Allah that we were standing there. And I knew that the reason that I'd been punished was due to my disobedience to my mother.

"I love you so much, ma!" I snatched my mother little tail up into my arms and twirled her around in the middle of Downtown Baltimore, kissing on her soft cheeks.

"Franklin, boy, if you don't put me down." She looked around embarrassed as my siblings laughed and joked.

Honor your parents Prophet Muhammad had said before going on to instruct us to honor our mothers three times, after Allah before honoring our fathers.

I had honored all the wrong people when I was on the streets. People who betrayed me. Yet, the one person who truly deserved my honor, loyalty and love. The one person who never left my side was the person I failed.

"No more, ma!" I shouted. "No more!"

"No more what?" My mother questioned confused as I carefully put her down.

"Don't worry about it." I kissed her again. "Just know that I love you."

"I love you too son."

I gave Dakaron some love and got the out of there. I didn't know what the judge was thinking releasing us. But I wasn't about to stick around to find out.

My sisters and little brother took me straight to the mall and started playing dress up. They had me in all kinds of gear I'd never even heard of. Skinny shit at that! In the end, I stepped out in a green and white Alexander McQueen Logo Tape Sweatshirt, some Purple Denim Vintage Spotted Black Wash Jeans, and a pair of green, white and black, Air Jordan DMP 1 Retro High with a nice ass Rolex Gold Daytona Green Dail.

I knew I was killing it because a bunch of women started flocking to me. I even ran into one of my old flames and booked or should I say, got the cellphone number of a fine, beautiful Muslim sister by the name of Bayyinah Bushrod or B as I decided to refer to her. Because she was so fucking beautiful and she had a thick body to match.

Chapter 26

Frank

Gotdamn! I thought as my head fell back on to the headrest. I bit my bottom lip, looked back down between my legs and pushed Mynesha's red and yellow locks over her shoulder. I wanted to get a good look at her pretty face, as she continued to give me that monster head.

The minute my sisters started posting pictures of me being home, the internet began buzzing and it wasn't long before old bitches I used to fuck were DMing my sisters. Mynesha being the main one. Now, of course, I had no intentions of fucking with no bitch who'd left me for dead. But I would be lying if I said that I wasn't curious about what that head and pussy was like. Especially considering the fact that her shit had been a torch back in the day.

After a brief phone conversation, I decided to let Mynesha 'break me in' as she said. I waited for Meek to leave for work before I texted Mynesha her address out in Annapolis and went to get ready. I was dying to sample that pussy and head again.

When Mynesha showed up, I was fucked up at first. I mean, you know how a nigga be hearing things in the joint. This bitch right, shorty fucked up now, and more. Yeah well, I'd heard about Mynesha getting some work done. But man, let me tell you. When I opened that door and laid eyes on this bitch, I immediately started second guessing my position. After all, it wasn't like she was my main girl or nothing when I went in.

Mynesha didn't waste no time. Bad bitches never do. She strutted pass me into the house and I quickly began struggling with the locks, trying to secure the door.

What I saw when I turned around was enough to make me forget about all the bullshit Mynesha had done while I was away. Mynesha was holding her coat open, revealing nothing except a sexy ass black negligee and matching heels. "You like that?" Mynesha teased allowing the long trench coat to fall from her shoulders.

I couldn't speak. All I could do was stand there hypnotized by her body. *This bitch body is sick!* I slowly licked my lips.

I knew that Meek was going to be at the hospital late. So, I was ready to pounce on her ass like a lion who hadn't eaten in months.

I slowly ran my eyes up and down Mynesha's torso, taking in every fucking inch carefully. I didn't remember her being so bad, so confident and so damn seductive.

Mynesha wet the tips of her fingers with her tongue and started playing with her own nipples. Then, she snaked one of her hands down to her pussy. That was when I noticed the pot of gold tattooed around her pussy with a clouds hovering above. The cloud had a rainbow extending from it that curved over Mynesha's soft hip and disappeared around to her back somewhere.

"I'ma make you fall in love boy," Mynesha assured with a devilish grin as her eyes narrowed. "You think this pussy was something before you went to jail." She gently patted her pot of gold. "Wait until you get some of this grown woman wet-wet."

Before I knew what was happening, I was moving towards Mynesha, taking off my clothes at the same time. I pushed her up against the wall and let my hands run wild. I wanted to touch and taste every part of her. I started ripping her negligee open, dying to get a piece of her.

"Slow down baby," Mynesha cautioned me as I went crazy. "Let me welcome you home first. That way, when you get up in this pussy, you can be there for a while." With that said, Mynesha walked me over to the couch and told me to sit down.

Then, she removed my jeans from around my ankles, forced my legs apart and took my dick into her hands.

"Hhhhhh, mmhhhh, mmmhhhh." Mynesha smiled up at me. "I'ma enjoy this big motherfucker." She slowly jerked my dick as she looked at it from all angles. And just when I was about to bust, Mynesha kissed the head and stood up to get out of her half torn negligee.

After she was completely naked, Mynesha turned her back to show me her fleshy ass cheeks before using her thighs to make them bounce and jiggle. I also discovered exactly where the other half of her rainbow tattoo landed. It traveled across her pretty, soft looking, left butt cheek directly to her ass crack.

When she backed up right into my face and bent over, I read the words that were stretched professionally around her asshole.

Taste the Rainbow, they read, and I did. I stuck my tongue right into Mynesha's ass and twisted it around, before attacking her mouthwatering looking pussy. This bitch really tasted like Skittles, I admitted to myself taking a mouthful of Mynesha's pussy into my mouth.

But again, Mynesha had other plans, which is how I ended up on the couch, getting the best head of my life.

"I just wanted you to taste what you have been missing." Mynesha looked over her shoulder and withdraw her pussy out of my mouth. "Now, I'ma let you feel it."

Mynesha got on her knees between my legs and took me back into her super soft, well-manicured hands. A woman had never looked sexier holding a dick in her hand.

"Close your eyes," she instructed but I shook my head. I was enjoying the view too much.

"Okay, but don't cum too fast," she warned leaning forward to take me into her mouth.

Man, let me tell you something. When Mynesha's mouth made contact with my dick, I couldn't do nothing but close my eyes. Then, she had the nerve to deep throat it. No gag-reflex or nothing.

When I opened my eyes to watch Mynesha's work, I knew that it wasn't going to be long. First of all, she took her time and used her mouth to make love to me. Secondly, she had this intoxicated look on her face as if she was getting pleasure out of sucking my dick. That shit was so fucking sexy.

Mynesha knew she had me too. The bitch even smiled when she felt me shiver and reached down to make sure my toes were curled. Plus, she kept talking shit. Mumbling little nasty things that sent chills up my spine.

Every time I came close to busting, Mynesha would order me to open my eyes and look at her as my dick slowly disappeared down her throat. Never losing eye contact.

I watched Mynesha come up for air, saliva and spit hanging from her mouth and hands as she slowly, long stroked me. "What the fuck are you doing to me?" I managed between shivers and heavy exhales.

"You ain't seen nothing yet," Mynesha whispered before dipping her head beneath the underside of my dick to slowly drag her tongue back and forth. "Mmmmmmh," she moaned licking my balls carefully as she firmly squeezed and stroked my dick.

"Bitch, I swear to God!" I don't know what came over me. But I reached down, grabbed Mynesha by her throat and began choking her. I wasn't trying to hurt her. I just wanted her to know how good she was sucking my dick. She must've known because she just grinned up at me.

"Yes, choke me daddy," Mynesha encouraged intensifying her attack.

The more I squeezed Mynesha's neck, the more passionately she sucked. I wrapped her locks around my fist and started shoving my dick deep down her throat and she loved every second of it.

"I'm about to bust!" I warned standing up so that I could fuck her face.

"Spit in my mouth." Mynesha begged opening her mouth to stick out her tongue.

Fuck it, I thought in the moment, spitting in Mynesha's mouth. I loved a nasty bitch anyway.

"Now, cum all over my face," Mynesha encouraged rubbing my dick all over her face.

I grabbed Mynesha's head and began fucking her throat again. And I swear by Allah, it felt like she had a tight, wet pussy in her throat.

I forced my dick down her throat over and over again, until spit and saliva was hanging from my nuts. Each time Mynesha's lips made contact with my balls. I felt like a porn star. Then, I felt a fire start in my stomach as my entire body got hot. And before I knew it I nutted deep in Mynesha's throat.

"Stick your tongue out," I commanded through clenched teeth, pulling my dick free just as the second blast of cum shot across Mynesha's pretty face completely missing her tongue.

"Stay still," I ordered gripping Mynesha's locks in one hand and stroking my saliva coated dick with the other as she wiggled her tongue wildly.

The next blast of sperm went across the side of Mynesha's cheek and tongue. After that, she just grabbed my dick and ate the nut off the tip as it spilled out. That shit drove me crazy.

After a while, my legs began to shake and I collapsed on the couch. Mynesha's nasty ass sat there on her heels, licking my nut off of her wrist and hands before using her fingers to push the cum on her face into her mouth like it was the best thing she'd ever tasted.

"Your cum taste good daddy." She twirled a cum string around her finger and stuffed it into her sticky looking mouth. "Now, I want you to stretch this pussy out."

"Hold up, give me a second to get myself together." I pleaded. I was quickly beginning to realize that fucking in the streets was a hell of a lot more serious than sneaking off for a jailhouse quickie.

Once I got myself together, I got up and bent Mynesha over the back of my sister's couch. Then, I mashed her face into the cushions because I wanted that phat ass all the way up in the air while I drilled it.

When I slid into that pussy, I was no more good. I mean, that motherfucker was titillating tight, super soaked and dangerously deep.

"Ssssss, yes daddy," Mynesha cried out as I went balls deep.

I slapped her across the ass aggressively and told her to shut up as I watched that pretty motherfucker shake. Then, I grabbed two handfuls of ass and spread that phat motherfucker wide open, so that I could get another good look at the end of that rainbow.

I spit right in Mynesha's asshole. *Bullseye!* I smiled as my spit saturated Mynesha's ass before rolling down the crack to her booty. I took my finger and smeared the spit around before pushing it into her asshole.

"You can have it however you want it daddy," Mynesha submitted looking over her shoulder.

I don't even got to tell you what came next. You know that I got up in that ass nice and good. I had to. I was a conqueror and I loved dominating bad bitches.

"Make me yours daddy! Make me yours!" Mynesha shouted over and over as I held her waist steady and tried to knock the bottom out of her asshole. I didn't want her to be able to sit down for days.

"Pull my hair while you pound it daddy. Stretch me wide open! That's how you make me cum!"

I tore Mynesha's ass up and she enjoyed every minute of it. I even made her squirt twice.

In the end, I had to admit that her pussy was still a torch. But her asshole and head game was a straight up missile.

"I missed you so much," Mynesha uttered softly out of the blue teasing my nipple as she had her head laid across my chest.

We were lying on the floor, sweaty, enjoying the aftermath of our sexcapade. At least I was. Until she started with the dumb shit.

I just continued to stare up at the ceiling. Why bitches always get emotional after they get some good dick? I wondered.

"You heard what I said?" Mynesha looked up into my face. I really didn't want to have this conversation.

"Franklin!" Mynesha punched me in the side and shot up on one elbow to look directly into my eyes. "I know you hear me."

"Yeah, I heard you," I mumbled still trying to avoid fucking up my good mood.

"Well," Mynesha pressed the issue.

"Come on, Cuz, chill with all that."

"Chill with all what?" Mynesha twisted her grill up. "Wasn't no chill with that when I was sucking your dick like crazy."

"Bitch!" I sat up. Now, I was mad. "You should be lucky I even let you sample the dick after all the fuck shit you did while a nigga was behind the wall."

"Fuck shit?" Mynesha repeated like she was surprised. "What fuck shit?"

"Fucking Jamaine for one bitch!" I got to my feet and started grabbing my clothes. I didn't even know why I had even entertained this bitch. The past had destroyed any chance we ever had at a future. To be honest, now I was surprised that I was even in the same room with this bitch. Let alone having sex or a conversation with her.

"So, you blaming me for some shit your phony ass friend did?"

"What? Bitch are you serious?" I just stared at her. She had to be joking. "It takes two to tango."

"You know what the fuck I mean nigga! I was hurt you were gone and that nigga caught me at a weak moment and took advantage of me." She tried to justify.

I just continued to stare at her. Then, I thought about something AbrasX always said about Muslims always showing the greatest intelligence. He said, they even argued in the best manner.

"Look Cuz, I think we were both kids who didn't understand what we were asking each other to do," I admitted sincerely.

"We both had our own set of rules Franklin," Mynesha retorted.

"Yeah, but there was no law," I explained still trying to humble myself. "And without law, there can be no order. So, we made shit up as we went along to justify our lack of faith and actions. And in the long run, it caused us to go and grow in different directions."

"So, what now? That's it? You can't fuck with me? I came over here and sucked your dick for nothing?" Mynesha asked with an attitude.

"It wasn't for nothing. You owed me that?" I laughed and tried to lighten the mood.

"Fuck you nigga!" Mynesha got up and snatched her trench coat up off the floor. "You think you're something because your home? You're a nobody." She marched towards the door slipping into her coat. "And for the record nigga, I fucked Jamaine a lot more than once!" She fired snatching the front door open.

"You think I didn't know that you dumb bitch?" I yelled behind her as she stormed out. "Why do you think both of you of bitches been dead to me?" I added just before the door slammed shut.

I picked up the remote and turned the flat screen on to see what was on TV. I flipped through the channels until I realized that there was nothing on but a bunch of old ass repeats. The only thing new on was The First 48 and I damn sure wasn't about to watch that. I hated that show. All it did was proved to me that America looked at us as entertainment and nothing else.

I laid there in my own thoughts for a while, just thinking. I didn't want to run around fucking a bunch of dumb, dizzy bitches with nothing going on in life. I was too old for that shit.

I wanted to find a good woman and settle down. Get married, maybe have some little ones. I wanted a woman I could love who would love me back. But what was love without freedom, justice and equality?

I thought about something the Prophet said about finding a good wife being half of your Islam and decided to call the beautiful Muslim sister Bayyinah I'd met the day I came home. *That's what I need. A good woman,* I thought reaching for my phone.

Chapter 27

Frank

The next year was crazy. First, Dakaron allowed Monique's son and his little crew to bait him into a pissing match. Although, I kept telling him to let them kids have it. But they didn't make it any better by fucking with Chanae's son, Darrien. Dakaron was hands on when it came to his family. Especially, his mother and daughters. Needless to say, once the peace treaty was violated, I couldn't talk Dakaron off the diving board. I definitely tried though.

I asked him when were we going to begin to live what we'd been preaching? I wanted to know why we weren't applying what we knew or enforcing what we said.

My argument was the fact that we claimed to know better. Promised to do better. We even professed to want better while we were still trapped in prison. Yet, when Allah blessed us to see daylight, we went right back down the path of ignorance and self-destruction.

Dakaron wasn't trying to hear none of that though. In his mind, Venique and his little crew were more dangerous to him and his family, than the Covid-19 pandemic.

Of course, this left me with a tough decision to make. But as always, I choose my nigga. So, after going back and forth for a few days. Dakaron and I hatched a plan to start putting Venique's little pups to sleep. A crazy plan, if you asked me.

The first kill was as easy as one, two, three. The second kill was a little more difficult. The kid Chimel didn't have a lot of hangups. So, he didn't do a lot of slipping up. We had to really work hard to box this kid in. We actually almost fucked around and got jammed up. Chimel really reminded

154

me of this black and Philippine joker named Fat Khy and his Mexican homeboy Jefe we tried to grab back in the day. But he never really slipped.

The crazy thing though was when, this silly ass nigga Dakaron decided to go to Chimel's vigil against my wishes.

It was the dumbest shit in the world in my mind. I mean, in the streets, when you really were responsible for putting the dirt over a nigga, you didn't attend his prayer vigil, wake, funeral, pay for no coffins or none of that other shit. That was some movie shit! But Dakaron had always had a reckless fetish for the spotlight.

On the day of vigil, I called Dakaron and tried to talk him off the ledge. I tried to make him understand that he may very well be jumping into something that could affect both of us.

" .... you do this Cuz, it is not about your family no more," I disputed. "It's about you and your ego. The great Dakaron."

"It always is," Dakaron chimed.

"You always have to win," I fired.

"I always do." Dakaron boasted.

I continued to challenge Dakaron's plans. But again, he was blinded by his own ego. So, I just cursed his dumb ass out and hung up the phone heated. *This dumb ass nigga going to send us back to prison watch,* I thought shaking my head in frustration.

For the rest of day, thoughts of being back in the box, trapped control my mind. I had to shoot over to B's house to try and ease my mind. Because honestly, she was the only thing that brought me peace. I found solace in her company; she was my sunshine.

Yet and still, when I left B's spot, I still felt like I had to do something. Even if it meant protecting Dakaron from himself. I couldn't just sit back and let Dakaron crash out. Especially, knowing that I was in the car with him.

I'ma take the wheel from this silly nigga, I told myself on the ride home.

I knew that Dakaron was going to buck any idea I had that kept him away from the vigil. So, I just decided to be at the vigil without being in it.

When I got back to my new apartment, I headed directly to the hall closet. I reached inside, behind my coats and pulled out the golf bag that was leaned up against the wall.

I carefully carried the golf bag into my bedroom and laid it across the bed. Then, I pushed a few golf clubs around and dug inside, carefully removing the burgundy Drako with the gold spray-painted clip that I'd got up off of the D.C. nigga, Buckey Fields, that Dak fucked with cousin.

I slid the golf bag out of my way and laid the Drako on top of the bedspread and just stared at it. I couldn't believe that I was about to pick the gun back up.

"Name your price," My mother had told me when I first came home and vowed to stay away from the streets. "And if it ever becomes more than you're willing to pay, walk away," She had added.

I thought about walking away, letting Dakaron figure shit out for himself. But I just wasn't cut like that. Dakaron was my nigga. My right-hand man. More importantly, he was my family. We'd road life and death together and made it back. So, I wasn't about to turn my back on him now.

I stuffed the Drako back into the golf bag, slung it over my shoulder, took it downstairs, sat it by the door and went to get some wheels.

For a moment, I thought about jumping in an Uber and putting the driver in the trunk. But I wasn't trying to keep having to clean up behind the mess Dakaron had made. The entire situation was already dirty enough. So, I just went and copped a rental.

I parked outside of Chanae's spot and waited for Dakaron to show his face. I still didn't understand how he had ended back up with Chanae. Especially, after all the shit he talked and all the stuff they'd been through. I just couldn't get over the last situation where she started vibing with a nigga. Then, turned around and came to Dakaron as if his opinion really mattered. It was like a slap in the face.

I honestly felt like Dakaron deserved a fresh start. But that was another story.

When Dakaron finally came bouncing out of the house, he had A'myiah, Nydeer and Sha'Nyiah with him. Once him and the girls were in the car, he pulled off and I followed closely behind.

I didn't really have to play him too close because I basically knew exactly where he was going.

At least he's smart enough not to park in plain sight, I thought pulling into the parking spot a few cars behind Dakaron.

Once Dakaron and the girls were gone, I got out of the rental and quickly removed the temp tags. Then, I pulled my hoodie up and headed for the vigil.

I played the background, making sure Dakaron or the girls never saw me. I brought a ten dollar RIP Chimel T-shirt from a pretty chocolate sister I assumed was Chimel's mother and slipped it on to blend in even more.

I watched Dakaron and the girls like a hawk. I was kind of surprised that he didn't sense my presence. But then again, he was focused on Venique and his crew.

At some point, Dakaron and Venique began exchanging words. I wasn't sure what was being said. But I could tell it wasn't friendly. Whatever it was, Venus had to intervene.

Damn! I thought instantly recognizing Venus. She was still bad as a motherfucker after all these years. I couldn't help but to reminisce about how wild Dakaron use to brag her sex game was.

Again, I couldn't figure out what Venus and Dakaron were discussing. But I knew something was up because Dakaron had that signature smile on his face. The one that left you unsure, if he was smiling at you, with you or simply baking you a cake. I tailed Dakaron until he rounded the girls up. Once I realized that he was about to leave, I got out of dodge and headed for the rental.

I sat in the car surprised that Venique or none of his little puppies had tried anything. I definitely hadn't expected that.

My feelings were short lived though. Because while I was sitting there waiting for Dakaron to show up, I saw Venique's little crew pull alongside Dakaron's car looking around. Before one of them jumped out and ran up to the corner to keep lookout.

I grabbed the Drako from beneath the front seat, laid it across my lap and got that bitch ready to work. *These little kids think they're about to ambush my nigga. But I got something for their little asses!* I grinned, pulling my mask down.

I was just about to get out and walk them little niggas down gangster style, when the kid up at the corner signaled for them to circle the block.

I looked into the rearview mirror and realized that Dakaron and the girls were coming from the far end of the block.

"Shit!" I fired quickly slouching down as Dak and the girls strolled by. I started the rental up and kept my eyes on the wing-mirror, waiting for the mini van with Venique's little pups inside to spin the bend. I was going to cut them little niggas off and wear their young asses out. However, the van never turned the corner. That's when I realized that I had misread something. These little niggas had other plans.

158

As Dakaron pulled out of his parking spot, I clocked the little kid at the top of the block, signaling I assume that Dakaron was on his way.

At that moment, I threw the rental in drive and pulled out.

However, before I could swerve pass Dakaron, he cut me off and sped up the block.

As soon as he stopped at the corner, I pulled up behind him, threw the car in park and jumped out with the Drako ready.

I came around the car just as the minivan slid to a stop and the side door slid open. I didn't even waste time making sure it was a hit. I already knew what time it was. So, I just aired that motherfucker out. I didn't even give them niggas a chance to let off.

I saw sparks jumping off the frame of the minivan as I let the Drako go. Tires burst, windows exploded, and metal shredded but I kept squeezing.

When the minivan began to burn rubber in an attempt to peel off, I could literally see niggas scrabbling for cover, trying to dodge death. But it was no use. The rounds I had in the Drako was strong enough to go through steel.

Once I finished with the minivan, I turned to get the lookout, but his little ass was gone.

I locked eyes with Dakaron for a second. And I'm not even going to lie to you. I thought about splitting his wig too. Only for a split second though.

Then, I ran back to the rental, tossed the Drako on the passenger's seat as I climbed inside, threw the car in drive and took off.

Dakaron peeled off in one direction and I went in the other. I sped right through the intersection where the minivan had crashed into the side of a MTA bus. For a moment, I considered pulling over to finish the job, But there were already too many witnesses around. So, I just stayed low and kept on driving. I wanted to be as far away as possible when the police showed up and started asking questions.

Chapter 28

Dakaron

A week had passed since the candlelight, prayer-vigil shooting, and everybody was still on edge. Chanae had a million questions and Venus wouldn't stop calling my phone. Then, there was Mikenzie Phrost, an energetic Fox 45 News reporter, who kept speculating about why the shooting had happened in the first place. This little white, blue-eyed devil wouldn't let up. She had a theory about Chimel's death, and the shooting being tied together and that made me nervous. Especially, when she started talking that, "Sources close to the investigation" shit. I remained calm though. Always cool under pressure. I didn't hate Mikenzie or nothing. I actually found her quite attractive. However, the general consensus in prison was that her, most of her co-anchor, and the Uncle TomsFoxx 45 had out in the field were racist. I didn't know, but I knew what that since I'd been locked up, all I ever saw them do, was use disgraced white man and misguided, self-hating blacks to jump on people inspiring to do something for the City of Baltimore. Especially the black community.

But again, I'd weathered worst investigations. Besides, the only thing that was certain at the moment, was the fact that there had been three heavily armed juveniles inside the minivan. Two of whom had been gravely injured, including the driver who still remained in critical condition at the University of Maryland Medical Center. However, no names were being released due to the ages of the victims. That didn't stop authorities from offering a reward and asking anyone with information to call Metro Crime Stoppers.

I looked at the screen of my cellphone and saw the nameless number again. I knew it was Venus, but I refused to take it. There was nothing else to talk about. It was obvious that she couldn't control her son. And I damn sure wasn't

Delmont Player

about to keep conversing recklessly about it over the phone. Especially, when I already knew what had to be done.

"Frank is outside," Chanae snuck up on me. I was zoned out, listening to one of my favorite prison anthems by Boyz II Men.

"Huh?" I pulled one of the ultra-loud earbuds out of my ear and turned the volume down on the *I'm Doing Just Fine* song, because I knew Chanae hated it for one reason or another. "What you say?"

"I said, Frank's out front," she repeated trying to eye my cellphone.

"Aight," I snapped holding the phone up against my chest. "He's not on my phone." I affirmed staring at her until she got the message.

"Oh, I can't see your phone now?" Chanae questioned with an attitude.

"Look, we're not about to start nothing new," I declared slipping my cellphone into my front pocket as I stood up. "Especially, not after you had a fit when I asked to hold your phone for thirty days, when I first came home."

"Yeah, whatever!" Chanae rolled her eyes and exited the room mumbling something slick.

Yeah, that's what I thought! I grabbed my burner and shook my head. All that 'no secrets' in our relationship shit sounded good until I came home and cracked for her cellphone and password. That's when all the boundaries and having trust talks started.

I laughed to myself thinking about Chanae's reaction. She almost had a panic attack when I cracked for her phone and password. She started breathing all hard, looking around, sweating and shit. It got so bad that I just decided to drop the subject. I mean, I didn't want her to fuck around and have an asthma attack. I never forgot her reaction though. Because if she really didn't have anything to hide as she claimed, she

162

would've handed that phone and password over with no problem.

But as always, Chanae thought that she was slick. When the truth of the matter was, she wasn't. I'd been on to her shenanigans for year. Being in prison and having the ability to converse with countless men had really exposed all of women's bullshit in general, not just Chanae's.

"I'll be back later!" I informed heading for the door. As bad as I wanted to, some shit I just couldn't discuss with Chanae.

"What's up?" I climbed into the passenger's seat of Frank's car and gave him some love.

"You tell me," Frank countered pulling off before I could even completely close the door.

"Ayo, we're not about to go through that again," I assured, hoping that he hadn't come all the way out to Owings Mills to continue arguing about the vigil shooting. Because I wasn't for it. I was already on edge too.

Don't get me wrong. I wasn't mad that Frank had shown up when he did because he'd basically saved my life. But we weren't about to keep talking about it either. Especially, when I hadn't asked his ass to be there.

"You hear anything else?" Frank changed his tone slightly as he slowed down at the corner, looked both ways and made a left.

"Nah." I shook my head. "Nothing you don't already know."

There was a long uncomfortable silence before Frank spoke. "I don't like this Cuz. If these little kids clam up and start talking it's over!" Frank ran his hand over his graying bread. "I'm not going back to prison Cuz."

"Them little kids not talking to no police," I said confidently.

They were too busy playing gangster. "And even if they did, what are they going to say? They were about to ambush me and got ambushed? Come on now. Plus, you were masked up anyway. So, you're in the clear. A'myiah and them didn't even recognize you."

"I told your dumb ass not to go down there, Cuz!" Frank fired back. "I told you that shit wasn't a good idea." He shook his head in disappointment. "Now this shit might bring a bunch of unnecessary heat."

"Yo, I didn't ask you to do what you did! You did that shit on your own!" I retorted honestly. He had a choice and he made one. Now he had to live with it, come what may.

"What are you going to say, if the folks take you in for questioning?" Frank appeared to ignore my last statement as he took his eyes off the road for a moment to look over at me.

"What the fuck you mean what I'm say?" I eyed Frank strangely, hoping that he wasn't questioning my gangster. Because I only knew one way to answer that.

"What are going to say?" Frank repeated.

"Nothing!" I barked kind of insulted. "The same thing I always say nigga." I was angry now and Frank knew it because I'd stopped using the N-word a long time ago.

"Don't look at me like that," Frank twisted his face up and placed his eyes back on the road.

"Nah yo, you're throwing me off with your little interrogation." I studied him.

"Nah, you're throwing me off Cuz," Frank countered sharply. "Out here acting like a fucking cowboy."

"Pull over," I requested suddenly as calmly as I could trying not to reveal my attitude.

"What?" Frank glanced at me again.

"Pull the fucking car over!" I ordered grabbing the steering wheel.

"Whoa, Cuz!" Frank shouted whipping over to the curve. "Fuck is you doing?"

"Look at me nigga!" I demanded using ignorant language again to emphasize just how serious I was. "Have I ever betrayed you?" I asked when Frank looked at me.

"Nah," Frank admitted.

"Have I ever not had your back?"

"Of course not," Frank replied reluctantly.

"Have I ever snitched on you, cooperated with the police or made you think that I would sell my soul or not carry my own weight?"

"Come on, Cuz, you're tripping now." Frank grabbed the steering wheel with a grin like he was about to pull back into traffic.

"Nah yo, I'm serious." I grabbed his arm. "Because I need to know that you still trust me."

"Stop playing Cuz, you already know what it is," Frank exclaimed. "I trust you with my fucking life."

"Aight then, stop acting like I don't know what happens to the fish that opens its mouth," I directed, knowing that I'd never ever allow either one of us to end up back on that hot plate.

"My bad Cuz, you know I didn't mean it like that. I was just saying … "

My cellphone rung again as Frank began explaining his position.

When I looked down and saw Venus nameless number again, I couldn't help myself anymore. I was tired of avoiding her calls.

"Hold that thought for a second." I held my finger up to stop Frank from continuing.

"Why the fuck do you keep calling my phone?" I answered the phone on speaker ready to curse Venus silly ass out. "You're starting to be a real fucking nuisance."

"First of all, as-salaam-alaikum!" Venus greeted.

"Look man, I ain't trying to hear all that." I had forgotten all about the fact that she was all of a sudden a Muslim now. "Why you keep calling my phone?"

"Cause I'm trying to save my son's life Dakaron!" She confessed making Frank and I lock eyes.

"Don't talk to her over that phone Cuz." I read Frank's lips.

"Where are you at right now?" I asked staring directly at Frank.

"Home, why?" Venus inquired curiously.

"Meet me downtown in an hour." I insisted before I realized what I was saying and saw Frank nod his head in agreement.

"Where at?" Venus sounded anxious. "You know downtown big as shit."

I thought for a second before looking to Frank after drawing a blank. But he only hunched his shoulders. "What about the aquarium?" I suggested impulsively.

"Boy won't nobody go to the aquarium no more." Venus laughed. "I keep forgetting you were lock up forever."

Yeah, I don't, I thought. "Where you want to meet then because I don't know all these new spots."

"Have you been to the H-K Fish House on Charles Street yet?"

"Nah," I admitted unfamiliar with it.

"You're not hipped to H-K Fish House?" Venus questioned like she couldn't believe it. "Boy, they got the best Peace Half and Halfs on the East Coast."

"Okay," I mumbled nonchalantly. I mean, it wasn't a date. I didn't give a fuck about no half and half. "That's where you want to meet?"

"Yeah," she replied. "Somebody got to put you back in the loop. Especially since your little girlfriend's cousin always performs down there."

"Who girlfriend?" I inquired confused.

"Your little girlfriend," Venus snapped before sucking her teeth.

"I'm lost," I admitted.

"Mmmm hmmm, I bet you are." Venus mumbled sarcastically. "N-E Way, I'm talking about that little, red, bitch Tinika Jones you use to be chasing all up and down Sergeant Street. Yeah, I bet you remember now."

"Yo, you're tripping." I smiled at Frank, amused that Venus was still acting jealous about Tinika.

"Whatever," she replied and I just knew she probably rolled her eyes. "Like I said, N-E-Way, her cousin Samone's sister Margo be performing down there a lot."

"Margo?" I repeated to be sure.

"Yeah, Margo the Comedian to be exact," Venus explained. "Although, I can't stand that bitch Tinika, her cousin funny as shit. She be opening up for everybody. Kevin Hart, Dave Chappelle, Mike Epps."

"And you say this spot downtown on Charles Street?" I looked over at Frank and his face was lit up. He'd been after Margo since we were kids.

"Yeah, right on Charles Street. Not too far from North Avenue," Venus replied.

"Aight, I'll meet you there in an hour."

"One hour it is then." Venus agreed. "And Dakaron," She began, but I ended the call on her ass.

"I don't know if this a good idea Cuz," Frank confessed. "What if it's a setup?"

"Man, Venus not crazy. She knows it'll be a whole lot of slow singing and flower bring fucking with me," I rationalized with confidence. "The question is what do we do when she shows up?"

"Find out what the hell is going on and figure out a way to squash this little beef." Frank pulled back out into traffic.

"I'ma let you do most of the talking since you're more diplomatic than me," I explained.

"Shiiid, fuck if you is! I ain't going up there," Frank assured. "I don't even want Venus to know that I'm involved."

"Come on now yo, you know damn well that if I'm involved, Venus knows you're involved," I argued.

"Yeah well, I won't **$** be confirming nothing for her. Speculation and confirmation are two different things."

"What if somebody sees me and runs back to Chanae?" I questioned knowing how motherfuckers were snapping photos and shit of dudes out cheating on their girls, posting them on social media.

"Didn't nobody tell your silly ass to agree to meet in a popular location," Frank fired.

"Oh, that's fucked up!" I said shaking my head as we headed towards downtown.

Chapter 29

Frank

What the hell am I doing? I thought, sitting outside, across the street from the *H-K Fish House* waiting for Dakaron to finish his meeting with Venus. I had already circled the block twice. But I was still on edge, paranoid as a motherfucker, watching everything moving.

How in the world had I allowed Dakaron to drag me back into the streets? *Once I find out exactly what Venus knows, I'm finished!* I vowed to myself again.

Venus showing up in full garb, dressed like a Muslima had me thinking that Allah was testing me. And I wasn't about to keep playing with fire until I got burned.

What the fuck? I spotted a uniformed officer exiting the fish house looking around. A few seconds later, a patrol car came out of nowhere and pulled in behind me.

This bitch set us up! My heart started beating extremely fast as my eyes began darting back and forth between the side door and the rearview mirrors. Then, I noticed that the officer who'd came out of the fish house was making his way across Charles Street towards me and started sweating.

I slid my hand down in between the seats and gripped the handle of my biscuit. I wasn't going back to prison. Not without a gunfight. *That was close*, I exhaled with a sigh of relief when the police officer nodded and walked on by. *Fuck*! I needed to calm the hell down. I was making myself crazy. I checked the rearview mirror again and saw the officer opening the passenger seat's door to climb into the patrol car. His partner had his head down, playing on the phone.

Man, I'm geeking. I admitted noticing the H-K Fish House bag in the officer's hand for the first time.

The patrol car pulled off, but I still felt uneasy like something was off. The whole situation just wasn't sitting right with me. Then the uniformed officers had the nerve to look at me as they cruised by.

I should've never come was my only thought. *What if Venus tries some dumb shit and Dak split her wig in there?* The police knew I was there now. So, they could spin that anyway they wanted to.

I looked at the entrance of the fish house again. There was no sign of Dakaron or Venus. So, I pulled out my burner phone and sent Dak a text message about needing to bounce.

Then, I waited a few minutes to see if he was going to come out.

When he didn't I pulled off, I wasn't about to be nobody's sitting duck.

That was when it hit me that I hadn't gotten rid of the fucking Drako. Not only that, but it was in my trunk. Broken down and wrapped up. But in my trunk nonetheless.

"Shit!" I pounded the steering wheel. I couldn't believe that I'd slipped up like that. Riding around with a fucking Drako I'd supposed to have dumped two days ago. Then, I had the nerve to be sitting outside of popular food spot. The police would've had a field day with me in court.

I stepped on the gas and headed for one of my old dumping sights to finally get rid of the only thing linking me to the South Baltimore shooting.

Chapter 30

Dakaron

I had read stories in prison about what mother's would do to protect their young. She would summons her inner strength to fight off a bear, run into a burning building or jump into alligator infested waters. But Venus took the cake. She was ready to go above and beyond to save her son's life.

When we first sat down inside the H-K Fish House, Venus went on and on about how Venique had come to her crying about trying to get me killed. She said that he was scared, claimed he was just a baby.

At first, I just listened, taking in all the information I could, trying to make sure Venus wasn't trying to set me up. But once I realized that she was being authentic, I explained the situation.

"Shorty made the vital mistake of missing me twice. To add insult to injury, I had the kids in the car the second time," I explained. "Had I not been trained to go and did what I do, all of us would be dead."

You know I had to stunt a little bit. I wouldn't be Dakaron if I didn't.

"What if I offered you twenty-grand to walk away?"

"Come on Venus, twenty thousand?" I challenged as if I wasn't impressed. "You're going to need more than that. Them little bastards almost killed my daughter."

"What else you want? That's my entire savings." Venus stared at me curiously.

"I want more than twenty bands I know that. Your son and them out there getting it."

"Don't even worry about my son. He's on his way to stay with my sister out in Denver," Venus proclaimed. "You ain't never got to worry about Venique again. I can promise you that."

"That's the same thing you said the last time," I reminded.

Venus continued to try and convince me that this time was different, because Venique had come to her. But I remained silent and kept my poker face on. I was6n't buying it.

"Look Dakaron, I can't read your mind. I don't know what else it is that you want from me. I told you that I can handle my son."

"You really want to know what I want to end this shit?"

"That's why we're here, Dakaron," Venus retorted. "So just tell me what it is. So we can make it happen and get this shit over with."

"First, I want that twenty grand," I admitted. "Then, I want to fuck you one good time, for old time sake."

"Nigga please, you know I got a man," Venus spat but I could see that old fire still burning in her eyes. "Plus, I thought you couldn't stand me?"

"Look, that's my price. You can take it or leave it." I laid a tip on the table and stood up to leave.

Truth be told, I still had a sweet tooth for Venus. I always had, probably always would.

"Hold up." Venus grabbed my hand with an unsure look on her face.

"Sit back down for second. Maybe we can come up with something else."

That was almost three hours ago. Now, I had Venus on the eleventh floor of the fully mirrored Downtown Marriot, pressed up against the floor to ceiling window, blowing her back out. And man, let me tell you. That pussy was still as good as Sunday Church Service.

I remembered Tupac saying something about revenge being the sweetest joy next to getting pussy. Which told me that he I'd never sampled them spontaneously like I now was.

I stepped back, withdrawing my dick from the amazing comforts of Venus' wet pussy and sat on the plush bed. I watched Venus slowly turn around and push her hair over her right shoulder.

Damn, I thought, as Venus stood there in nothing but a pair of sexy, six-inch stilettos. She was still one of the baddest bitches I'd ever had the pleasure of fucking; And if I was really being honest. I still loved her trifling ass.

"You know the drill." I bit my bottom lip as she seductively strutted towards me. "There's nothing in the world sexier than a confident woman in high heels." I confessed honestly.

"Is that right?" Venus stopped in mid-stride and spun around to tease me again.

I licked my lips and took my cum coated dick into my hand and slowly started stroking it.

"I'ma make you regret choosing Chanae over me." Venus peeked at me over her shoulder with a devilish smiled and shook her soft looking ass from side to side.

"Please tell me that you know how to twerk," I begged never taking my off of her intoxicating form.

"Ain't nobody twerk for you since you been home?"

"Nah," I admitted shaking my head.

"Not even Chanae?" She inquired.

"Nope," I confessed honestly.

"You're in for a real treat then," Venus suggested with her devilish grin. Then, she made her ass sit up by popping her legs backs.

"You ever heard of the City Girls?" Venus asked slightly shaking her leg to make her ass and thighs shake.

"Nah, who's that?" I replied curiously.

"You ever seen that music video where Cardi B got the body paint on twerking?" Her ass and thighs continued to shake like they had a mind of their own.

"Fuck yeah!" I confessed with my tongue hanging out of my mouth. "That's the joint that fucked me up! I ain't never seen no shit like that in my life. I loved that shit!" I railed thinking about Cardi B and the two other bad ass bitches from the music video.

"Yeah well, I'm about to show you what I did to win their twerk contest." She revealed bending completely over at the waist until she could place her hands flat on the carpet. Then, she slide all the way down into a full split.

After that, she went to work. I mean, she was doing shit with her ass cheeks that made it appear as if they weren't attached to her body. When she started making her cheeks move like a water wave, I was no more good.

I sat there craving Venus more than I'd probably ever craved any woman in my entire life. I mean, seeing women twerk on television in music videos was one thing. But seeing that shit in real time, live, up close and personal was next level. However, it wasn't until Venus locked her legs, leaned forward until her body was pressed into the carpet and made her pussy open and close like a back catcher's mitt that I lost it.

I couldn't take it no more. I got up, walked over to scoop Venus up off the floor and tossed her on the bed. Then, I pinned her in the position that I wanted her in and tore that pussy out the frame.

I fucked Venus hard, deep and fast. I wanted to stretch that pussy out of shape for all the shit I'd been through behind her ass. I wanted to punish her for the shit she put me through with Quincey, Chanae, Monique and now her son. Plus, I wanted to prove to myself that I could still make that pussy talk back to me.

I made Venus cum instantly. Then, I hit that g-spot over and over again until she came two or three more times. I had that pussy talking like old times. Venus begged me to eat her pussy. But of course, I wasn't having that. At one point, I had to stop. I needed my breath. So, I stretched out on the bed and allowed Venus to suck my dick until every trace of her cum was gone.

After that, I tried out this deep throating thing, I'd recently seen this bad bitch name Jasmine Banks do in one of her Fansonly.com videos.

I basically had Venus lay across the bed on her back, with her head hanging off, directly in between my legs, so that I could fuck her right in the mouth like it was a pussy.

I swear, I still loved her ass. There was nothing in the world like a nasty, sexy ass, smart woman who knew how to fuck.

After a while, I spun Venus back around and picked her up in the air. Then, I carried her all over the room as she held on to my neck like she was on a merry-go-round and bounced up and down on my dick until we both came.

Fuck it! There's no reason to lie. Ain't no shame in my game.

After that, I laid Venus on the bed, held her legs completely back and ate that pussy for the first time too. I couldn't help it. The combination of bomb ass sex and beauty was enough to emasculate the strongest man.

When Venus let me put it in her ass, I instantly remembered one of the reasons why I could never get enough of her. She was in a class all by herself and she knew it too. Venus got up on that dick and road me into submission. I bullshit you not, all I could do was keep running my hands over my face and throwing my head back as her asshole squeezed me like a compression sock.

"You going to make sure my son okay?" Venus slowed down to a steady pace.

"Yeah, shorty good!" I agreed. To be honest, at that moment, I would've agreed to kill for her son.

"Tell me you didn't miss this while you were gone." Venus used the headboard to balance herself as she professionally continued to slowly gyrate her hips. "Tell me!" She taunted knowing damn well I couldn't.

I wanted to lie. I wanted to buck her challenge. But I couldn't find the words to speak. Not while my eyes were locked an Venus' super wet asshole, wrapped tightly around my cum-streaked dick as she skillfully bounced and slide her ass up and down the length of my dick.

"Slide to the edge of the bed," Venus instructed crawling forward until my dick slipped from the soft comforts of her silky asshole. "I want to show you something."

I sat on the edge without hesitation as Venus crawled over and got up off the bed. I was ready to comply with all of her commands. My tongue was still in knots. But my body spoke a language of its own.

I slowly stroked my dick a few times as Venus stepped in front of me and back up until she was standing directly over top of me. Then, she carefully took my dick into her soft hand and intentionally ran the head back and forth across her asshole, letting me feel the heat and wetness before holding it steady and slowly sitting down until her ass cheeks touched my nuts.

"Ssssss," I moaned as her asshole opened up and engulfed me.

"Tell me there's another bitch that can fuck you better than me!" Venus fired carefully bouncing that pretty ass in my lap. "Tell me or I'ma stop!" She threatened withdrawing my dick all the way to the tip. "Let me hear you say it," she snapped twining on the head.

"It's not," I confessed honestly.

Venus looked over her shoulder satisfied and dropped all of her weight down on me until my dick completely disappeared into her amazing asshole again.

I love this bitch, I said to myself as she sat there and did something to my dick with her muscles until I nutted.

"I hate you bitch!" I fired because no other woman had ever been able to turn me out like Venus. But just when I thought that it couldn't get any better, Venus got up, crawled between my legs and started sucking my dick again.

I got to call Frank, I thought, reaching for my cellphone as my eyes began to roll back into my head again.

"Boy, you can't record this." Venus suddenly stopped and came up for air. "I told you I got a whole man at home."

"Man, ain't nobody trying to recording your cheating ass," I retorted. "I'm calling Frank." I explained, and Venus went back to work.

Frank's phone went straight to voicemail. So, I just told him to come to the Marriot as soon as he got my message. "I'm at the joint right across from the Inner Harbor. Eleventh floor, room fourteen." I managed as best I could before dropping the cellphone as my cum shot down Venus' throat.

"I hope you don't think that I'm about to fuck Frank?" Venus paused to wipe her mouth off.

"Hold up yo, we got a deal," I challenged.

"Exactly, we as in me and you." Venus pointed from herself to me.

"Yeah well, the deal just changed." I snapped knowing how bad Frank had wanted to fuck Venus back in the day. "Me and Frank going to tag team that pussy when he gets here."

"Nigga, you got me fucked up, if you think I'ma let you and Frank run a train on me!" Venus got to her feet and walked across the room to gather her things. "You must really be out of your fucking mind," she vented reaching for her garb.

"Bitch! What the fuck you think you doing?" I jumped up off the bed and went over to snatch the garb out of her hand. "You aren't going nowhere until I'm satisfied," I warned tossing the garb across the room.

"So, what are saying? You're keeping me here against my will?" Venus studied me.

"Man, I'm not trying to hear that shit. We made a deal and you're going to live up to your end or I'ma bring your son's life to an end." I grabbed a chair and pulled it over near the window. Then, I sat down and gestured with my finger for her to come to me.

"Bitch don't make me get up," I advised.

Venus reluctantly walked over and stood in front of me with a defeated look on her face. "The deal is off," she informed.

"The deal is off when I say it's off." I grabbed her by the wrist and pulled her down to her knees. "Now be a woman of your word and finish showing me a good time," I encouraged, leaning back in the chair, spreading my legs wide as I looked out the window like a king.

Chapter 31

Frank

After getting off the elevator and making my way down the well-kept, brightly lit hall, I knocked on Dak's hotel room door and waited. It had been about an hour since I first heard his message.

"Who is it?" I recognized Dakaron voice instantly.

"It's room service. "I joked a second before the peephole went dark and the locks began to rattle.

"Man, do I got a surprise for you." Dakaron opened the door with a huge smile on his face.

"Fuck took you so long?"

"Some shit came up with sis," I lied. I'd actually went to the Mosque to offer salat and seek Allah's guidance. "Plus, I wasn't able to check my messages until I got home. You know, I only been carrying the burner lately. What's good though? What happened with Venus?"

Dakaron closed the door and was about to say something when I noticed Venus stretched out across the hotel bed with her hands and feet tied.

"Yeah, that's how I do it!" Dakaron walked pass nodding his head proudly as he noticed the surprised look on my face. "I makes dreams come true shorty."

"What the fuck is this Cuz?" I looked from Venus to Dakaron confused.

"Fuck you mean, what it look like? It's pussy on a platter." Dakaron smiled.

"You tripping Cuz," I looked at him like he was crazy. "I know you're not in here raping that girl?"

"What?" Dakaron shot me a deadly look. "Nigga don't ever insult me like that," he warned. "I don't got to rape no bitch!"

"You geeking, Cuz." I walked over to the bed, snatched the gag out of Venus' mouth and then began untying her wrist.

"Fuck is you doing, man?" Dakaron rushed over to stop me.

"Untying her, Cuz." I pulled my arm free and began untying Venus's wrist again. "You got this sister in here like this."

"Sister?" Dakaron repeated looking at me as if I'd lost my mind.

"Yeah Cuz, *sister!*" I barked staring back at him. Now I was mad. "She's a Muslim, Cuz."

"I don't give a fuck!" Dakaron snapped reaching for my arm again.

"Move Cuz!" I shoved him back.

"You move nigga," Dakaron retorted, pushing me into the nightstand next to the bed. "I ain't finish with this bitch yet. I got this pussy all night."

"I'm not going to tell you again Cuz. Move!" I stepped into Dakaron's personal space ready for whatever.

Dakaron held his ground for a minute. But he wasn't stupid. He knew that he couldn't do nothing with me with the hands. He never could. So, he retreated and allowed me to finish untying Venus' wrist.

"This your last warning," Dakaron declared coming up behind me a second before I heard the unmistakable sound of the hammer of a gun being cocked back. "Don't make yourself my enemy."

I stopped untying Venus's ankle and turned around slowly to find Dakaron standing there, holding a 357 Bulldog down by his side. "You pulled a gun on me, Cuz?" I stared at him hurt. "After all the shit we done been through. You go and pull a gun on me?"

"I invited you up here to party and you come in here on some sucker shit!" He tried to justify his actions. "As bad as you used to say you wanted to fuck this bitch back in the day."

"Not like this Cuz ! Not while she's all crying and shit," I argued. "Look at her Cuz, she is scared."

"Man, that bitch ain't scared. She's playing you." Dakaron rationalized.

"Cuz, I'm taking this sister home." I reached for Venus' leg again.

"She made her choice. Now, you got to make yours." Dakaron brought the gun up and aimed it at me.

I studied him. This was my right-hand man. My childhood friend.

The only motherfucker I trusted with both my life and freedom. The only male besides my little brother who I'd gladly give my life for. Yet, here he was, standing in the middle of a hotel room, pointing a gun at me.

I'd always known that Dak's honor was bigger than his heart. But I never suspected that it was bigger than me. Especially, if it put us at odds with each other.

"You're tripping Cuz," I backed up.

"Nah, you're tripping!" Dakaron rebutted.

I stood there and stared at Dakaron like a wild dog who needed to be put down. Then, I turned and headed towards the door. "From here on out, you're on your own Cuz," I informed opening the door.

"I don't give a fuck nigga! I thrives on my own anyway. I don't need nobody!" He shouted in anger.

"I hope you're right Cuz." I walked out of the room shaking my head before turning around to look at Venus. "I'm sorry sister."

Dakaron marched over to the door and slammed it in my face. "Fuck you nigga!" He shouted from the other side securing the locks. "You know how I got down!"

I stared at the closed door. I wasn't sure if I was angry or hurt.

Whatever the case, I knew that me and Dakaron's relationship had just changed forever.

Chapter 32

Dakaron

"Call the lawyer!" Were the first words out of my mouth when I saw the flashing red and white lights in the rearview mirror and realized that we were being pulled over. "Look for the name George Smith," I uttered passing Chanae my cellphone as my eyes darted back and forth between the rearview and wing side mirrors.

One of the first things I'd done after coming back from seeing Buckey Fields cousin out in Washington DC again, was rehire the attorney who'd secured my freedom. Because I knew that if I was going after Venique and his little squad of toy soldiers, I'd best get lawyered up just in case.

"He's not picking up," Chanae alerted after turning the music down. "You want me to call Frank?"

I thought for a second. Even though Frank and I had gotten pass the hotel situation, I was still upset with him for allowing Venus to play us against each other. I'd even told Buckey Field's cousin not to fuck with him just in case he got on some of that extreme Muslim shit and tried to come see me.

"Nah, George probably in court," I replied trying to think for a moment. "Let it keep ringing."

"It's going to voice mail."

"Put it on speaker," I ordered watching two plain clothes officer climb from a unmarked Copo Camaro in tactical vests in the rearview mirror.

Chanae sat the phone up on the dashboard just as I heard Mr. Smith's voice instructing the caller to leave a message at the sound of the tone.

"What are you doing?" I stole a quick look at Chanae and saw her thumbs moving as fast as a spider spinning a web. It was something I still had not gotten used to.

"Texting A'myiah to let her know what's going on," she replied without stopping just as the plain clothes officers approached the car from both sides.

"Tell her to call my lawyer," I instructed nervously. I knew A'myiah had the number because she'd hit George on the three way a hundred times when I was still locked up.

The plain clothes officer on my side of the vehicle, walked right up to the door and tried the handle.

"Unlock the door!" He tapped on the glass with the back end of what appeared to be a black, metal flashlight.

"What's going on?" I questioned bringing the window down a few inches.

"Unlock the door, Sir," he directed again. This time a little more aggressively.

"I'm trying to figure out why you're pulling me over?" I inquired noticing that he hadn't even asked for my license or registration.

"I said open the door!" he shouted but I didn't flinch.

"I don't have to open the door until you tell me what's going on." I explained calmly keeping my eyes locked on my hands, so that they wouldn't move. "I know my rights," I added.

"Ma'am, put the phone down." I heard the other plain clothes officer talking to Chanae.

"Oh, you're a smart ass huh?" The officer on my side of the car fired before trying to force his hand inside the car to unlock the door himself. However, I hadn't brought the window down that far. I wasn't that green.

"Can you please just tell me what this is all about officer?" I questioned calmly again, making sure my hands remained on the steering wheel in plain view. All I could think about was the increased number of unjustified police shootings around the world lately.

It almost seemed like every other week a cop was shooting somebody down, choking somebody out or so-called mistakenly pulling the wrong equipment. It didn't matter if you were walking, celebrating, panhandling, coming from the store, jogging, sleeping, already in police custody, laying on the ground in broad daylight on a crowded street being arrested or simply being pulled over. If you were doing it while you were black, there was a great chance that you could end up losing your life for it.

The worst part was, there were barely any consequences. The rapper, Lil Baby had released a song called the 'Bigger Picture' and a lot of people still didn't see the picture he'd painted. The song had went over their heads.

"Unlock the door, Sir!" The officer held the door handle and pointed towards the latch.

"For what?" I asked glancing at him.

Ignoring me, the officer leaned down enough to see into the car.

"Open her door!" he shouted ordering his partner to open Chanae's door after noticing that the latch was up.

"Man, you'll can't do that!" I snapped knowing my rights as the other officer opened Chanae's door. I'd been studying law for the last fifteen plus years.

"Please, step out of the car ma'am." The plain clothes officer on Chanae's side reached into the car to unbuckle Chanae's seatbelt, before grabbing her arm and hauling her from the car.

"Hold up man, she's pregnant!" I reached for my seatbelt. "Don't fucking grab her like that!" I barked watching the way the officer was handling Chanae.

"Don't move!" was all I heard before I turned back around and realized that the officer on my side had drawn his service weapon and trained it on me.

"Open the fucking door now!" He demanded yanking on the door handle like he wanted a piece of me. I started wondering if I knew him or whatnot.

I heard Chanae telling him to calm down, informing him that I didn't have anything. This time I complied by slowly reaching one hand for the safety lock. "I'm letting you know now that my lawyer is on the phone recording everything," I revealed, opening the door staring down the barrel of his service weapon, after removing my seatbelt.

The instant the driver's door came open enough for me to exit, I was yanked out of my seat, wrestled up against the car and placed into a plastic pair of zip-tie handcuffs before being punched.

Chanae started going off.

"You want me to put her in the car, Serg?" The other plain clothes officer acted as if he hadn't seen the assault.

"Yeah, maybe that will shut her up," he replied walking me around the car and sitting me down on the curb.

I watched in pure frustration as Chanae was lead to the Camaro and placed in the backseat. I didn't know what to think. My mind was all over the place. But my biggest concern at the moment was Chanae. She was pregnant and already under enough stress. Especially since Venus' trifling ass had taken to social media about our little Marriot rendezvous, posting photos I hadn't realized she had.

It was the first time I'd been in a fight that I couldn't figure out a way to win. The only good thing that had come out of Venus's little stunt was the fact that Frank now knew that she'd played him at the hotel.

I sat there watching with tears rolling down my face as the plain clothes officers taunted me and tossed all of the toys and baby stuff we'd just purchased at Walmart out onto the sidewalk. It was the only thing that I could do to keep from killing one of them whores when they took the cuffs off.

"Y'all some wild bitches!" I fired unable to keep my thoughts to myself any longer. "That's some straight coward shit y'all doing." I added watching them as they continued to perform.

After they tore the car up, I saw one of them nod to the other and watched in horror as he sneakily removed a small caliber weapon from behind his vest and looked around. I instantly tried to get to my feet and stumbled sideways and fell.

"Serg, Serg," the partner alerted as he sat me back down and warned me to sit still.

"Man, y'all bitches trying to set me up! Y'all about to plant something on me!" I argued trying to get up again.

"Serg!" His partner called out when he drew his fist back to punch me again. "Six o'clock."

"Huh?" The Sergeant stopped himself.

"We got a problem," his partner gestured with his head and they stepped off to the side as the Sergeant tucked the weapon back into his vest.

"Don't look now. But there's a motorist across the street on your six, sitting in a green Karma Revera recording the entire stop," the partner tried to whisper. But I could hear him as clear as day.

I looked across the street and saw the luxury plug-in Hybrid and thanked Allah.

"Fuck!" The Sergeant fired and looked around as if to think for a minute. "Did you do anything?"

"Nah, I was waiting on you."

"Okay, good. Let's wrap this shit up for now. But get me that motherfucker's phone!" He directed as they moved back over to me. "It's your lucky day asshole. You're free to go." The sergeant mumbled unhappy kneeling down behind me to cut the plastic cuffs off with a small pair of pocket scissors.

Suddenly, the partner darted out into traffic in an attempt to cross the street and almost got his stupid ass run over by several cars. I stood up in time to witness the motorist speeding off as he pulled out his cellphone and began recording.

"I got that motherfucker's tag numbers." He returned holding up his cellphone as he headed for the unmarked Camaro.

He tossed the cellphone through the open passenger's side window and opened the back door to help Chanae out.

After Chanae and I gathered all our stuff off the curb and climbed back into the car and got ready to pull off, the unmarked Camaro pulled alongside the car and stopped.

"You know why I stopped you right?" The Sergeant had his hand hanging out the window as he laid back in the passenger's seat like he was a boss or something.

I just stared at him. Had he caught me nine, maybe ten years ago, under different circumstances, I would've given his bitch ass everything he was looking for.

"Because I could nigga." He smiled.

I grinned. But not for the same reason.

"Since you can't seem to stay the fuck away from Venus." He finally played his hand. "The next time I see you, I'ma show you why we own this city," he warned aggressively.

We locked eyes for a long moment, both knowing that the next time we crossed paths, would be the last one way or the other. Then, he smiled at me and told his partner to pull off.

"You okay baby?" I turned my attention to Chanae.

"Here we go with this bitch Venus again." Chanae shot me an accusatory look. "When is it going to stop Dakaron? I mean, seriously, don't you get tired of breaking my heart?"

"I'm not going to keep explaining the same shit to you over and over," I snapped.

188

I had already confessed my demons to her. I mean, there was no sense in lying. Especially since Venus was on social media telling everything anyway.

"So what, you're beefing with the police now?" Chanae had that old worried look on her face. The one she got when she thought that I couldn't control my emotions. But that Dakaron had died in prison years ago. The new Dakaron, thought five times before he did or said anything. He also understood the proper way of handling people.

"Man, I don't even know that clown," I admitted honestly.

"I assume he's Venus boyfriend though."

"So what does that mean Dakaron?"

"I don't know, you heard that clown threaten me though."

"So, you're going to feed into that shit? Fuck me and the kids right?" Chanae stared at me intensely.

"Yo, don't even do that."

"Yo?" Chanae, repeated, shaking her head.

I could feel myself started to get agitated. But I humbled myself. "Baby, you know that you and the kids are the most important thing in my life. But at the same time, I'm not about to sit back and let nobody use me for target practice. This cop…"

I tried to explain, but Chanae simply just leaned over and turned the music up before looking out of the window, ignoring me.

At that point, I just left it alone because I didn't give a fuck no more. I was tired of motherfuckers trying to dictate how I responded to shit. Frank, Chanae, every fucking body! I didn't owe nobody shit! I had took my time like a champ and stood up the entire time. Even when nobody was there to hold me in my toughest moments.

There had been times when I laid in the cell broken. Where was everybody with their opinions and help then?

Nowhere to be found, which meant, I didn't have to kiss nobody's ass.

I started the car and pulled off. I knew how stubborn Chanae could be. That was one thing about her that hadn't changed. To be honest, it had gotten worst. Because when she got mad, she couldn't see or hear nothing but her own rage.

My mind went back to the police and his threat. I had to find a way to clip his nuts. *Maybe I should grab that bitch Venus*, I thought as my cellphone began to ring.

Damn! I had forgotten all about the phone I thought reaching for it, wondering just how much my lawyer's voice mail had picked up.

Chapter 33

Frank

"Where are you at Cuz?" I questioned the moment Dakaron answered his phone.

"On the way back to the house, why?"

"I need you to pull over real quick." I suggested constantly checking my mirrors to see if I was being followed.

"What? Look yo, now's not the time. I got Chanae in the car and it's a bunch of wild shit going on!"

"Cuz, pull over!" I ordered. "I just found a fucking tracker underneath my car."

"What do you mean a tracker?"

"A tracker Cuz, like some James Bond shit! It was all wrapped up in some type of tinfoil and attached to the side of my gas tank."

"How the hell you find that out?"

"I took the car for a checkup and the mechanic dude found it," I replied.

"Hold up yo, when all this happen?"

"About an hour ago," I glanced at the dashboard timer and tried to calculate an exact time. "I tried to call you."

"Yeah, I was probably still inside Walmart. But hold up yo, I just got pulled over and threatened by some pigs. These bitches were about to try to frame me too. Plain clothes suckers in a silver Camaro."

"You said a silver Camaro?" I questioned to be sure because that was exactly the color and type of car that had been lurking around the auto mechanic shop. "Did it have mirror tints?"

"Absolutely," Dakaron replied. "One of the chumps was Venus' boyfriend. Sucker told me next time we meet, it's game over."

It was all starting to make sense now. The G. T. T. F letters engraved on the back of the tracker. The city wide jurisdiction the mechanic guy told me they had. "You say you're on your way to the house?"

"Yeah."

"When you get there, make sure you check underneath the car and wipe the it down real good," I instructed not wanting to discuss anything else over the phone. "I'll meet you there."

"Aight, bet. But what am I wiping the car down for?"

"Because if these are the motherfuckers I think it is. I remember reading a case about them that got overturned, where during investigations, they would conduct traffic stops and intentionally touch the truck of the car to leave a fingerprint in case anything ever happened. The suspect would be on the hook as coming in contact with them or some shit like that. I don't remember everything about the case." I tried to remember but had too much on my mind. "Just wipe the car down, Cuz and I'll see you when I get there."

"Say no more," Dakaron ended the call.

What the fuck is going on? I wondered stepping on the gas. Was the police coming for us behind Venus? And if so, what in the world were we going to do about it?

Chapter 34

Dakaron

When I pulled up in front of the house, Chanae immediately climbed out of the car and stormed into the house while I busied myself looking for a tracker. I was just about to give up and work on getting the toys and stuff out of the car, when I spotted what looked like a small black box tucked off between some pipes running beneath my car and *grabbed it.*

What the fuck? I stood up analyzing the box in my hand. I couldn't believe these bitches had really put some shit underneath my car. I had honestly thought Frank was tripping. But now I knew he wasn't. I also knew that these pigs weren't bluffing.

I mean, to go through all of that just to threaten me didn't make sense. Which meant, we had to get them before they got us.

I looked around the neighborhood, wondering what to do with the box. I thought about throwing it up on the roof. But I knew I needed that motherfucker to remain mobile. Then, I spotted my neighbors yellow, purple and red Jeep JLU Wrangler Rubicon and snuck over and placed it on the inside of the frame just above the rainbow colored back wheel. I didn't like his fruity ass anyway.

I walked into the house with my arms full of toys and instantly knew something was wrong. First of all, all of the lights were out, and Chanae knew I hated that shit. It was another effect that prison had had on me. Another part of the monster the system had created. However, before I could think twice, two masked men were all over me.

One popped out from behind the door and the other came out from behind the couch. The Walmart bags fell from my arms and hit the floor, sending the contents everywhere as we began to work.

Before long, we were slipping on toys and baby clothes. But I was trained to go. If prison hadn't prepared me for nothing else, it had prepared me for hand to hand combat and unexpected attacks. So, we were going to touch everything up in that motherfucker before I gave up.

I dropped the attacker in front of me first and spun around to square up with his man. I had always been nice with my mitts. I mean, I had been throwing them since my cousin David and I use to scrap in the basement of my mother's house up Park Heights. But over the years, I'd gotten even nicer. I could dance circles around the average joker and sting anybody who stepped in front of me.

So, after going toe-to-toe for a moment. I worked the second attacker over with a wicked body combination that my brother, Detauwn had taught me when I was still a kid.

I reached down on the floor, scooped up one of the scattered steak knives that had fallen from the new knife set Chanae had just purchased at Walmart for the kitchen, and went to work. And let me tell you, once I got to slinging that bitch, I was back on the penitentiary yard. All I saw was Monique, Doogy and all the other motherfuckers who'd made the mistake of sleeping on me.

I stabbed the second attacker in the center of his chest twice before he could grab my arm. But it was too late, and I could already tell that it was over.

First of all, blood was squirting all over the place, which made me as slippery as a snail. Secondly, I was too strong. So, I snatched my arm free and started stabbing him with all kill shots.

I couldn't say for sure if it was the six or seventh blow. But eventually he stopped trying to defend himself and collapsed to the floor.

Next, I turned on his friend's ass. He saw me coming and tried to run. I sent him to the ground with a nasty back wound and quickly climbed his body like a tree.

"You broke into the wrong house motherfucker!" I assured rolling him over onto his back. "Now, I'ma kill you and beat it in court," I added, drawing the knife high.

"Dakaron!" I heard Chanae's pleading voice and looked up to see another masked intruder holding a gun to the side of her head.

"If you stab my man one more time, I'ma put your girl's brains all over the place!" he warned, pressing the gun up against Chanae's temple.

I instantly dropped the bloody knife and slowly pushed up off of his homeboy as he scoured to his feet.

"Bitch ass nigga!" The *should be* dead attacker snapped before striking me. "Hand me that tone dummy," he demanded snatching his mask off, reaching for the gun.

"Man, nigga, move!" The intruder holding Chanae waved the second attacker off before removing his mask too. "Didn't nobody tell your dumb ass to jump on him anyway," the intruder I now realized was Dhakiy argued. "Click the damn light on!" He added.

When the light came on, I checked my lip for any signs of blood. "You hit like a bitch shorty," I taunted, spitting on the carpet. Then, I noticed all the blood over near the front door where I'd stabbed the first attacker to death.

Before I could say anything else, somebody clapped their hands and I turned around to see Venique standing in the doorway, clapping his hands.

"Y'all old niggas tough. I'll give y'all that." Venique commended with a smile.

I was so happy that A'myiah had taken her brothers to the city to see their grandmother. The thought of someone hurting them was too much to bear. "Aight shorty, you win. You the man. Now, let my children's mother go. She's pregnant," I pleaded wondering if Venique could see the murder in my eyes.

"We got some business to discuss first O.G.," Venique declared walking over to sit down on the living room couch.

"Come on shorty, she doesn't have anything to do with this. You got me." I appealed again thinking about something Frank had said to me a while ago. Protecting your family isn't always about taking a life, sometimes it's about giving yours.

"Let's talk about the twenty bands you extorted my mother out of first. Then, maybe we can discuss who walks out of here and who doesn't."

"Oh, so that's what this is all about? Twenty-grand?" I couldn't help but laugh as the kid I'd stabbed in the back shoved me to the living room floor.

"That and the truth about my homies," he revealed referring I assumed to Chimel and the other kid I'd put the dirt on.

"For the move you just made, you better have the answer to that question," I warned getting back to my feet.

"Nah nigga, you better have the answer," Dhakiy fired walking Chanae right in front of me.

I looked at Dhakiy and smiled. He was going to be the first one I killed if I made it out of there alive.

"Oh, you think I'm sweet huh? You think shit a game?" Dhakiy stared at me before hitting Chanae upside the head with his gun. "You think a nigga won't crack your bitch right here?" Dhakiy stepped back and jammed the gun into Chanae's head. "Did you kill my cousin or not?"

"Chill dummy," Venique tried to calm him down.

"Nah yo, niggas not going to keep asking his bitch ass the same thing over and over again," Dhakiy retorted. *I'll trash this bitch right here."*

"I said chill!" Venique instructed, and Dhakiy lowered his gun.

I did my best to maintain my composure. "Shorty, I'ma torture you when this is all over for putting your hands on my children's mother," I threatened sincerely. "I'ma make it real painful. I'ma bleed you out real slow so it'll last too. I promise you that."

Out of nowhere, Venique hit me across the back of the head with the butt of his gun.

"Tie both of their asses up!" He ordered.

I shook my head and tried to regain my focus. My vision was blurry. But I knew that I had to figure a way out of this shit. Because there was no way that I could allow these kids to tie me up. Not while Chanae was still with me. I had to save her somehow.

"Let my children's mother go shorty. She's pregnant." I tried to shake off the dizziness again. "This is between you and me."

"Nah." Venique shook his head. "It was between you and me. Then, you went and involved my homies and my mother," he corrected. "I told you how we were coming O.G. Remember? Nobody's off limits."

"Listen to me shorty," I pleaded as my vision came back into focus. "If you hurt my family, my peoples are going to slaughter everything you love. I'm talking about babies, parents, everybody. They aren't going to show you no mercy," I warned hoping that Venique would take heed and not take our beef beyond the streets. "They're not going to stop until they hunt your entire family tree down."

"Who you talking about Frank or your brothers Detauwn and Antauwn?" Venique questioned with a smirk. "Yeah, I know all about your folks," he revealed with a look of amusement on his face. "Don't worry though. Frank's probably laying in a ditch by now too. I'll deal with your brothers later."

"I'll give you the money and tell you whatever you want to know." I surrendered.

"In fact, I got more money," I confessed. "You can get all of it. Just please let my children's mother go," I begged trying to convince Venique to spare Chanae's life.

"You hear this old nigga?" Dhakiy looked at the second attacker. "All the bitch coming up out of him now. And here it is, I thought this nigga was an O.G."

"I'm not leaving you," Chanae interjected. "If you're staying, I'm staying! We're dying together!" she declared like we were still kids.

"I like that gangster shit baby girl." Venique shook his head in admiration. "Aren't too many real bitches like you left. That is that Queen and Slim shit." He smiled. "But check it, before we get into all of that, we're going to tie y'all up and talk about this money."

"Let her go first." I directed as the little kid I'd stabbed in the back began looking around for something to restrain Chanae and I with.

"Like I said, we'll deal with that once we got the money, and you tell us about Chimel and—"

"I'm not stupid shorty," I fired cutting Venique off. I'd been playing the game a long time and I knew exactly what happened once you got tied up. "I know if you tie her up, it's over."

I don't trust Venique for one second. Especially not with the lives of my first love and unborn child.

"Come sit in this chair right here," Dhakiy instructed pulling Chanae by her arm. "Sit him over there." He pointed to another chair on the other side of the room.

"I'm not sitting nowhere!" Chanae bucked.

"Chanae!" I snapped ready to talk some sense into her. Now wasn't the time to be breaking bad. I needed to think and she wasn't helping.

"Don't Chanae me! Ain't nobody tying me up!" She proclaimed snatching away from Dhakiy. "Whatever y'all going to do. Y'all going to have to do it right here."

"Chanae, please," I begged as a tear rolled from my eye. I was trapped between living and dying for love. "Just do what he says. I promise it will be okay."

I looked at Chanae. She was still my heart. I know, I talked a lot of big shit but the truth was that Chanae was still the only woman that had ever had all of me. She was my past, my present and now she was carrying my future. She was my Coretta, my Betty, my Michelle, my Khadijah, and my very own Dr. Ava Muhammad all wrapped up in one.

So, despite all the things we'd went through, she still meant the world to me, and I'd gladly give my life to save hers.

"I love you baby." My voice began cracking up. "You know that. I have always loved you."

"Prove it!" Chanae shouted. "Fucking prove it!" Chanae challenged before spinning around to hit Dhakiy with a two-piece that forced him to stumble into the couch before anybody realized what was happening.

My mind went into overdrive. I instantly went into survival mode and tackled Venique over the couch. We crashed into the floor and immediately began exchanging blows before I began slamming his head into the floor with all my might, putting him out.

I had to give it to him though. He had heart. More than his father to be honest. But heart and warrior skills were two totally different things.

I quickly got to my feet and stumbled around the couch in time to see Chanae going down. My killer instincts kicked in and I zeroed in on Dhakiy as he took aim.

The first shot went wild as Dhakiy and I bumped into the table. I hit Dhakiy with a slew of punches and tried to get the gun. I grabbed his wrist and forced the gun above our heads as two more shots rang out.

"Get the gun! "I yelled to Chanae, still tussling with Dhakiy.

However, she ignored me, picked up the knife and began stabbing him until his grip relaxed and I was able to pry the gun from his hand.

The moment I got my hand around the handle of that gun and finger behind the trigger, it was go time. I pressed that mother fucker right up against Dhakiy's face and blew the whole left side of his face off.

"I told you that I was going to get you shorty," I spat as his body bounced off the table, hit the chair and smashed into the floor.

Venus and her punk ass boyfriend next, I thought wiping Dhakiy's blood and brains off of my face. *I'ma drive down South Baltimore and slaughter them bitches, watch!* But first, I had to deal with Venique's other little partner.

The fact he'd froze up meant nothing to me. He'd entered my sanctuary and violated my peace and for that, he too, would pay with his life.

"You okay?" I rushed to Chanae's side as she held her stomach.

"Don't worry about me. Find out what he knows and handle your business." She gestured towards the kid standing over in the corner shaking like he had Parkinson's disease making me smile. She was the real gangster.

I was just about to turn around and focus my attention on the second attacker when I heard a loud bang and felt something rip through my lower back, before knocking the inside of my stomach out, sending me to the ground.

I rolled over in time to see Venique propped up on one arm, peeping from behind the couch about to take aim at Chanae.

I used every ounce of strength I had left to get to my feet and dive in Venique's direction just as he pulled the trigger again.

The first bullet breezed by me, hit Chanae in her shoulder and made her do a complete spin. The second one ripped through my upper chest while I was in mid-air. But I landed on top of Venique, nonetheless.

"You little bitch!" I mustered enough strength to bring my hands up to his neck.

Venique jammed the gun into my side and pulled trigger again. This time my hip dislocated. But I opened my mouth wide and bit down on a chunk of his cheek and a part of his lip.

"Ahhhhh!" Venique squealed as I started pulling and shaking on his cheek and bottom lip like a blood-thirsty Pitbull.

"Dakaron!" Chanae cried out for my help.

I pulled, jerked and shook as Venique continued to yell out in pain, until I was able to rip a chunk of flesh off of Venique's face and lip and spit it out.

"Dakaron!" Chanae cried out again.

Looking up to see Chanae tussling with the second attacker I'd stabbed gave me a boost of strength. I tried to get up. But I'd already lost so much blood.

I have to save Chanae and our unborn child were the only thoughts running through my mind as my adrenaline continued to dwindle.

"Hold that bitch!" I heard Venique command pushing me out of the way, getting to his feet.

All I could do was lay there, wishing I had the strength to defend the only woman besides my mother that I'd ever loved with all of my heart. I froze in fear as Venique aimed his gun at the back of Chanae's head and prepared to pull the trigger. "I want you to see me kill your supposed-to-be future nigga."

"No!" I hollered closing my eyes just as the front door burst open and shots rung out.

When Venique's body collapsed to the floor a few feet away, I stared at the blood bubbling from the side of his head and noticed the awkward look on his partial missing face and managed to smile.

Then, I saw Frank stepped over top of him and nailed his head to the floor with a few more rounds. And for some reason I could see every bullet entering his head in slow motion.

Chapter 35

Frank

When I pulled up outside of Chanae's house and heard the gunshots, I instantly knew what was up. So, I threw the car in park and hopped out with it on my mind.

I pulled my biscuit out as I ran around the car towards the front door. There was no time to waste. So, I just kicked that motherfucker in and knocked the noodles out of the first person who wasn't supposed to be there.

I didn't realize that it was Venus' son until I stepped over top of him and issued three more shots. The lower portion of his cheek and bottom lip was missing and all the skin where his sideburns once were had peeled back from the first shot.

"Please," the kid wrestling with Chanae begged as I turned my attention to him. "Please, it wasn't my idea. It was Vee and his mother's boyfriend," he confessed dropping to his knees with his hands up in surrender.

I eyed him for a moment. Almost as if I was contemplating what to do next.

In that instant, Chanae picked up Venique's gun off the floor and shot the kid in the head twice at point blank range.

"Dakaron!" She screamed dropping the gun to rush to his side.

"Oh shit, Cuz!" I exclaimed finally noticing him. "Hold on Cuz!" I encouraged pulling out my cellphone as I got to his side.

"No," Dakaron reached out and grabbed my shirt. "No!" He strained to pull me closer. "Give me the gun."

"What?" I questioned confused.

"Give me the gun!" He ordered again barely able to hold on to my shirt.

"Cuz, you're tripping. You done lost too much blood." I went to dial *911* again as Chanae held his head gently in her hands.

"No." Dakaron knocked the cellphone out of my hand. "You got to get out of here," he warned gesturing towards his gun.

I realized what Dakaron was saying and stood up. I couldn't be there when the police arrived. They'd surely throw me back in prison. But Dakaron and Chanae would never be charged. Not for protecting themselves.

"I love you Cuz," I said stuffing the guns in my dip. "I'll see you at the hospital."

"Frank, go!" Chanae shouted waving me off as the dispatcher picked up and she began shouting into the phone.

Dakaron winked at me as I slowly backed up towards the door. I pulled my hoody up and ran outside to my car as Chanae explained to the dispatcher how some guys had broken into her home and shot her children's father.

Since I was double parked, all I had to do was climb behind the wheel and get out of there.

I couldn't believe Venus' son and boyfriend had pulled some fuck shit. I was going to kill that motherfucker. Maybe Venus ass too.

I hugged all back streets until I was able to exit Owings Mills, Maryland and head back into the city. I didn't want no traffic cams or nothing to see me leaving Chanae's house. I couldn't afford to have to explain myself. Not when there were three died bodies on the floor.

I drove to the house of the only woman, besides my mother that I trusted more than anything and parked outside. Then, I sat in the car trying to figure out what in the hell had I gotten myself into fucking with Dakaron.

I don't know exactly just how long I'd been sitting there zoned out but, the knock on the passenger's side window scared me half to death.

"Cuz, you scared the fuck out of me," I admitted as Meek opened the door after I popped the lock. "I was just about to come in."

"Boy, where you been?" Meek stuck her head inside the car. "Me, Kim, Cindy, everybody been calling you."

"What's up? What's going on? You good?" I inquired noticing that she'd been crying.

"Mommy died in her sleep last night," Meek managed to say through a broken voice before her tears started again.

"What you mean mommy died?" I questioned unable to register what she'd just laid on me. I mean, I knew that my mother had been sick. She'd been in and out of the hospital my last few years in prison. But she was strong. My mother had always been a fighter. She was so close to Jesus, she often joked about whipping Lucifer on his behalf.

"She died in her sleep last night," Meek whispered. "Pooch, found her this morning."

Tears started falling from my eyes without warning. I thought back to all the time I'd missed. Then, I began thinking about all the people who let my mother down when she'd first gotten sick. All the motherfuckers she had bent over backwards for and gave her last to. They all turned their backs on her and went on about their lives. The same way they had done when I'd gone to prison. *Fake bitches, fake friends and fake family!* They were all the same.

I thought about my mother staying over my sister house. Living in the basement with a dog. A fucking Pitbull at that! I thought and began to get upset. I couldn't help it. This woman had given us the world. Went without just so we didn't have to.

I began to cry harder. My mother was one of the few people I never stopped having faith in.

"Get out Cuz," I whispered.

"Huh?" Meek stopped crying for a moment.

"Get the fuck out!" I snapped starting the car up. I needed to be alone.

"Fuck you nigga, don't take that shit out on me. She was my mother too!" Meek climbed out of the car and slammed the door.

I pounded the steering wheel repeated as tears continued to pour from my eyes.

"Fuck! Fuck! Fuck!" I shouted. Somebody was going to pay. Nurses. Doctors. I would even settle for a paramedic. Then, it hit me. The system had done this to me. They had essentially buried me in prison for something I'm sure they knew for a fact that I hadn't done. I could still remember the carefree look that cracker had on his face the day Dakaron and I got sentenced.

It was the same carefree look he had when we got released. The same carefree look that every privileged cop had rather they were kneeling on ours necks or withholding exculpatory evidence. It was a look that said rather I'm right or wrong. I'm protected.

Not anymore, bitch! I threw the car in drive and pulled off. It was time to go find out if all the Baltimore City homicide detectives still parked in the Fayette Street Parking Garage.

Chapter 36

Frank

"Why do you always put your shirt on like that?" Bayyinah asked from the bed as I continued to dress far Dakaron's Janazah.

"Like what?" I looked towards the bed curious.

"Like you're always in a hurry," she replied. "You do it every time too. You roll your shirt up until the collar and tail is touching. Then, you pulling it over your head real quick."

"Oh," I smiled for the first time in days. "That is a habit I picked up in prison. It be so much going on you don't have time to be swimming around inside your shirt, feeling for arm-sleeves and stuff," I explained. "I done seen guys get stabbed up like that."

"I guess that makes sense," Bayyinah mumbled in agreement before yawning tiredly and rolling back over to snugged up with her pillow.

Damn! I thought watching her soft, light-streaked butt cheeks wiggle as she turned over on her stomach. *She's even bad after sex.* I hadn't ever had nothing like Bayyinah Bushrod. A dime to say the least. A queen by far.

I just shook my head and continued to get dressed. First Dakaron, then my mother. Which was something I had refused to deal with. I mean, I couldn't. At least not now. I'd go crazy. I had already been riding around the city, looking for the retired detectives on my case. One thing for sure and two things for certain though, once I buried my right hand man and laid my queen, Evon Johnson— the most precious thing in my life— to rest, I was going to cut up something serious.

I slipped into a fresh, crispy white, Jalabiyyah and matching kufi.

Then, I stepped into a pair of light blue, soft-bottom Prada slip-ons and grabbed my accessories. After that, I kissed Bayyinah on her beautiful face and headed for the door.

I climbed into my car and sat in the silence for a moment to clear my head. I still couldn't believe that both my mother and my right-hand man were gone.

I'd overestimated Allah's patience for me and underestimated Venique's power in the streets and it had cost me more than I ever wanted to lose. Now, I was going to murder any and everyone who I felt like caused the pain.

I pulled out my cellphone and looked up the video footage of Dakaron and Chanae's traffic stop. Someone had released the video a few days after Dakaron was murdered and it went viral. As it turns out, the two gun trace Task Force chumps in the video had somehow been linked to another illegal traffic stop that ended in death. Not exactly like Dakaron's case. But death, nonetheless.

I studied the one Chanae said was Venus' boyfriend and locked his face in my memory bank. Then, I tossed the phone on the passenger's seat, started the car and pulled off in route for Dakaron's Janazah or funeral.

I won't bore you with all the Islamic Rituals and eulogies. I'll just tell you that Dakaron's funeral was lit. I mean, leave it up to Dakaron to have already planned his own Janazah. He had a will, guest list and everything. Of course, everybody came out to pay their final respects. Family, friends, a few local celebrities, and a handful of foes. I even ran into a couple of Dakaron's old flames.

Dakaron's brothers, Detauwn and Antauwn, his cousins Little Phil, myself and the twins Clifton and Clinton were all pallbearers.

"Frank let me holler at you for a minute." I looked up to see Dakaron's cousin Little Phil and another short, brown-skin dude walking up on me after the burial.

I was sitting underneath a large oak tree, far off from everyone else, lost in deep thought, wondering about the future.

"What's up?" I questioned making no attempt to get up.

"Ain't too much." Little Phil sat down on the ground beside me. "I just wanted to holler at you."

I didn't respond at first. To be honest, I was tired of talking.

Tired of telling old prison and childhood war stories about Dakaron. Tired of seeing how much pain his death caused to his family. Especially his mother and daughters. It made me think about my mother too much. And that was one thing I didn't want to think about right now.

"I ain't trying to be rude, Little Phil." I paused to stare at him humbly. "But I don't got the energy to keep reminiscing about Dak."

"Shiiid, me either," Little Phil admitted. "Chanae just almost killed me with the story about feeling Cuzzo's heart stop."

"She hit you with that joint too?"

"Ain't no question," Little Phil nodded. "You know she is crazy like that glue." He added.

"Anyway, I didn't come over here to reminisce. I came over here to talk about retribution for what niggas did to my little cousin."

"Is it true that some bitch police boyfriend might be involved?" the short dude inquired.

"Oh damn, my bad Frank," Little Phil saw the look on my face and spoke up. "This me and Dak's cousin, Clyde." He gestured towards the short brown-skin dude. "Clyde meet Frank."

"What's good?" He extended his hand, and I accepted it, noticing the unique birthmark on his face for the first time.

"All is well," I replied without going any further. Dakaron's family or not. I didn't just go trusting motherfuckers because they had family ties. I knew a lot of niggas who'd made that mistake.

Now, I personally knew Little Phil. We'd been in the penitentiary annex together and I knew how Cuz got down. I both seen and heard about his work in the trenches. But Clyde had to grow on me.

"So, is there any truth to that?" Little Phil questioned. "I mean, I saw the video of Cuzzo and Chanae getting pulled over. But you know how people just be saying shit."

"Nah, that's legit," I confirmed with a head nod. "Them bitches had trackers and everything under my car. They some kind of city gun trace squad."

"Yeah, Clyde just hipped me to 'em," Little Phil confessed rubbing his bald head. "Said they corrupt as hell too."

"They are," Clyde confirmed. "Them bitches be turning their body cams off and everything. Last month they spanked a nigga outside of Hip Hop Fish & Chicken for stealing from the BP Gas Station and got away with it."

"How the fuck them bitches get city wide jurisdiction?" I wanted to know. Shit like that was almost unheard of.

"I'm not sure," Clyde admitted. "All I know is like almost three hundred and fifty motherfuckers got cracked in twenty-nineteen and twenty-twenty, and the next thing I know, the Sergeant chump, Bruce Baker who leads the task force rolls out a new Body-Worn Camera Program and these bitches start popping up everywhere."

"Who is Bruce Baker? He in the video?"

"Yeah, he's the one calling the shots," Clyde explained. "He is a wild bitch too. One time they grabbed my man and took him to a lonesome, old, bombed out building in East Baltimore and fucked him over real bad."

"Hold up," Little Phil interjected eyeing Clyde. "Did you say Bruce Baker?"

"Yeah, why?" Clyde and I both looked at Little Phil curiously.

There was no way he could know him. Little Phil hadn't been home a hot ninety days.

Maybe he was on Little Phil's case back in the day, I thought.

"As in former Homicide Detective, Bruce 'Bunchy' Baker? The one whose partner got killed some years back in a shootout?"

"Yeah, that's him," Clyde confirmed.

"Wow." Little Phil grinned. "It's a small world."

"What's up?" I pried staring at Little Phil. "Don't keep me in the blind. You know him or something?"

"Nah, hearing that name just gave me an idea. Especially, if y'all niggas talking about going at the police," Little Phil explained looking at Clyde. "Is that what we're really talking about Cuzzo? Going at the police? The biggest gang in the city?"

"Cuzzo, you already know blue ain't never trump black in my eyes. So, it damn sure doesn't trump blood," Clyde fired. "What them young boys say now? Drag your nuts?" he continued. "Yeah, well, I'm trying to drag my nuts."

"What about you? "Little Phil directed his attention to me.

"That's how you want to play this too? Make sure you think about what you're saying. Because once we ring that bell, it's no turning back."

Instead of answering, I just stared at the human-size headstone of Jesus being crucified on the cross above the gravestone in front of me, until Little Phil and Clyde got the picture.

I'd lost everything I truly cared about behind the police in one sense or another. So, I was ready to take the entire force up to Calvary.

Chapter 33

Frank

It took Little Phil and Clyde a few days to get back with me. But they assured me that everything was a go. Little Phil had even hollered at his man, and he jumped at the opportunity. Said he was all the way with it. According to Little Phil, he had some unfinished business with Sergeant Baker. So, we were all supposed to hook up Friday after Ju'mah service at Clyde's house.

I reached out to Dakaron's man, Buckey Fields folks to get some heavy metal. But he never got back to me. So, I ended up having to deal with my little cousin's boyfriend. A kid by the name of Double-O who was allegedly moving major armory over on Eager and Caroline. Cha'de said he was one of the Feldmans. So, I decided to take my chances. After all, I was out of options.

Of course, I didn't know Double-O from a can of paint. But his family's name was stamped in the streets. Especially over in Deakyland. His older cousin Steven had been my man back in the day. Besides, if all else failed and Double-O tried to run game. He fucked with my little cousin. So, his young ass wouldn't be hard to locate.

When I pulled up in the nine block of Caroline, it seemed like some type of celebration was taking place. There were motherfuckers everywhere. I climbed from the car looking for Cha'de and spotted her standing over near a stocky, little nigga with waves in his funny shaped head.

It had damn near been twenty years since I'd seen Cha'de, but she still had her mother's pretty face.

"What's up little cousin?" I walked up on Cha'de and the stocky young boy with a smile.

"Oh my God! "Cha'de lit up and jumped into my arms when she realized it was me. "Frank! What's up family?"

"You," I replied breaking the embrace to step back and check her out. She'd been a tiny, little thing when I first left the streets. "All grown and shit."

"Yeah." She blushed.

"I heard you got a kid and everything," I revealed.

"That's what happens when people grow up," she joked. "Oh, Frank this my boyfriend, Double-O." She gestured towards the stocky kid. "Double-O, this my cousin Frank I was telling you about."

"What's good Unc?" Double-O nodded.

Unc? I ain't no motherfucking Unc, I thought before I replied. "That's what I'm trying fine out," I confessed looking from Double-O to Cha'de and back. "My little cousin tells me you're in the music business."

"I dib and dap." He smiled knowingly.

This little kid too slick, I smiled. "Good, I need something to rock and roll with."

"What type of party we talking about? What's the size of the guest list?" Double-O inquired.

"Don't worry about the guess list. Just provide the equipment and I'll take care of the rest." I assured.

"It's your party, Unc. I just figured you may have wanted certain drums and stuff." Double-O looked around.

"Just make it heavy." I encouraged.

"Give me twenty minutes." Double-O stepped off before I could say anything else.

"What's going on out here?" I questioned finally able to take in the scenery.

"Oh, it's a celebration for Double-O's little brother Poody. He got shot and died a few years ago."

"I respect that." I nodded and continued to look around. Everybody had on Poody Gang t-shirts with a single bullet laying on the ground.

I stood there talking with Cha'de about the family, life and the future until Double-O returned.

"Let's take a ride, Unc." Double-O requested strolling by.

I hugged Cha'de told her that I loved her and followed Double-O to a black Lexus coup.

"How much paper you working with Unc?" Double-O questioned the moment we were alone in the car.

"Twenty-five," I admitted.

"That's it?" He smiled. "Come on, Unc, what are you trying to have a baby shower?"

"Things are tight right now," I explained. "I just buried my right-hand man and paid to lay my queen to rest. That's why I came to Cha'de. I'm in a jam."

Double-O started the car. "Don't worry I'ma look out. I got you. Any family of my baby. Is family of mines." Double-O said pulling out into traffic.

Chapter 37

Frank

After Double-O made sure I was war ready, my sisters and I laid our queen to rest. I had to duck my little brother out because he wanted me to go out of town with him. But the only thing on my mind was retaliation.

When Friday finally rolled around I couldn't sit still in Ju'Mah to save my life. I don't believe I heard one word of the entire Katbah. I was ready to hook up with Little Phil and them and do some damage.

The police had been getting away with their bullshit for too long. Playing both sides. Clocking-in to protect and serve, only to service themselves.

I pulled up in front of Little Phil's house and hit the horn. It was time to issue some old fashion street justice.

Little Phil stumbled out of the house tongue kissing a fine ass, thick joint who I assumed was his wife.

"Be safe baby!" I heard her encourage as she waved.

"Ain't no question," Little Phil yelled back as he came around the car and climbed into the passenger's seat.

"Cuz, I hope you didn't tell your wife what we're about to get into," I said studying her carefully. She looked so familiar.

"Who Danny?" Little Phil questioned.

"Yeah," I confirmed, turning to see a confused look on his face.

"Fuck no!" He snapped as his facial expression changed to one of insult. "But trust me nigga, If I did, she'd be trying to slide with us." Little Phil guaranteed. "My wife ride or die for real! And I'm not just talking about during my bid. Danny a fucking gangster. Fine as a hell. But a gangster nonetheless."

"I heard that." I took one more look at her before she disappeared into the house and pulled off.

"Cuz, was your wife's last name Simpkin?" I probed when it hit me why she looked so familiar.

"Nah, Green why?" Little Phil secured his seatbelt as we came to the corner.

"Nah, I don't want to sound crazy or nothing. But she looked exactly like this M-C-E supervisor named Ms. Simpkin I use to have a serious crush on when I was down Patuxent."

"It's all good, "Little Phil smiled. "I know my wife bad. That's one of the reasons I married her."

"So, where are we heading?" I asked wanting to change the subject.

"North and Braddish," Little Phil directed.

"So, tell me about your man," I suggested.

"Oh yeah, Billy Lo a soldier. The last time we were together was the first time I won a new trial. We were cell-buddies over the jail. I gave that crazy nigga something that resembled a chainsaw to cut a little hopper he was having static with down," Little Phil explained.

"I heard that name before," I confessed, running it through my mental rolodex.

"Yeah, his shit was definitely ringing before he got found guilty and went with the feds. They tried to tie him to a bunch of shootings and stuff with the Muslims and Italians."

"That's where I heard the name," I revealed when it hit me. "That's the dude who got into it with the community."

"Yeah, a lot of bodies dropped behind that beef." Little Phil confirmed. "But it wasn't only Billy Lo though. Shorty had a team of young goons who weren't going for nothing. Little project kids." Little Phil continued to tell me about the life and times of Billy Lo until we arrived at Clyde's house.

"You're going to fuck with Billy Lo though watch. Y'all the same caliber of niggas." That was the last thing

216

Little Phil said before we climbed from the car and made our way inside.

Chapter 38

Frank

"Billy Lo's pulling up now," Little Phil revealed peeping out the window.

I got up off the couch and made my way over to the curtain. I wanted to see what all the hype was about. I mean, I had come up underneath gangsters like Marlow and Timmir. But I'd been hearing Billy Lo's name since I became Sunni Muslim and got into the folds of Islam. He was like the boogey-man.

Brothers in the community talked about him like he was the big bad wolf. They said he stayed on some big monster, bad man, BGF, guerrilla shit! However, when I saw the egghead, slim joker with the half slick limp climb out of this car. I wasn't impressed. At least, not by first observation.

I sat back down as Clyde went to open the door for Billy Lo.

"Men," Billy Lo greeted Clyde and I with a nod entering the house before going straight to Little Phil and embracing him like a long last brother. "What's up jack?"

"Slow motion. You know me," Little Phil replied as they stepped apart.

"It's good to see you again jack," Billy Lo confessed.

"Likewise." Little Phil turned to me as Clyde locked the door.

"This Frank," Little Phil introduced me. "Frank. Billy Lo. And of course, you already met Clyde."

"As-Salaam-Alaikum," I fired with a head nod, intentionally letting Billy Lo know that I was a Muslim.

Billy Lo glanced at Little Phil.

"He already knows," Little Phil admitted. "But he also knows you're family."

Billy Lo gave a satisfied nodded and we all headed to the kitchen to sit down and discuss business.

We compared notes. Billy Lo and Clyde appeared to know the most, which made sense, especially since Little Phil and I had been in prison roughly the last twenty years.

Billy Lo explained how Sergeant Baker joined the gun trace task force after he'd escaped conviction on his state case and ended up with a sweet federal deal that guaranteed he'd see daylight. "That bitch tried to take me down. But I beat them bitches at their own game-" Billy continued.

"Shiiid, that's too much bad blood for me," I disclosed. "I'd have been got out of the city."

"Yeah, me too." Clyde seconded. "Especially when I'm fucking with a detective who has a history of playing games."

"I thought about it. But honestly, the city is all I know," Billy Lo admitted. "So, I just started keeping taps on his ass. Making sure I knew where to find him at if I ever needed to."

"You been doing more than that," Little Phil stated with a grin.

"Well, ahhh, I guess you can say I been keeping him off balance every now and then." Billy Lo laughed. "But you know jack, when you're at war with somebody, you got to keep them emotional, frustrated and angry. That's how you keep them from thinking. The angrier they are, the less they think. And we both know the advantage you have when a man's not thinking."

"True." Little Phil nodded.

We continued to plot, plan and scheme. Billy Lo and Little Phil wanted to strategize, draw up blueprints and shit. But I wasn't with all that. We had all the information we needed, and I was ready to work.

"I got some heavy shit in my trunk right now," I proclaimed.

"What a couple handguns?" Billy Lo challenged. "We aren't talking about corner boys jack. These police officers. Tactical officers at that. They train for hostile situations."

"Yeah, ain't no way we can just walk down on no police. At least not today." Little Phil paused. "We'd need bulletproof vests and some more shit first."

I knew what Little Phil and Billy Lo were saying was right. But I still wasn't ready to surrender. Especially not while I knew that the police were already hunting me. "So, if we can get some vests we're on?" I looked from Little Phil to Billy Lo thinking about my little cousin's boyfriend Double-O again.

Little Phil and Billy Lo stared at each other for a while. Then, they both looked back at me and nodded.

"Aight." I shot to my feet. "I'm about to start working on that now." I pulled out my phone and headed for the door.

"Hold up Frank," Clyde stopped me in my tracks. "Come with me," he added moving towards the basement door.

Little Phil and Billy Lo got up from the table as I followed Clyde down the basement stairs.

"Watch your step," Clyde reached above his head, pulled the chain link, light switch and the room lit up.

There was nothing in the basement except an old, dirty, yellow refrigerator and a matching deep freezer. I was about to ask Clyde what was up when he walked over to the back wall and slid it to the side like it was a curtain.

"What the fuck?" I took a step back as two very aggressive looking, blue Pitbulls cautiously made their way forward like lions about to feed.

"What's up with the dogs?" I bumped into Billy Lo.

"Don't let them sense your fear," Clyde mumbled nonchalantly walking over to the refrigerator. "And wherever you do, don't run. They hate sudden movement."

I backed up against the wall and stayed put. Clyde opened the refrigerator and reached inside to pull out an extra-large slab of raw meat to toss on the floor. The Pitbulls instantly began circling the raw meat as they watched each other. One was so low that his heavy jaws were dragging on the concrete. The other just growled.

"Feed!" Clyde shouted and the pitbulls charged forward and smashed into each other, both trying to gain the advantage as they tore into the raw meat. I mean, they devoured that raw meat. And when it got down to the last piece, they fought over it until one of them was able to rip it from the other's mouth, flung it up in the air and catch it in its mouth.

After that, they both retreated to their previous positions and began licking the blood off of their own lips, paws and bodies.

"Damn!" Billy Lo exclaimed getting my attention. "Now, that's what I'm talking about."

When I looked up and saw what Billy Lo was referring to, my dick almost got hard. The back wall of Clyde's basement was loaded with shit. Bulletproof vests, army Swiss knifes, SK's, Drakos, AR's, handguns, and all kind of crazy equipment. I even seen a futuristic machine gun that only had one button like an Atari.

"I been dying to get my hands on some artillery like this," Billy Lo confessed picking up a pretty ass, white AK off the rack. "I can work with this."

"Now, you know what the dogs are for," Clyde stated as I slowly moved towards the wall. "They're the only bitches I trust with my guns."

I walked up to the wall and picked up a silencer. I had been wanting to use one since I'd seen the movie 'Killer' as a kid. I grab a bulletproof vest and tried it on. "This the type of shit you were saying we needed right?" I looked at Little Phil and he nodded.

"Cuzzo, what the fuck is all this?" Little Phil inquired turning to Clyde.

"Preparation for Armageddon," Clyde replied.

"Aight, so let's go separate the good from the bad," I suggested.

It took us a little longer than I'd expected to get ready. But that was only because Clyde had to go and jack some wheels. Once he pulled up with the stolen family-size van, we turned our cellphones off, grabbed our accessories and jumped into the van Grand Theft Auto style.

The location Clyde knew about was like Fort Knox. But Billy Lo knew the exact bar where Sergeant Baker and all the members of his gun trace task force squad hung out. It was small sports lodge over in Little Italy called Todd's.

So we rolled into Little Italy and parked on the next block over, just off of Albemarle Street and tried to decide who was going to go to the lodge.

Little Italy was a small community where everybody knew everybody.

So, we knew standing around looking strange wasn't even an option. And going inside a police after hour spot looking for cops, crooked or otherwise damn sure wasn't a thought.

In the end, it was decided that Billy Lo and I would carry out the mission for two reasons. One, Billy Lo knew all the G.T.T.F. players. Two, I looked the youngest.

When we got to the lodge, Billy Lo instantly noticed that Sergeant Baker's silver Camaro wasn't parked outside. But he said we were in luck. "You see that BMW Motorcycle right there?" Billy Lo pointed out one of those new model Nmoto Nostalgia BMW RT's Motorcycles sitting just inside an alley way and I nodded. "That's one of Baker's newest recruits."

That was all I needed to hear. We stood outside, up the street from the sports lodge and waited. When the new rookie recruit stumbled out of the lodge looking a little tipsy, I instantly recognized him.

"I know that motherfucker Cuz," I confessed. "He clocked me outside of H-K Fish House when Dakaron met with Venus."

"Well, at least we know we got the right motherfuckers," Billy Lo said as we took off for the van.

"He's on the move!" Billy Lo exclaimed as we climbed back into the van with Little Phil and Clyde.

"So, he was there?" Clyde sounded surprised.

"Nah, one of his boys was though," Billy Lo replied as Clyde started the van.

"So what are we doing?" Clyde asked pulling off.

"Grabbing the rookie," Billy Lo instructed. "He's going to take us right to Baker."

"Which way are we going?" Clyde asked driving down the block.

"When you get to the corner, make a right," Billy Lo directed. "Fawn Street is a one way. So, he's going to be coming straight at us."

Clyde arrived at the corner just in time to see the Nmoto Nostalgia fly by.

"Follow his ass!" Billy Lo ordered. "We can take him near Central Avenue."

Clyde made the right and followed the rookie as I looked around the van for something to crack him upside the head with. "What are you doing?" Billy Lo quizzed as I pulled the rug up in the back of the van and removed the crow bar.

"Getting something to crack him over the head with," I confessed.

"He has a helmet on, jack." Billy Lo smiled at me and shook his head. "Just let me handle it."

Billy Lo waited until the perfect moment to tell Clyde to pull up and cut the rookie off. When he did, Billy Lo instantly slid the side door back and stuck the business end of his Mossberg into the rookie's face.

"Get your bitch ass off the bike and climb in the van before I knock your whole head off," Billy Lo demanded through clenched teeth.

At first, the rookie began to explain that we had the wrong person. He was a Baltimore City police officer, he confessed. He told Billy Lo that if he pulled the shotgun back in the van and took off, he would forget the entire incident. Billy Lo laughed, jammed the Mossberg into face and informed him that he had one second to get in the van or he'd leave his brains all over the street.

The rookie must've recognized the seriousness in Billy Lo's voice or something. Because he dropped his brand new bike like it wasn't worth every bit of one hundred and fifty thousand and climbed into the back of the van with me.

"You guys are making a big mistake," he warned as Billy Lo pulled the door shut. "I'm apart of special police unit—"

"The gun trace task force." I finished his sentence for him. "We know exactly who you are," I informed leaning forward until he could see my entire face.

I smiled when his eyes got big. "You remember me?"

"Hold up man, please." He went for the door as Clyde peeled off.

"Wrong move!" Billy Lo advised slipping his arms around the rookie's neck.

"Please," the rookie begged struggling to get free as Billy Lo began to choke him out.

The rookie clawed, moaned, tussled and fought until Billy Lo choked him to sleep.

"Find somewhere quiet so we can talk to this bitch," Billy Lo instructed tossing the rookie's body to the floor. "He's going to tell us everything we need to know," Billy Lo assured going through his pockets.

"Here," I tossed Billy Lo a pair of the zip-ties I'd gotten from Clyde's. "Put them on him."

Billy Lo removed a photograph from the rookie's wallet and stuffed it into his own. Then, he rolled the rookie completely over on his back and placed the zip-ties on. It was time to go find out what we needed to know.

Chapter 39

Frank

"Hold up." Little Phil grabbed my waist just before I pulled the latch down and popped the door open. "Slow down for a second," he cautioned.

"For what? We know everything we need to know," I rationalized. We'd gotten all the information we needed out of the rookie before I blew his brains out.

"Let Billy Lo get a good look around first. Make sure everybody's where their supposed to be."

I paused for a moment to study Little Phil. But I never removed my hand from the latch. "Why Billy Lo?" I questioned curiously.

"First of all, he's the smallest." Little Phil justified.

"Secondly, all of us can't go snooping around somebody's house in this neighborhood."

"That definitely makes a lot of sense." Clyde took the words right out of my mouth.

"You picked my pockets," I admitted looking at Clyde to let him know that we'd been thinking the same exact thing.

"I won't be long," Billy Lo assured before sliding past me, stepping over the front seat, and getting out of the passenger's side door of the van.

I peeped out the side window of the van and watched Billy Lo disappear into the hedges.

I could not say for sure exactly how long Billy Lo was gone. It may have been ten minutes. But it could've been just as easily twenty. Whatever the case, all I knew was that I sat impatiently in silence until he returned.

"What it look like out there?" Little Phil inquired as soon as Billy Lo climbed back into the van.

"We're good. All four of them are in the house like the rookie said." Billy Lo revealed. "It looks like they're eating and playing cards. I can't be sure because of the angle of the kitchen window. I would've had to get up on the back porch."

"Did you see any weapons?" Clyde picked my pockets again.

"Not from my position. But like I said, I didn't get all the way up on the porch. I did see what looked like the strap of bag hanging on the back of a chair though," Billy Lo described.

"What about the rest of the house? Anybody else in there?" I wanted to make sure Billy Lo had cleared the house. I wasn't trying to walk into a trap.

"Ain't nothing else moving in that bitch." Billy Lo guaranteed. "I peeped through all the windows before I went around the back."

"Aight, let hit it then." Little Phil rallied sliding the side door to the van open.

I was the first one out of the van. I glanced around, tugged on the edge of my leather gloves to make sure that they were extremely secure. Then, I quickly darted into the hedges and ducked down behind the wall running down the side of the house, before anyone noticed.

Billy Lo, Clyde and Little Phil weren't far behind. Once we were all in position Billy Lo began to lay out the plan.

"Aight listen, there's a window on the back porch. But there's no way of getting to it without being exposed. So, I'ma climb up on the porch from the blind side and post up outside the window." Billy Lo detailed. "Once y'all get up on the back door, I'ma fire through the window to throw them off and y'all rush in and finish the job."

"Who's going in first?" Clyde questioned excitedly.

"I don't know, you," Billy Lo replied. "Just make sure you give me the signal. Because I want to shoot first. Any questions?"

Billy Lo looked around and waited for one of us to reply. Nobody did.

"Good, let's get it in," he instructed and began leading the way. "Stay low," he whispered over his shoulder.

I held the SK at the ready as we made our way down the side of the house towards the back yard like Seal Team Six.

When we finally reached the backyard, Billy Lo signaled for us to keep going around to the steps. Then, he carefully slid the Mossberg underneath the banister before, pulling him up and quietly climbing over it.

I waited until Billy Lo pressed his back up against the house, and edged his way over to the window before I nodded to Clyde.

We could hear the gun trace task force chumps inside, talking shit as we got into position outside the back door.

When everybody was ready, I signaled for Billy Lo to set it off and he immediately, stepped out in front of the window and let the Mossberg go.

The first blast sounded like a cannon going off as it lit the night up and knocked the entire back window from its frame. It looked like balls of flames were jumping out of the Mossberg as Billy Lo stood in front of the window, firing into the safe house.

I wanted to let him unload. But Clyde suddenly jumped up and kicked the back door in. Then, he rushed inside without warning.

"Cuzzo!" Little Phil hollered running behind Clyde and of course, I wasn't far behind.

When I came through the door, the first thing I spotted was Sergeant Baker, slumped over at the kitchen table, laying face down next to a half-eaten steak with the whole back of his cranium missing. I saw Little Phil step over another chump whose guts were hanging out.

Two more shots echoed in the kitchen, and I looked over to see Clyde standing over another young-looking officer near the sink smiling. "He was still moving," he defended.

I was just beginning to wonder where the fourth task force joker was when I noticed slight movement out the corner of my eye. I looked just in time to see the fourth task force joker rolled from beneath the kitchen table and knock Clyde off of his feet with what sounded like a .50 caliber Desert Eagle.

I immediately turned the SK loose on him and ate his ass alive before he could fire another shot. His body bounced, spun and rolled across the kitchen floor like a barrel being hit by rapid gunfire.

"Make sure all them motherfuckers dead." Little Phil ran to Clyde's side, as Billy Lo entered the house and started issuing headshots for verification of death.

"How the fuck you miss that Cuz?" Little Phil helped Clyde up. "You were the first one through the door."

"Yeah, I know. I was slipping." Clyde grimaced as he got to his feet. "Fuck," he whined holding his chest in pain. "I think my fucking ribs are broken."

"You're lucky that's all he broken," I criticized as he picked up a knife off the table and began to cut the straps off of his bulletproof vest to inspected the damage.

"We got to move!" Billy Lo directed going over to the counter. "Check these bags!" He instructed tossing everyone a bag. It was a total of five including the one still hanging off the back of Sergeant Baker's chair.

There was a few stacks of money in my duffle bag. "Money! "I declared holding the bag down by my side.

"Money," Clyde confessed looking inside the duffle bag.

"This one a little heavy," Little Phil pulled the one off Sergeant Baker's chair and sat it on the blood-covered kitchen table. Then, he unzipped it and stuck his hand inside.

"It looks like jewelry, guns and prescription pills," he revealed shifting the contents around. "This the Sergeant chump's bag."

"Why you say that?" I questioned curiously.

"Because it got his keys in here." Little Phil held up a set of house keys with a micro-miniature Copo Camaro attached to the keychain.

"Let me get those," I requested taking the keys out of Little Phil's hand as an idea popped up in my head.

"This one got money in it too," Billy Lo disclosed. "Aight, leave the jewels and shit," Billy Lo flung the second money bag to Little Phil. "We don't need nothing tracing back to us."

"Don't touch nothing, Cuzzo!" Little Phil warned Clyde. "And hold on to that knife."

"Yo, we gotta move," I echoed Billy Lo's sentiment to remind everybody that we'd just slumped four Baltimore City police officers in the middle of Hamden.

"Y'all go ahead. I'ma set this bitch on fire." Little Phil directed and I slung the duffle bag over my shoulder and started moving. He didn't have to tell me twice.

"Nah, we're going out the front door." Billy Lo urged as I moved towards the back door.

I spun around, walked in front of him and headed for the front door with the quickness with Clyde and Billy Lo in tow.

"Watch out!" Clyde warned a split-second before I felt the cold steel being pressed up against my temple and Billy Lo grabbing me.

Boom!

I heard a loud bang and saw a burst of fire just before my body smashed into the wall and I went down as the second shot went off.

My ears were ringing like shit. And I could not hear nor see nothing. I cried out for help as I held my head and tried to get to my feet. I stumbled and fell again.

When I was finally able to gain my vision, I saw Billy Lo stretched out across the hallway floor with a paint ball-sized hole in his face not far from another Tom Hanks looking mother fucker.

"What the fuck was that?" Little Phil dashed into the hallway with his gun drawn.

"Nah, it was another cop in here hiding behind the wall." As Clyde began to explain what had actually happened. I couldn't even believe it.

I hadn't even seen nobody step from the shadows. Nor had I felt Billy Lo tackle me into the wall as he took the brunt of the .44 Magnum shot to the head for me.

We suddenly heard the wounded cop moan out in agony.

"Oh, you still breathing bitch?" Clyde cordially walked over to him, aimed his gun and pulled the trigger. *Click.*

Clyde studied his gun with a strange look before trying to fire it again. *Click.* Then, he just stuffed the gun back into his waistline, drew the knife he'd taken from the kitchen and started butchering the half dead cop until the only thing moving on the floor was his blood.

"We got to move!" Little Phil pushed me towards the door crouching.

Smoke was now pouring from the kitchen. I grabbed Billy Lo's duffle-bag and went out the door.

"We should be good. Nothing traces back to us. Not even Billy Lo," Little Phil said as I passed him one of the two bags I had slung over my shoulder.

"What the hell are you doing?" Little Phil questioned as I headed for Sergeant Baker's Camaro.

"I got one more stop to make," I replied.

"What?" Clyde stared at me like I was crazy. "We just killed five pigs."

"I know, but if I don't handle this, I'll have to answer for every last one of them," I assured.

"Aight, you're on your own." Clyde gave me some love. "Take care of yourself, family."

"Of course."

"You're crazy like that glue," Little Phil exclaimed climbing into the stolen van.

I took Sergeant Baker's keys out of my pocket, opened the car door, tossed the duffle bag on the passenger's seat and climbed in. Then, I started that motherfucker up and pulled off.

Damn, I thought adjusting the rearview mirror and driver's seat. I could literally feel the horsepower.

Chapter 40

Frank

I knew that I was working with borrowed time when I pulled up across the street from Venus house and hit the horn until she looked out of the window. She couldn't see me behind the mirror-tints of Sergeant Baker's Camaro so I stayed calm.

When she finally opened the door, I cracked the window just enough to wave her over. I didn't know what I'd do if she didn't come. But I knew she had to go tonight if I wanted to stay out of prison, So, I tapped on the horn again. As luck would have it, Venus peeped out the door. Probably checking for neighbors. But strangely, nobody was out on Cross Street.

So, she wrapped her skimpy pink robe tightly around her body, tied it up and stepped out into the cool night air.

I could see the beautiful shape of her body as she sashayed towards the car looking all cute. Her pretty little foot and toenails were showing through her sheer bedroom slippers.

"Why didn't you just use your key?" Venus began as I rolled the window down and extended the silencer outside of it.

When she saw me, she froze up like a rodent caught in the gaze of a snake. "Judgement Day, bitch!" I fired with a smile.

I didn't waste any time. I pulled the trigger and hit Venus in the chest twice. When she fell to the ground, I extended my arm out the window and shot her about six or seven more times. Then, I ran over her body as I pulled off.

Since I wasn't trying to be riding around in no dead cop's car and knew South Baltimore so much, I drove straight out Washington Boulevard until I hit State Park. Then, I pulled the Camaro off the road and drove as far as I could into the woods.

I popped the trunk and found something to wipe the car down real good with. After that, I stuffed a cloth into the gas tank until it was wet with gasoline. Then, I flipped it around and stuffed the opposite side in the gas tank. Next, I pushed the car-lighter in, removed my extra clothes and waited.

Once the car lighter popped out, I grabbed my duffle bag, lit the end of the cloth hanging from the gas tank, toss the car-lighter inside and took off running.

It took a minute for me to hear the loud explosion and see the smoke and fire lighting up the sky. By then, I was already out of the park.

I walked along the side of the road and watched my past go up in smoke.

I'd entered the game to take care of my family. Now, I was leaving it behind to be with them. What was more gangster than that? I'd lose my closest friend and probably met the only woman I ever loved.

I took one more look at the sky as fire trucks sped by, lighting up the night.

"Long live Dakaron nigga!" I mumbled to myself with a smile. "Rest in power and may Allah have mercy on your soul," I added knowing that I'd killed all of his enemies.

I entered Tim's twenty-one-dollar motel parking lot and made my way to the front desk.

I paid for the weekend in cash and tipped the cashier very nicely.

Then, I headed to the room and called Bayyinah.

"Hello," she answered on the fifth ring. I could tell that she'd been asleep.

"Hey baby, this Frank," I said.

"What's going on baby? Are you okay?" She sounded concerned.

"Yeah," I could tell she'd probably sat up. "I just wanted to see you. I was thinking—"

"Just tell me where you are baby and I'll be there," she interrupted me before I could finish and made me smile.

She was exactly the type of woman I needed. The type I deserved. Ride or die.

I told Bayyinah exactly where I was at, and she kept me on the phone until she pulled into the parking lot.

Once we were back inside, I broke my burner phone up and flushed it down the toilet.

Bayyinah didn't ask no questions she just stretched out across the bed and asked me what I planned to do with her all weekend.

"Netflix and chill," I joked making her laugh.

"Netflix and chill it is then." She agreed and I knew right then and there that, I'd probably found the only woman who made me want to give up the gangster shit and be a better man.

THE END

Before I go though. Before I move on with my life, I have to thank all the people who counted be out, wrote me off or traded be in. I could not have ever become who I am without you. Or in the words of my right-hand man, Dakaron: *fuck you and I'm still standing!*

The Death of a Gangster

After reading so many gangster novels, most of which were pure garbage, one-sided, unrealistic and or too glamorizing, I felt like it was time to expose the truth behind this gangster persona. Time to close the casket on the hidden hand created pandemic that has left countless men and woman dead or in prison and continues to be self-promoted by the very people whom it effects the most.

I felt like it was time to close the gap between the OGs of the past and the Men of today and prove that there's no difference. I say that because I do not want anybody to think that I am excluding them. Because trust me, I am not!

Now, as I stated before, due to the oversaturation of propaganda when it comes to being a gangster, I decided to bring people a lot closer to the dangers, truths and myths that make up 'The Game' we've become so infatuated with. It's time to separate the facts from fiction. Because only the truth can lead to peace on our inner-city streets.

I have remained silent for years as men and women glorified and promoted The Game and gangster persona in music, movies, television series, books and magazines. Shiiid, I've even force fed it to a few of the Men who followed me in my ignorance. However, the truth is, much of what is being written, produced, shown, promoted and digested is an illusion.

This is the main reason why I felt like it was by far time that, I used my experience, voice and platform to speak the truth regardless of the consequences. Besides, who else is going to do it?

I mean honestly, who else is worthy? Surely not none of the wannabes, has-beens or certified rats still running around playing The Game themselves. Nor any of the so-called gangsters or men who are benefiting from it the most. Not only do they not have the heart, balls, history or intellect to be worthy. But they haven't seen what I've seen or survived what I've been through.

I played 'The Game' on both sides of the fence. And some people — especially if they are real — will tell you that I was good at it. I don't say that to sound slick nor brag because I too was *sick*. I just say that so you will know exactly how qualified I am on the topic.

I did a lot of dirt, caused a lot of pain and made a lot of bad decisions out of peer pressure, pure ignorance and adolescence. Because I didn't understand the science behind the pre-frontal cortex of the brain and how it responds to situations and circumstances differently than that of an adult. This is why I have to expose The Game for exactly what it is, an illusion designed by unimaginable forces to keep the poor and disenfranchised more focused on what they don't have instead of what they do.

I have regrets and I wish that I could take a lot of things back.

But Allah knows best. So, I strive daily to make amends and educate the unlearned. Because The Game that killed me is now killing our future. Because it was designed to place value on what you have and not who you are. 'The Game' keeps us focused on the type of clothes we put on our bodies. So that we never concern ourselves about what goes into them. We love what is happening outside of our communities as opposed to taking the time, energy and resources we have to build up our own. This is the real game.

Who's snitching. Who has the most money, the nicest whips or the finest woman means absolutely nothing in the real scheme of things. That's why 'The Game' doesn't stop no matter who's on top, who's hot, who gets shot, who got popped or regardless of whose body drop.

It's time to shine the light on the dark sides of 'The Game' that continues to destroy us and everything in it its path. You see, The Game is loyal to no one, and it will never love you back no matter how much you give. You can dedicate your time, sacrifice your family and freedom, even claim it as your own. But the minute you fall, The Game will choose someone to take your place on it's wall. To be honest, The Game will swallow you whole and spit you out in pieces.

I've witnessed 'The Game' turn friend into rivals, gangsters into rats and men into shells of themselves. I've seen the innocent become blood sucking parasites of their own community and drugs drain the life out of people. However, the most tragic thing I believe that I've witnessed 'The Game' do was destroy families. Especially my own.

'The Game' has left my daughter fatherless. Forced my sons to become men long before their time and sucked at the very dignity of my relationships with women, until the foundation which they were once built on fell out. Furthermore, for almost seventy-years not one male in my family has attended college. If that's not enough, for almost forty none even graduated high school. Everybody ran the streets getting high, partying, hustling and sticking-up until they went to prison or got murdered. That's not living!

I threw my life away, destroy an entire family and ruined the future of the only real friend that I ever had. To be fair to myself though. Back then, everything in 'The Game' was a test and or testament to my gangster. And when it came to being a gangster, I passed all the test. I would've died to be the best. In some sense, I actually did.

But gone are the days of honor and respect. Gone are the accepted golden rules, if there ever were any, that had helped to keep the 'The Game' in check and the streets in order. I mean, there has never been anything morally right about 'The Game'. Just think about it, everything about 'The Game' is fake! So fake that there's no right or wrong way to play.

Greed, betrayal and GAMICIDE = intentional killing of the game, has always existed. Snitching on your partner, snaking him out for some bread, creeping with his woman or leaving him for dead didn't just begin trust me. There's nothing new under the sun. Certified men have been trying to weed the imposters out since the beginning of time. But whenever you mix the truth with falsehood, there will never be a safe way to play The Game. How do you think the cemeteries and prisons got so packed?

I am warning you. No! I am begging you to let *this* SERIES be a cautionary tale to you. 'The Game' is dead! All that gangster shit is phony. Obtaining knowledge, wisdom, understanding and education is what real gangsters do. Then, they put it into practice. That's the only key to success.

You may not have actually known the players in this book. But I am sure that you are very familiar with their characteristics. They live in every neighborhood, hang on every corner, join every gang and walk any given cellblock. They are our brothers and sisters. Our family and friends. In many cases, they're our reflections. Simply meaning, we have all been them at one time or another.

Before I woke up, I really thought that I was something. I wanted to be nationally known for putting in work and would have done just about anything to be labeled the number one gangster. I can still remember the first time I hit the jail. I was antsy, anticipating the action. Now, I know that I was a damn fool! I didn't know any better. So, I didn't want any better. Nobody told me the truth about The Game. They just pushed me to go hard and encouraged me to never cooperate with the authorities. Not even if it was to *man up* and cut an innocence man free. That was the ceiling in life. Nothing more, nothing less.

A gangster was all I ever wanted to be and all that I ever thought that I could do. And I refused to let anyone, or anything stand in the way or tell me different. Even at the expense of my own life. That's how bent my mind was at that time. It's the same *sickness* and mindset that continues to plague the youth of our communities.

'The Game' and the gangster thing is so fake! Like I said, I threw my life away for it and guess what happened? All my so called friends — even the older ones who encouraged me to be like them. The ones I just knew had my back. They threw me away or wrote me off. And all the women disappeared. Even the ones that claimed to love me. That's the real game.

'The Game' that nobody really talks about. Anybody can talk a good game. That's why the game is so messed up today. Everybody's running game. Playing on the ignorance of our children. That stops now!

Let's stop lying to each other and get real. Stop acting like we're winning. Our community is feeding off of itself. We're killing each other at an alarming rate, disrespecting our woman, sacrificing our children, leaving the community unprotected and undervalued. What's so gangster about that?

More importantly, let's stop lying to our children. Stop making them think that 'The Game' is something it's not. Stop allowing them to be raised by social media and given their principles and value systems by rappers and television characters. They're our future! Now, I know we cannot change the past. But we can certainly learn from it, so that our children can be better prepared for the future. We can also do something today that will definitely have a major impact on what takes place with our children tomorrow. The number one thing being, SPEAK THE TRUTH. No more mixing the truth with falsehood. After that, we must forgive ourselves and each other for all the broken promises, the unkind words, the unintentional and intentional pain and the forgotten task.

If we do that, I think that we'll do better both individually and collectively. After all, the fate and future of our children, community and world depends upon it.

Stay tuned! Your man coming with something crazy next!

Lock Down Publications and Ca$h Presents
Assisted Publishing Packages

BASIC PACKAGE	UPGRADED PACKAGE
$499	$800
Editing	Typing
Cover Design	Editing
Formatting	Cover Design
	Formatting
ADVANCE PACKAGE	**LDP SUPREME PACKAGE**
$1,200	$1,500
Typing	Typing
Editing	Editing
Cover Design	Cover Design
Formatting	Formatting
Copyright registration	Copyright registration
Proofreading	Proofreading
Upload book to Amazon	Set up Amazon account
	Upload book to Amazon
	Advertise on LDP, Amazon and Facebook Page

***Other services available upon request.
Additional charges may apply
Lock Down Publications
P.O. Box 944
Stockbridge, GA 30281-9998
Phone: 470 303-9761

Submission Guideline

Submit the first three chapters of your completed manuscript to ldpsubmissions@gmail.com, subject line: Your book's title. The manuscript must be in a .doc file and sent as an attachment. Document should be in Times New Roman, double spaced and in size 12 font. Also, provide your synopsis and full contact information. If sending multiple submissions, they must each be in a separate email.

Have a story but no way to send it electronically? You can still submit to LDP/Ca$h Presents. Send in the first three chapters, written or typed, of your completed manuscript to:

LDP: Submissions Dept
Po Box 944
Stockbridge, Ga 30281

DO NOT send original manuscript. Must be a duplicate.

Provide your synopsis and a cover letter containing your full contact information.

Thanks for considering LDP and Ca$h Presents.

NEW RELEASES

SOSA GANG 2 by ROMELL TUKES
KINGZ OF THE GAME 7 by PLAYA RAY
SKI MASK MONEY 2 by RENTA
BORN IN THE GRAVE 3 by SELF MADE TAY
LOYALTY IS EVERYTHING 3 by MOLOTTI

Delmont Player

Coming Soon from Lock Down Publications/Ca$h Presents

BLOOD OF A BOSS **VI**
SHADOWS OF THE GAME II
TRAP BASTARD II
By Askari
LOYAL TO THE GAME **IV**
By T.J. & Jelissa
TRUE SAVAGE **VIII**
MIDNIGHT CARTEL IV
DOPE BOY MAGIC IV
CITY OF KINGZ III
NIGHTMARE ON SILENT AVE II
THE PLUG OF LIL MEXICO II
CLASSIC CITY II
By Chris Green
BLAST FOR ME **III**
A SAVAGE DOPEBOY III
CUTTHROAT MAFIA III
DUFFLE BAG CARTEL VII
HEARTLESS GOON VI
By Ghost
A HUSTLER'S DECEIT III
KILL ZONE II
BAE BELONGS TO ME III
TIL DEATH II
By Aryanna

KING OF THE TRAP III
By T.J. Edwards
GORILLAZ IN THE BAY V
3X KRAZY III
STRAIGHT BEAST MODE III
De'Kari
KINGPIN KILLAZ IV
STREET KINGS III
PAID IN BLOOD III
CARTEL KILLAZ IV
DOPE GODS III
Hood Rich
SINS OF A HUSTLA II
ASAD
YAYO V
Bred In The Game 2
S. Allen
THE STREETS WILL TALK II
By Yolanda Moore
SON OF A DOPE FIEND III
HEAVEN GOT A GHETTO III
SKI MASK MONEY III
By Renta
LOYALTY AIN'T PROMISED III
By Keith Williams
I'M NOTHING WITHOUT HIS LOVE II
SINS OF A THUG II
TO THE THUG I LOVED BEFORE II
IN A HUSTLER I TRUST II
By Monet Dragun
QUIET MONEY IV
EXTENDED CLIP III
THUG LIFE IV
By Trai'Quan
THE STREETS MADE ME IV
By Larry D. Wright

Delmont Player

IF YOU CROSS ME ONCE III
ANGEL V
By Anthony Fields
THE STREETS WILL NEVER CLOSE IV
By K'ajji
HARD AND RUTHLESS III
KILLA KOUNTY IV
By Khufu
MONEY GAME III
By Smoove Dolla
JACK BOYS VS DOPE BOYS IV
A GANGSTA'S QUR'AN V
COKE GIRLZ II
COKE BOYS II
LIFE OF A SAVAGE V
CHI'RAQ GANGSTAS V
SOSA GANG III
BRONX SAVAGES II
BODYMORE KINGPINS II
By Romell Tukes
MURDA WAS THE CASE III
Elijah R. Freeman
AN UNFORESEEN LOVE IV
BABY, I'M WINTERTIME COLD III
By Meesha

QUEEN OF THE ZOO III
By Black Migo
CONFESSIONS OF A JACKBOY III
By Nicholas Lock
KING KILLA II
By Vincent "Vitto" Holloway
BETRAYAL OF A THUG III
By Fre$h

248

THE MURDER QUEENS III
By Michael Gallon
THE BIRTH OF A GANGSTER III
By Delmont Player
TREAL LOVE II
By Le'Monica Jackson
FOR THE LOVE OF BLOOD III
By Jamel Mitchell
RAN OFF ON DA PLUG II
By Paper Boi Rari
HOOD CONSIGLIERE III
By Keese
PRETTY GIRLS DO NASTY THINGS II
By Nicole Goosby
PROTÉGÉ OF A LEGEND III
LOVE IN THE TRENCHES II
By Corey Robinson
IT'S JUST ME AND YOU II
By Ah'Million
FOREVER GANGSTA III
By Adrian Dulan
GORILLAZ IN THE TRENCHES II
By SayNoMore
THE COCAINE PRINCESS VIII
By King Rio
CRIME BOSS II
Playa Ray
LOYALTY IS EVERYTHING III
Molotti
HERE TODAY GONE TOMORROW II
By Fly Rock
REAL G'S MOVE IN SILENCE II
By Von Diesel
GRIMEY WAYS IV
By Ray Vinci

Available Now

RESTRAINING ORDER **I & II**
By CA$H & Coffee
LOVE KNOWS NO BOUNDARIES **I II & III**
By Coffee
RAISED AS A GOON I, II, III & IV
BRED BY THE SLUMS I, II, III
BLAST FOR ME I & II
ROTTEN TO THE CORE I II III
A BRONX TALE I, II, III
DUFFLE BAG CARTEL I II III IV V VI
HEARTLESS GOON I II III IV V
A SAVAGE DOPEBOY I II
DRUG LORDS I II III
CUTTHROAT MAFIA I II
KING OF THE TRENCHES
By Ghost
LAY IT DOWN **I & II**
LAST OF A DYING BREED I II
BLOOD STAINS OF A SHOTTA I & II III
By Jamaica
LOYAL TO THE GAME I II III
LIFE OF SIN I, II III
By TJ & Jelissa
BLOODY COMMAS I & II
SKI MASK CARTEL I II & III
KING OF NEW YORK I II,III IV V
RISE TO POWER I II III
COKE KINGS I II III IV V
BORN HEARTLESS I II III IV

The Birth of a Gangster 4

KING OF THE TRAP I II
By T.J. Edwards
IF LOVING HIM IS WRONG…I & II
LOVE ME EVEN WHEN IT HURTS I II III
By Jelissa
WHEN THE STREETS CLAP BACK I & II III
THE HEART OF A SAVAGE I II III IV
MONEY MAFIA I II
LOYAL TO THE SOIL I II III
By Jibril Williams
A DISTINGUISHED THUG STOLE MY HEART I II
& III
LOVE SHOULDN'T HURT I II III IV
RENEGADE BOYS I II III IV
PAID IN KARMA I II III
SAVAGE STORMS I II III
AN UNFORESEEN LOVE I II III
BABY, I'M WINTERTIME COLD I II
By Meesha
A GANGSTER'S CODE I &, II III
A GANGSTER'S SYN I II III
THE SAVAGE LIFE I II III
CHAINED TO THE STREETS I II III
BLOOD ON THE MONEY I II III
A GANGSTA'S PAIN I II III
By J-Blunt
PUSH IT TO THE LIMIT
By Bre' Hayes
BLOOD OF A BOSS I, II, III, IV, V
SHADOWS OF THE GAME
TRAP BASTARD
By Askari
THE STREETS BLEED MURDER **I, II & III**
THE HEART OF A GANGSTA I II& III
By Jerry Jackson
CUM FOR ME I II III IV V VI VII VIII

Delmont Player

An LDP Erotica Collaboration
BRIDE OF A HUSTLA **I II & II**
THE FETTI GIRLS **I, II& III**
CORRUPTED BY A GANGSTA I, II III, IV
BLINDED BY HIS LOVE
THE PRICE YOU PAY FOR LOVE I, II ,III
DOPE GIRL MAGIC I II III
By Destiny Skai
WHEN A GOOD GIRL GOES BAD
By Adrienne
THE COST OF LOYALTY I II III
By Kweli
A GANGSTER'S REVENGE **I II III & IV**
THE BOSS MAN'S DAUGHTERS I II III IV V
A SAVAGE LOVE **I & II**
BAE BELONGS TO ME I II
A HUSTLER'S DECEIT I, II, III
WHAT BAD BITCHES DO I, II, III
SOUL OF A MONSTER I II III
KILL ZONE
A DOPE BOY'S QUEEN I II III
TIL DEATH
By Aryanna
A KINGPIN'S AMBITON
A KINGPIN'S AMBITION **II**
I MURDER FOR THE DOUGH
By Ambitious
TRUE SAVAGE I II III IV V VI VII
DOPE BOY MAGIC I, II, III
MIDNIGHT CARTEL I II III
CITY OF KINGZ I II
NIGHTMARE ON SILENT AVE
THE PLUG OF LIL MEXICO II
CLASSIC CITY

The Birth of a Gangster 4
By Chris Green
A DOPEBOY'S PRAYER
By Eddie "Wolf" Lee
THE KING CARTEL **I, II & III**
By Frank Gresham
THESE NIGGAS AIN'T LOYAL **I, II & III**
By Nikki Tee
GANGSTA SHYT **I II &III**
By CATO
THE ULTIMATE BETRAYAL
By Phoenix
Boss'n Up i , ii & IIi
By Royal Nicole
I LOVE YOU TO DEATH
By Destiny J
I RIDE FOR MY HITTA
I STILL RIDE FOR MY HITTA
By Misty Holt
LOVE & CHASIN' PAPER
By Qay Crockett
TO DIE IN VAIN
SINS OF A HUSTLA
By ASAD
BROOKLYN HUSTLAZ
By Boogsy Morina
BROOKLYN ON LOCK I & II
By Sonovia
GANGSTA CITY
By Teddy Duke
A DRUG KING AND HIS DIAMOND I & II III
A DOPEMAN'S RICHES
HER MAN, MINE'S TOO I, II
CASH MONEY HO'S
THE WIFEY I USED TO BE I II
PRETTY GIRLS DO NASTY THINGS
By Nicole Goosby

Delmont Player

TRAPHOUSE KING **I II & III**
KINGPIN KILLAZ I II III
STREET KINGS I II
PAID IN BLOOD **I II**
CARTEL KILLAZ I II III
DOPE GODS I II
By Hood Rich
LIPSTICK KILLAH **I, II, III**
CRIME OF PASSION I II & III
FRIEND OR FOE I II III
By Mimi
STEADY MOBBN' **I, II, III**
THE STREETS STAINED MY SOUL I II III
By Marcellus Allen
WHO SHOT YA **I, II, III**
SON OF A DOPE FIEND I II
HEAVEN GOT A GHETTO I II
SKI MASK MONEY I II
Renta
GORILLAZ IN THE BAY **I II III IV**
TEARS OF A GANGSTA I II
3X KRAZY I II
STRAIGHT BEAST MODE I II
DE'KARI
TRIGGADALE I II III
MURDAROBER WAS THE CASE I II
Elijah R. Freeman
GOD BLESS THE TRAPPERS I, II, III
THESE SCANDALOUS STREETS I, II, III
FEAR MY GANGSTA I, II, III IV, V
THESE STREETS DON'T LOVE NOBODY I, II
BURY ME A G I, II, III, IV, V
A GANGSTA'S EMPIRE I, II, III, IV
THE DOPEMAN'S BODYGAURD I II

254

The Birth of a Gangster 4
THE REALEST KILLAZ I II III
THE LAST OF THE OGS I II III
Tranay Adams
THE STREETS ARE CALLING
Duquie Wilson
MARRIED TO A BOSS I II III
By Destiny Skai & Chris Green
KINGZ OF THE GAME I II III IV V VI VII
CRIME BOSS
Playa Ray
SLAUGHTER GANG I II III
RUTHLESS HEART I II III
By Willie Slaughter
FUK SHYT
By Blakk Diamond
DON'T F#CK WITH MY HEART I II
By Linnea
ADDICTED TO THE DRAMA I II III
IN THE ARM OF HIS BOSS II
By Jamila
YAYO I II III IV
A SHOOTER'S AMBITION I II
BRED IN THE GAME
By S. Allen
TRAP GOD I II III
RICH $AVAGE I II III
MONEY IN THE GRAVE I II III
By Martell Troublesome Bolden
FOREVER GANGSTA I II
 GLOCKS ON SATIN SHEETS I II
By Adrian Dulan
TOE TAGZ I II III IV
LEVELS TO THIS SHYT I II
IT'S JUST ME AND YOU
By Ah'Million
KINGPIN DREAMS I II III

Delmont Player
RAN OFF ON DA PLUG
By Paper Boi Rari
CONFESSIONS OF A GANGSTA I II III IV
CONFESSIONS OF A JACKBOY I II
By Nicholas Lock
I'M NOTHING WITHOUT HIS LOVE
SINS OF A THUG
TO THE THUG I LOVED BEFORE
A GANGSTA SAVED XMAS
IN A HUSTLER I TRUST
By Monet Dragun
CAUGHT UP IN THE LIFE I II III
THE STREETS NEVER LET GO I II III
By Robert Baptiste
NEW TO THE GAME I II III
MONEY, MURDER & MEMORIES I II III
By Malik D. Rice
LIFE OF A SAVAGE I II III IV
A GANGSTA'S QUR'AN I II III IV
MURDA SEASON I II III
GANGLAND CARTEL I II III
CHI'RAQ GANGSTAS I II III IV
KILLERS ON ELM STREET I II III
JACK BOYZ N DA BRONX I II III
A DOPEBOY'S DREAM I II III
JACK BOYS VS DOPE BOYS I II III
COKE GIRLZ
COKE BOYS
SOSA GANG I II
BRONX SAVAGES
BODYMORE KINGPINS
By Romell Tukes
LOYALTY AIN'T PROMISED I II
By Keith Williams

The Birth of a Gangster 4
QUIET MONEY I II III
THUG LIFE I II III
EXTENDED CLIP I II
A GANGSTA'S PARADISE
By Trai'Quan
THE STREETS MADE ME I II III
By Larry D. Wright
THE ULTIMATE SACRIFICE I, II, III, IV, V, VI
KHADIFI
IF YOU CROSS ME ONCE I II
ANGEL I II III IV
IN THE BLINK OF AN EYE
By Anthony Fields
THE LIFE OF A HOOD STAR
By Ca$h & Rashia Wilson
THE STREETS WILL NEVER CLOSE I II III
By K'ajji
CREAM I II III
THE STREETS WILL TALK
By Yolanda Moore
NIGHTMARES OF A HUSTLA I II III
By King Dream
CONCRETE KILLA I II III
VICIOUS LOYALTY I II III
By Kingpen
HARD AND RUTHLESS I II
MOB TOWN 251
THE BILLIONAIRE BENTLEYS I II III
REAL G'S MOVE IN SILENCE
By Von Diesel
GHOST MOB
Stilloan Robinson
MOB TIES I II III IV V VI
SOUL OF A HUSTLER, HEART OF A KILLER I II
GORILLAZ IN THE TRENCHES
By SayNoMore

Delmont Player
BODYMORE MURDERLAND I II III
THE BIRTH OF A GANGSTER I II
By Delmont Player
FOR THE LOVE OF A BOSS
By C. D. Blue
MOBBED UP I II III IV
THE BRICK MAN I II III IV V
THE COCAINE PRINCESS I II III IV V VI VII
By King Rio
KILLA KOUNTY I II III IV
By Khufu
MONEY GAME I II
By Smoove Dolla
A GANGSTA'S KARMA I II III
By FLAME
KING OF THE TRENCHES I II III
 by GHOST & TRANAY ADAMS
QUEEN OF THE ZOO I II
By Black Migo
GRIMEY WAYS I II III
By Ray Vinci
XMAS WITH AN ATL SHOOTER
By Ca$h & Destiny Skai
KING KILLA
By Vincent "Vitto" Holloway
BETRAYAL OF A THUG I II
By Fre$h
THE MURDER QUEENS I II
By Michael Gallon
TREAL LOVE
By Le'Monica Jackson
FOR THE LOVE OF BLOOD I II
By Jamel Mitchell
HOOD CONSIGLIERE I II

The Birth of a Gangster 4
By Keese
PROTÉGÉ OF A LEGEND I II
LOVE IN THE TRENCHES
By Corey Robinson
BORN IN THE GRAVE I II III
By Self Made Tay
MOAN IN MY MOUTH
By XTASY
TORN BETWEEN A GANGSTER AND A
GENTLEMAN
By J-BLUNT & Miss Kim
LOYALTY IS EVERYTHING I II
Molotti
HERE TODAY GONE TOMORROW
By Fly Rock
PILLOW PRINCESS
By S. Hawkins

BOOKS BY LDP'S CEO, CA$H

TRUST IN NO MAN
TRUST IN NO MAN 2
TRUST IN NO MAN 3
BONDED BY BLOOD
SHORTY GOT A THUG
THUGS CRY
THUGS CRY 2
THUGS CRY 3
TRUST NO BITCH
TRUST NO BITCH 2
TRUST NO BITCH 3
TIL MY CASKET DROPS
RESTRAINING ORDER
RESTRAINING ORDER 2
IN LOVE WITH A CONVICT
LIFE OF A HOOD STAR
XMAS WITH AN ATL SHOOTER

www.ingramcontent.com/pod-product-compliance
Lightning Source LLC
Chambersburg PA
CBHW071136260626
47162CB00003B/806